Praise for Robert J. Begiebing

The Strange Death of Mistress Coffin (1991, 1996)
"Mesmerizing. Slowly, subtly, the story twists on itself like a pinned snake. . . .Not since Kenneth Roberts has anyone written of early New England life in such vivid and convincing detail. . . .A gifted writer with an extraordinary feeling for the past."
　　—Annie Proulx, *The New York Times Book Review*

"Stereotypes we learned in grade school simply don't exist here; instead, there are passionate, complex characters, including unexpectedly strong and often rebellious women."
　　—*The Denver Post*

"Begiebing illuminates the dark and wonderful intricacy of the human heart."
　　—*Yankee Magazine*

"This is no ordinary mystery. Just imagine Peyton Place as Hawthorne would have written it."
　　—*Booklist*

"A great achievement of imagination and research."
　　—*Boston Magazine*

The Adventures of Allegra Fullerton (1999)
"Fascinating. . . Allegra describes her transformation from 'mere traveling face maker' to sophisticated associate of Margaret Fuller and John Ruskin .

. . .Allegra's insightful ruminations on the artistic life make up the lively heart of this book."
—*The New York Times Book Review*

"The green landscapes of nineteenth-century New England are beautifully evoked, and Allegra Fullerton is as keen to catch the play of light in language as she is in paint. . . . The pleasure of the novel derives from its careful specificities of time and place."
—*Times Literary Supplement (London)*

"Art, philosophy, religion, slavery, sexual propriety, suffrage—all are addressed with candid clarity. . . .Highly recommended."
—*Library Journal*, starred review.

"The meticulously evoked settings, dialogue and characters provide a seamlessly authentic entry into the era . . . .Saturated with vivid period detail, sprinkled with rousing feminist sentiments . . .the novel will keep readers engrossed in its intelligent heroine's adventures. A first rate tale."
—*Publishers Weekly*

Rebecca Wentworth's Distraction (2003)
"The Langum Prize. . . is awarded to Rebecca Wentworth's Distraction: A Novel as the best university press novel of 2003 to make the rich history of America accessible to the educated general public."
—*Prize citation, 2003*

Also by Robert Begiebing

NOVELS

The Strange Death of Mistress Coffin (1991, 2012)

The Adventures of Allegra Fullerton (1999)

Rebecca Wentworth's Distraction (2003)

CRITICISM

*Acts of Regeneration: Allegory and Archetype
in the Work of Norman Mailer* (1981)

*Toward a New Synthesis: John Fowles,
John Gardner, and Norman Mailer* (1989)

*The Literature of Nature: The British and
American Traditions* (1990)
(a critical anthology with V. Owen Grumbling)

DRAMA

Ernest and Norman: A Dialogue in Two Acts (2010)

The Turner Erotica

A Biographical Novel

Robert J. Begiebing

ILIUM
PRESS

Spokane Valley, Washington, USA
www.iliumpress.com

The Turner Erotica: A Biographical Novel

Copyright © 2013 by Robert J. Begiebing. All rights reserved.

This book has been composed in Garamond.

Cover design: Kenyon Sharp
Book design: John Lemon

The Turner Erotica / a biographical novel [by] Robert J. Begiebing.

ISBN 978-0-9833002-4-3 (pbk.)
ISBN 978-0-9833002-5-0 (ePub)

Library of Congress Control Number: 2012953957
Library of Congress subject headings:
1. Stillman, William James, 1828-1901 –Fiction.
2. Turner, J. M. W. (Joseph Mallord William), 1775-1851 –Fiction.
3. Ruskin, John, 1819-1900 –Fiction.
4. Stillman, Marie Spartali, 1844-1927 –Fiction.
5. Burton, Richard Francis, Sir, 1821-1890 –Fiction.
6. Painters –Fiction. 7. Biographical fiction. 8. Historical fiction.
9. England –Fiction.
I. Begiebing, Robert J., 1946 –   . II. Title

Published and printed in the United States of America by the Ilium Press,
Spokane Valley, Washington, U.S.A.

All books from the Ilium Press are printed on high quality, acid-free, book-grade
opaque paper stock that meets ANSI standards for archival quality paper. Binding
materials are chosen for strength and durability.

Visit the Ilium Press online at www.iliumpress.com.

For Jack Scovil, 1937-2012,
friend and agent,
who believed in this book.

Contents

That art which ... is specifically known as 'Christian,' erred by pride in its denial of the animal nature of man; — and, in connection with all monkish and fanatical forms of religion, by looking always to another world instead of this. It ... was therefore swept away ... by the strong truth of the naturalist art of the sixteenth century. But that naturalist art erred on the other side; denied at last the spiritual nature of man, and perished in corruption.

— John Ruskin, *Modern Painters*, vol. V

An Apparition

When I, William James Stillman, first heard of the unholy conflagration, this is how I imagined it.

In some damp basement room of London's National Gallery, a man of thirty-nine years—slim, sandy-haired, blue-eyed, of impeccable dress and deportment, his head leaning against one hand—sat opposite the Keeper of Collections, Mr. Ralph Wornum. The Keeper appeared to be the thin man's physical opposite: a veritable Hercules, judging from the muscular development shifting beneath his shirt and waistcoat. On the table before him lay a portfolio of sketches by the deceased painter Joseph Mallord William Turner. Through his own political exertions, the thin man, one Mr. John Ruskin, had been granted the task of arranging and cataloguing an enormous body of Turner's work, particularly sketch studies, left in the master's studio at his death.

As a well-stoked coal fire wavered in the grate, Mr. Wornum appeared to await some word from his colleague.

Finally Mr. Ruskin spoke. "Surely we have no other recourse."

Wornum replied as if further silence would be painful to them. "The authorities have not thought proper even to register them, sir, as you know."

Ruskin offered him the portfolio. The Keeper looked as though he dearly wished he had never heard of such sketches. One might have suspected that Wornum, who himself aspired to genius, would have been aware that they were preparing to violate a trust and alter the history of British art. And one might have suspected that Wornum—married to the former Miss Selden, one of the most perfectly formed women in London—was fully alert to the erotic pleasures of the work bundled before them.

But such suspicions are always complicated by deeper truths, for Wornum was himself bred a Swedenborgian and held that the physical world is the fictitious—or nonessential—one, and that the spiritual world to which we will one day fully awake is the real.

Finally, the Keeper untied the bundle and opened it on the desk before him. He tried not to look at the sketchbooks and studies on single sheets. But as he lifted the first sheaf and turned to the fireplace, his eyes fell on the ink and watercolor depiction—a glorious, dewy jewelweed blossom—of a woman's private parts in a state of flagrant availability.

After a moment's hesitation, he allowed the sheet to slide into the flames. Then he picked up another, and another, with gradually increasing fury, and pushed the works of art from his hand into the fire. He stopped from time to time to thrust an iron poker into the mass of paper to ensure incineration. Then he gathered another sheaf, even a whole sketchbook, and repeated the process.

Neither man spoke throughout the entire immolation. Only two years earlier, in 1856, Ruskin had completed the fourth volume of his defense of Turner as the greatest modern genius of British art.

When all the ashes had finally been stirred, Ruskin rose off his bench and walked over to the fireplace where Wornum stood, poker in hand.

"It's done," he said to the Keeper.

The Keeper didn't answer at first. He seemed spellbound by the ashes and the flames still leaping off the grate.

"It is indeed, Mr. Ruskin, done," the Keeper finally said.

"And it is good," Ruskin said. "They are, they were, an abomination against humanity. Against womanhood, surely."

"I pray you are right, sir. I pray we did the right thing."

"How can we doubt it? You're the very one, are you not, who maintained the illegality of anyone holding these compositions?"

The Keeper hesitated. "I no longer doubt," he said. "And it's too late to believe otherwise. As you say, it's done."

Ruskin offered his hand. Wornum took it firmly, as they looked solemnly into one another's eyes. "Good day to you, sir," Ruskin said.

Part I, 1850–1862

I have had a cloud upon me this year and don't quite know the meaning of it; only I've had no heart to write to anybody. I suppose the real gist of it is that next year I shall be forty, and begin to see what life and the world mean, seen from the middle of them—and the middle inclining to the dustward end. ... I believe there is something owing to the violent reaction ... after the excitement of the arrangement of Turner's sketches; something to my ascertaining in the course of that work how the old man's soul had been gradually crushed within him.

 —John Ruskin, Letter to Elizabeth Barrett Browning,
 October 24, 1858

Chapter 1

As a young art student abroad in 1850, I had the good fortune—I had the misfortune—to meet John Ruskin. I had been frequenting Thomas Griffith's London gallery, viewing some Turners, when Ruskin came in one day, as Mr. Griffith said he would. Griffith introduced me to Ruskin as "Mr. William Stillman, a young man with a particular interest in Mr. Turner's works."

Before me stood John Ruskin, about thirty years, the youthful English gentleman of mild countenance and manner. Where was the fire-eating dogmatist of *Modern Painters*? Where was the author who, by the nobility and power of his rhetoric, left the reader gasping in assent? I wondered that first moment whether Mr. Griffith were having a little joke on me, but soon realized it was none other than Ruskin himself. We began a quiet conversation before some of the Turners.

"I see you have knowledgeable appreciation of the master, Mr. Stillman," he said as we ended our talk. "Why don't you come down to Denmark Hill to see my father's collection." We set a date, and that was the beginning of my true education in Turner.

The way to Denmark Hill in the southern suburbs of London was lovely and very near open country, so I walked the road by Norwood to Addington, through a territory of field and wood, crossed here and there by winding lanes and a few smoother mail-coach roads. The seven acres of garden grounds upon which the Ruskin house was situated, with many peach, plum, pear, and hawthorn trees about, felt restorative in its reclusion. The ample dwelling, with attached hothouses, was covered in ivies, and around the veranda, wisteria. The entire scene before me was testimony to his father's success in the wine importing business.

Welcomed in, I asked Ruskin about the gorgeous camellia and azalea blossoms I had espied in the hothouses.

"Oh," he said, smiling and wistful, "those were mine to bestow on our female guests. Before my marriage."

Ruskin encouraged my peculiar appreciations of the old master's work, and asserted very little himself by way of how to see it. After tea with his parents, he invited me to visit him at 31 Park Street, Grosvenor Square—a street, I found, of small dull houses rather startling in contrast to Denmark Hill. Here too he greeted me at his door, wearing his trademark bright Oxford blue stock, dark blue frock coat with velvet collar, black trousers, and patent slippers. His wife Euphemia, or "Effie"—a woman of considerable charm and serenity—joined us for tea, but soon left us that he and I might resume the discussions begun at Denmark Hill. Beyond our fascination with Turner, we discovered shared similarity of backgrounds: our firm upbringing by mothers, on either side of the Atlantic, whose stain of Calvinism still marked us both.

"I was raised under a harsh regime of Sabbatarianism," I said to him, "my most ancient roots on my mother's side reaching back to the band driven with Roger Williams from Massachusetts to Providence Plantation. The utterly free rein of conscience there loosed extreme doctrines and the greatest variety of sects."

"But once you attained your education and reason," he suggested, "you began to rise above the bigotries of your upbringing."

"And you likewise?"

He laughed. "I've only begun my painful journey."

"But we moved to Schenectady, New York," I went on, "after my father's business failed in Rhode Island, to become hard-working laborers and farmers. Only my mother's complete absorption in the daily demands of domestic life saved her from religious insanity."

He nodded. I knew he grasped immediately the circumstances of my youth.

"And may have saved me too," I added. "For I began to follow my fascination with nature in scant leisure, wandering about the nearby woods and streams, learning to draw the unfolding leaves, the singing frogs, the returning birds in their succession. From the first bluebirds with their plaintive song, all the way through the cheery robin, bobolink, hermit thrush, and the whippoorwill."

"You learned to savor the natural world," he said in a strange yet sympathetic tone.

"Yes. And though I'd missed the advantages of my older siblings during my family's prosperity, I was precocious in my studies and draftsmanship. At my mother's insistence, to give her her due, I went on to a university education."

At that moment, as with every brief encounter, our empathy seemed to align. But I was soon due to return to America and Ruskin was so busy with his own researches that our acquaintance remained shallow. How could I have known then that he was to become the very engine of my ever more desperate peregrinations and obsessions?

Chapter 2

Later, in 1861, on one of my return trips to London, I received from Ruskin a playful note:

> I hear from mutual acquaintance you have returned! You will be amused when I tell you, my dear Stillman, that the debates which took place between 'Soapy Sam' Wilberforce, Bishop of Oxford, and Mr. Huxley ended, I cannot deny, rather in Huxley's—and therefore Mr. Darwin's—favor. The most singular highlight of which is now bandied among people of fashion and people of science. It is this: Wilberforce, after striding into the room like a god about to dispose of one merest mortal's folly, asked Mr. Huxley whether he were descended from an ape on his mother's side or his father's, received without the slightest decorous pause, this rejoinder from Huxley: "I'd rather have an ape for an ancestor than an intellectual prostitute like the bishop." You can imagine the uproar, the sheer fun and mayhem these remarks sparked. And that was just the beginning of it....

At that time, I still felt considerable warmth for the man, and I understood that his note was an overture in recompense for certain arguments we'd had a year earlier during our tour of Switzerland together. But paying my respects to him, I was much intrigued when he introduced me to a compatriot who happened, like me, to be visiting him while in London: the talented Mrs. Allegra Fullerton. Their friendship went back to their first meeting in a gallery in Florence, Italy, in the 1840s. As sometimes happens, you know a compatriot by reputation but never meet him, or her, until your two paths cross by chance while on separate excursions abroad.

In her early years, as a young widow, she pursued her liberty and her art across New England and Europe. Now she had escaped an America splitting asunder in civil war. While she was using the opportunity to exhibit and sell her paintings, she was, like me, pinning her hopes on the possibility that England, and conceivably Europe, would not be dragged into the American Armageddon.

One would hardly have guessed her age (which Ruskin gave me reason to believe was forty-some-odd years) from the preservation of her beauty. At her invitation I later went to her painting rooms where she kept a small exhibition gallery. Her oils were mostly portraits, of real accomplishment, and a few landscapes in early stages of development. She had been selling landscapes for some time, she told me when I inquired, based on her American and European travels, but had just begun this new work since arriving in London.

Though we differed by at least a decade in age, we had certain experiences in common. In her early years she had been an itinerant artist, while I had my first lessons from one, Mr. John Wilson. She had studied with a friend of Thomas Cole—George Spooner—while I had corresponded with Cole, an ardent student of Turner. Cole had agreed to take me on as his pupil just before his death in 1848. I had brief acquaintance with Asher Durand, as she had, while I was trying to become his pupil following Cole's demise, and then with Frederick Church, who, unlike Durand, had allowed me into his studio for the term of a single winter. And we had both taken our art studies abroad —she before me, of course—when I was hardly more than a youth.

We soon felt at ease in one another's company. While we sat in her rooms before ample windows, she asked about my friendship with Ruskin. I told her that for all the aberrations of his personal life, Ruskin was to my mind a man of wisdom (a man whose works, George Eliot would come to say, were "among the highest writings of the age").

"I see him as a prophet," I told her, "whose critique of the direction of European civilization only posterity, no doubt, will be able to appreciate."

She held her tongue, so I went on. "I'm still a little in awe of him, but I've been disillusioned somewhat as to our personal compatibility."

"Indeed?" she said, one eyebrow lifted slightly. "How so?"

"During my second return to England in 1860," I told her, "Ruskin invited me to join him in early June at Geneva—to travel together, along with his old guide Joseph Couttet. Ruskin believed I might be of help to him while my own sketching improved under his tutelage. We would pursue young Turner's July 1802 trip, following the peace between Britain and France when hordes of English travelers sallied forth to Paris. Turner and his friend, the amateur artist Newby Lowson, however, had passed through Paris and headed straight for Switzerland in high summer, as we were to do nearly sixty years later, when, as Ruskin promised, 'the Alps would be most visible in the bright air, the crags and rocks barest of snow, the grass greenest and sky bluest, and the mountain storms as sudden as they are omnipotent'."

She laughed. "Of course you joined him."

"Of course."

"But...?"

"But I had one doubt. You see, my fiancé Miss Laura Mack back in America hadn't expected I would extend my art studies in England to a trip without clear end on the continent. Nonetheless, I foolishly

14

persuaded myself that no self-respecting art student would decline this opportunity."

Not knowing Mrs. Fullerton at all really, I was unsure how to continue. Mrs. Fullerton's beauty was not that ferocious, intimidating kind. Rather it was more open and direct, as was her demeanor, as if she had long ago cast off all commonplace inhibitions and prejudices. Her very presence encouraged me to speak—even of my own folly. And since in this intimate memoir I am being honest judging the failings and virtues of others, I have promised myself to be brutally honest about my own.

I plunged forward, "Looking back on these events, I count as one of the great errors of my life the letter I wrote Laura begging her indulgence. We left before her reply would have had a chance to reach me."

"I believe there's a name for men who act like that," she said, a mischievous glint in her eyes.

"I hardly need reminding." I looked away. "Perhaps I'd better not go on."

"You have to go on, Mr. Stillman. You've begun to tantalize me with your tale of far travels with friend Ruskin."

I would have to hold back certain events, out of delicacy toward her sex, but I thought I might offer some sense of our rambles and disputes.

"Ruskin," I began, "proved from our first rendezvous—ten days at the Hotel des Bergues in Geneva—to be a most hospitable and kind companion. But our methods and temperament differed, as when we first climbed the Saleve to admire the distant view of Mont Blanc."

"Byron's monarch of mountains," she interposed.

"To be sure, Mrs. Fullerton. Anyway, I admired and proposed to sketch, instead, the flora, some soldanella and gentians immediate to us. As you no doubt know from your own travels, in such valleys the globe ranunculus, mixed in profusion with purple vetch and orchis, and the long grass waving over moon daisies, yellow pansies, scarlet poppies, and wild geraniums, can be so dazzling that I suppose one's eyes must finally lift to the creamy snow fields of Mount Blanc and its aiguilles for relief."

"Well said, Mr. Stillman."

"Soon thereafter we set out on sketching excursions from Perte du Rhone, and then on to Bonneville, to St. Martin on the Arve, and to Chamonix. Chamonix, Ruskin told me, since his first arrival there had always been the home of his heart."

"He once told me," she said, "that Chamonix was where he was inspired to write those four brilliant essays on political economy for *Cornhill.* To be collected as a book next year, I believe he mentioned."

"That inspiration doesn't surprise me. Still," I continued, "you see, I was unable to discipline myself to his workmanlike approach. I was motivated to study and sketch only that which caught my attention or moved me. As a result I turned in some bad work he had set me to, which caused considerable tension between us. I was restituted only when I happened on some tasks he set that I unexpectedly found inspiring. The results of these he rather admired."

"Was the incompatibility, then, due to your differing work habits?"

I could not then tell her how my mind during these Swiss excursions was oppressed by what William Rossetti had told me of Turner's "unseemly" work.

"The two of us," I told her instead, "would spend our evenings playing chess and conversing, often till midnight. Our congeniality made me careful not to do anything more that might disturb our peace. It became clear to me that Ruskin already had suffered from some degree of theological doubt. Judging from his remarks, I calculated that these pricks of negative conscience had begun to afflict him about 1858."

I did not say this was the very year Ruskin had discovered the master's salacious illustrations. Instead, I said, "Though ten years his junior, I now discovered I had freed myself before him from the coarser bonds of dogma and creed that enmeshed our two boyhoods."

She nodded her head. "The poor man's greatly afflicted from his mother's religious mania."

"He'd hinted at that. In any event, Charles Darwin's *Origin* had been one of his themes in our conversations—a kind of sore to which he constantly returned. He asked what I made of the 'wicked book.' Everyone had read the opprobrious prose launched against Mr. Darwin from Herschel and Sedgwick, accusing him, to reduce it to essentials, of 'rank materialism.' In our debates, Ruskin feigned support of Darwin's adversaries, which included the very captain of the *Beagle*, now *Admiral* Fitzroy, who outright disavowed his former shipmate and shook his Bible, like a saber, at him in public."

"Anyone who actually reads a little of Darwin," she offered, "recognizes his belief in divine force animating creation."

"I taunted him one evening, saying, 'I think the problem, at bottom, is fear of admitting our animal nature'."

She laughed. "How did he respond to that?"

"So you would have us nothing but animals, Stillman?"

She smiled, encouraging me to go on.

Sitting in her rooms, the afternoon light beginning to wane beyond the large windows, I began to feel overwhelmed by memory. My entire debate with Ruskin rose before me like an old dream I was dreaming all over again.

* * *

17

I once again saw myself arguing with Ruskin. "No. But animals as well as whatever's higher in us. I myself no longer take it as a matter of either-or."

"You no doubt embraced Robert Chambers as well!" he came back without a blink of hesitation.

"I was too young to 'embrace' Chambers, or Lyell earlier, or anyone else in the time of their public agonies." I laughed at my little joke. "I was a mere child and then an unthinking undergraduate."

When he smiled, I charged ahead. "But if there's any merit in Darwin's thesis," I went on, "then there must be credit to Chambers', whether or not one accepts Chambers' conclusion that we spindle-legged anthropoids can hardly claim the zoological superiority that millennia of theology have promised us." I myself was struggling with these questions at the time, but I began to take pleasure in debating my mentor.

"To deny us anything beyond the animal is to deny the possibility of art," Ruskin said.

"To deny our animal essence is to deny the possibility of civil life," I rejoined, "to tame our arrogant separation from the judicious proportions of nature. Which separation always breeds hypocrisy and corruption in the affairs of men."

"You Americans are so ambitious." He looked at me with more than a little consternation.

But before he could thrust home one more point, I parried with a hint of my real purpose. "Is that not, perhaps, my dear Ruskin, worthy of your hero's own understanding? Didn't Turner's endless versifications in his *Fallacies of Hope* connect humanity irrevocably with the earth—with all nature? Wasn't he teaching humility and self-restraint?"

"One must be on guard against one's own arrogance, William," he said.

He meant to go on, but I interrupted him. "I know you're speaking for the pleasures of argument, my friend. Rather than quibble, let's consider Turner's depictions of the human form," I suggested. "Our deformities and glories, but always the realities of flesh—flesh under the burden of labor, and flesh under the burden of passion."

* * *

A bell tower some distance off rang the hour, shaking me out of memory even as I was telling Mrs. Fullerton of my debate with Ruskin. She rose, consulted a mantle clock, and said, "You must tell me the rest of your tale, Mr. Stillman. But I've an appointment in about thirty minutes that requires preparation."

I therefore invited her to dinner the next Friday. She refused out of her habit of eating light throughout the day, so as not to interfere with her work, and take her main meal in the evening. I altered my invitation accordingly, and at her suggestion we arranged to meet at the Sabloniere restaurant in Leicester Square— an establishment frequented by artists and writers and where, the following year, Lizzie Siddal was to take her last meal with husband Gabriel Rossetti before going home to minister herself a fatal dose of laudanum.

* * *

That Friday evening we were sitting over our bottle of wine when Mrs. Fullerton returned us to my travels with Ruskin. "Did he begin to suspect you of some…ignoble purpose?"

I looked right at her and startled myself to realize I could not possibly continue down the road my tale had been heading. "Well," I said, biding time, "he didn't wish to speak of fleshy passions, as you can imagine."

"And your conversation ceased, but left bad feelings between you?"

"Yes," I said.

She merely looked at me.

"My ambitions are much reduced," I added.

"Is that what Ruskin meant when he said you're to be Consul at Rome—that you've gone on to another line of work?" Her look became sympathetic.

"More or less."

"Did Ruskin also have something to do with your loss of ambition? During those travels in Switzerland?"

I was sorely tempted to broach the destroyed Turner sketches in some indirect fashion. She was a good listener, and her striking frankness tempted me toward frankness in turn. As she turned her plate away to the waiting woman, there was a look about her demeanor reminding me that Mrs. Fullerton was known not only for her uncompromising paintings and the energy of her intellect, but for her rather notorious affairs of the heart. Surely, I began to believe, she was a woman of the world enough to tell without any crude explicitness about the destruction of the Turner studies. I screwed my courage.

"Well, as you recall, I had mentioned Turner's painting of flesh."

"You begin to repeat yourself."

"I confess I had a deeper purpose, about which Ruskin expected nothing."

"Deeper purpose?"

"You see, at first he appeared not to discourage our debate, apparently taking some pleasure in those evening discussions. But finally I prompted him into a disquisition of the masters from whom Turner had learned to paint flesh. But when I queried him on the naked human form, he grew hesitant."

I stopped, not sure how to continue.

"And?" she said. "Please go on, Mr. Stillman."

I now understood that I had backed myself into telling her what had really come between my mentor and me. I decided to trust her and plunged forward into my tale. My telling it, I had no way of knowing then, would lead me on a quest lasting for years. But I told it, all caution abandoned, as if I had known this woman all my life.

Chapter 3

In the very midst of my debate with Ruskin over Darwin, I had introduced the topic of Turner's painting of flesh, giving me an opening to confront Ruskin with a question I had been trying to find a way to ask. "William Rossetti said something about numerous sketches, rather shocking apparently...perhaps not worthy of preservation."

Ruskin regarded me closely. "Rossetti? Ah yes, he assisted me for a time with the Turner trust." His face resumed its mild demeanor, but I could tell there was some discomfort, something held in reserve.

"Did you retain them in the collection?" I asked.

His blue eyes turned quite cold. And then as if he had made a sudden decision, he rather matter-of-factly said, "No." He paused a moment. "They were not worthy of it, the products of a certain disease of the mind which afflicted him at times. I burned them. His mother spent her last years in the madhouse and incurable hospital. Such distraction, perchance, ran in the family."

My face must have revealed more than I intended. "You don't approve? Speak out, William!"

"I'm merely surprised, John. I hadn't known about the destruction," I lied. "But as you say perhaps it was necessary. Still, I can't imagine myself destroying a single line of his work. It feels, as we speak, a little like killing off some portion of his life. However dark a portion."

It was then that his lip curled, on one side only due to a childhood injury from a dog bite. His anger brought home my growing conviction that, finally, the time to go our separate ways was drawing near.

"I'm not ashamed of what I did!" he said. I believed, however, that he had his doubts as well now, this man whose central dogma had always been the necessity of absolute and uncompromising truth in art. Yet as every gossip knew, here before me stood the man whose wife—a most appealing woman—finally divorced him after enduring years of unconsummated marriage; she even returned the £10,000 he had settled on her. But I didn't press him further; there was no purpose in doing so. I didn't trust my own growing anger.

By way of mitigating our dispute—I think on reflection that the flaring of his own anger surprised him—he added that his curiosity about the lewder elements of his hero's madness led him to pursue the mystery briefly. "It seems that Turner used to leave his dwellings on Fridays or Saturdays to go to his property at Wapping till Monday morning. There he consorted with stevedores and sailors. And their women! A secret life, the extent of which none of us knew fully before our discovery of the sketches and other personal papers. Some people knew of certain illicit relationships. And other indiscretions—during gatherings at country houses."

"Well," I said, "he was a healthy man with normal appetites, with a sensual life within sanctioned marriage if possible, outside marriage if not. Isn't his way less hypocritical than the common practice of keeping a hidden mistress beyond one's wife?"

"For a long time he struck me as rather greater than most mortals."

"So it was his mortality that shocked you?"

"Well, let's say a hero exposed."

"Turner, I understand, agreed with Sir Joshua Reynolds that an artist can be married only to his art," I said. "Yet is there anyone who believes Reynolds didn't count even Angelica Kauffman among his conquests? And Sir Thomas Lawrence, an equal pillar of academic respectability and painterly accomplishment—and Turner's good friend—was famous for his defeat of female virtue. Why, like most men and women they find the life of the body where they can. Would you deny them that? Would you absolutely insist on marriage, even a bad marriage, for such men of genius?"

"Why not marriage or celibacy?" he said to me. But I had seen him flinch at my phrase "bad marriage," so I did not thrust again with a vexing phrase in my thoughts—"marriage *and* celibacy."

Then he added: "Listen, William. I hear that argument all the time: the polyandrous Michelangelo, Fra Filippo Lippi seducing a nun, Rembrandt's devoted mistress Hendrickje Stoffels; Titian, Delacroix, and so on. What does all that 'married to art' on the one hand and self-indulgence on the other excuse in any particular man's behavior? Look, all my life I had viewed Turner otherwise." He stood up and began to walk in agitation about the room.

"And I can tell you," he went on, "this discovery of obscene studies and the extent of his secret life laid a great burden on me. What would anyone have done? I spent some weeks in a misery of indecision, until it dawned on me that perhaps I was the only one capable of coming to a decision on such a matter. Perhaps my discovery of the despicable images was…well, chosen, if that's not too vain a word."

* * *

"Too vain!" Mrs. Fullerton interrupted me at this point in my tale. "Too vain!" she cried out.

I focused once again on her intelligent face.

"I think I understand the falling out now," she added, "but—"

"Looking back on it," I interrupted in turn, "it's fortunate we soon separated that summer."

"So it seems," she said.

24

I rushed to finish my story. "While drawing a view of Neuchatel at the end of a season of grinding work, my eyes gave out. Something seemed to snap behind my eyes, my vision almost completely left me, and the most debilitating headaches ensued. I could no longer sketch or view landscapes. After a rest at Basel and Laufenburg, my vision returned and I began work on the subjects of one of Turner's *Liber Studiorum* engravings. But my eyes gave out again, with similar pain. Then Ruskin decided suddenly, and without explanation, that he must return to England.

"I traveled under his care back to Geneva, where he set out for home, after he wrote a letter I dictated to my fiancé back in Cambridge, Massachusetts, deeply apologizing for my recuperative delay. I then set out for St. Martin, where I spent the rest of that autumn, hoping to heal my wounded eyes. It seemed as though my summer with Ruskin, for all its adventure, ended in catastrophe. I had abandoned my Laura and lost faith in myself as an artist."

She looked at me with a convincing empathy.

"And you married Laura?"

"Best thing I ever did."

"Then you are fortunate indeed!"

I had the feeling that for all her good wishes, she was hardly finished pursuing our Turner discussions. My intuitions, I've discovered, are often correct.

"Had you ever actually met the great J. M. W. Turner?" she asked.

"Yes, once only, a strange meeting."

"Strange?"

"I met him when he was an old man. The same year I met Ruskin, and in the same gallery. In 1850, I'd sailed for London. Among my letters of introduction was one to artist James Baker Pyne, a follower of Turner whom I esteemed above all others, save Turner himself. We got on well. I'd walk the six miles to Pyne's house from my lodgings on Bouverie Street on Sundays, and after an early dinner we'd talk art and artists the rest of the afternoon. He soon understood my desire to learn more of Turner, whom he told me had been quite ill. So he recommended me to Mr. Thomas Griffith, Turner's agent and a dealer in pictures.

"I had begun paying visits to Griffith's gallery and acquainting myself with the owner. For some reason he took to me, perhaps my boyish enthusiasm. Once I began to view Turner's work first hand, which I had known in America chiefly through the initial volume of *Modern Painters*, I understood Turner's greatness in comparison with Pyne. Pyne, I now understood, put all his work through the provenance and test of a theory, thereby restricting his art to little more than a prodigy of technique.

"I asked Mr. Griffith about Turner's illness. He appreciated my concern and explained that the artist was still well enough to keep an eye on every painting and sale; that, in fact, he even kept back some of his paintings if he did not approve the buyer.

" 'For example,' Griffith told me, mischief in his smile, 'his *Temeraire*, which he always called "my darling," Turner refused to sell to the American collector James Lenox, who had offered him £500! And then refused again when Mr. Lenox offered him a blank check!' He threw up his hands in mock exasperation and laughed."

"I've heard something of all that," Mrs. Fullerton said.

"Yes, well, a few days later Griffith sent me a note to say the old master was again ambulatory and coming into his shop on business at a certain time. The date he gave was on the eve of my sailing back to America, which circumstance he knew from my having told him.

"I immediately went to the gallery and, making myself inconspicuous over various prints, waited for the unsuspecting old gentleman to come through the door. Right on schedule he entered. Eventually Griffith called to me and I went over, whereupon he introduced me as 'Mr. William James Stillman, a young American artist who is making a study of your work, sir.'

"The old man with a beaked nose seemed ill and diminutive. Yet he fixed me with his penetrating eye, like an eagle about to eviscerate a rabbit, and stood utterly straight, almost leaning backwards. An aura of restless energy emanated from him, and I was humbled and confused as he fixed me there. I remained speechless, until I extended my hand. This he refused, placed his hands behind him, and peered at me with a sort of malicious good humor.

"I turned away, horrified at some gaffe I must have committed, and walked back to the corner whence I had come. But I glanced back to see that he now held out his hand. His eyes suddenly were kind as they examined my face, yet strangely luminous, like those of a clairvoyant. He indulged me in brief conversation and, finally, amidst a good deal of harrumphing and nodding, interposing, perhaps, an invitation: 'If you come to England again...' or some such incomplete statement."

"Wouldn't he have died shortly thereafter?" she asked.

"Yes, and before my return, so I was never able to take him up on his half-baked invitation; I doubt he'd have remembered me anyway. But that odd meeting didn't diminish my appreciation. For to my mind he's the greatest artist since Hogarth, Gainsborough, Constable, and Reynolds, and superior to them all. Indeed, even today I ask you with confidence, Mrs. Fullerton: Where is the original painter in all British history who surpasses Turner?"

"You shan't get an argument from me. Yet I wonder, Mr. Stillman: you said that William Rossetti first told you about the Turner sketches Ruskin destroyed. But you haven't told me how Rossetti knew Ruskin had done it and then came to reveal the destruction to you."

As we finished the wine, I could see now she was not going to let me off the hook. She wanted to grasp in its entirety the tale I had begun and returned to at her instigation. And I felt as if I had been cornered by this bewitching woman again and again into revealing far more than I ever intended to. Had I become helpless in her hands? As we finished our dessert, I revealed the story of Rossetti's first of several revelations that were to change my life.

Chapter 4

I should mention that in 1855, on Ruskin's recommendation, William Rossetti had become my English correspondent for the Crayon, an American journal of art and letters that John Durand and I founded with the encouragement of such New England luminaries as Appleton, Bryant, Lowell, Longfellow, and Norton. It was established on Ruskinian principles, but ran all too soon from immediate success to disaster, due to my broken down condition from overwork and my failure to garner the proper support of advertisers.

As I was renewing my acquaintance with Rossetti during an extended trip to England in 1860, he let slip something about Ruskin's discovery of "a large number of Turners, I assure you, Stillman, of a great degree of indecency." I asked what he meant. He demurred, but on my insistence began to open up.

Ruskin had admitted to him, he told me, that in one of the tin storage boxes he found the most disturbing images imaginable, the result of the master's darker, indeed madder, side—"some deep taint of vileness and vice, some diseased element of himself," as Ruskin had put it.

"He was so obviously troubled by his discovery," Rossetti continued, "that I encouraged him to confide in me as a tonic to his own distraction. 'I've always believed,' Ruskin told me, 'that the good and pure and beautiful—especially as to color and form—are manifestations of the divine.'"

Rossetti said that when Ruskin seemed unable to go on, he prompted Ruskin by suggesting that the study of the naked human form, of both men and women, throughout the ages, teaches us that the human body in all its postures and appurtenances is a fit subject for pen, brush, and mallet.

"He looked at me as if I were a schoolboy," Rossetti told me. "Then Ruskin said: 'Yet you haven't yourself seen the scurrilous objects of which I speak. I'm not speaking of a Michelangelo or a Phidias in this instance, I assure you'."

"And he described some of what he had found?" I asked.

"He finally blew out a breath," Rossetti explained. "Then went into a rant: 'Women, with men and without, in every posture of abandonment! Sketches of the pudenda of women, Rossetti! Like studies of flowers by the coldest prying eye....' He hung fire; the mere memory had defeated him." William Rossetti looked at me as if he wished to be done with it himself.

Studies of flowers? I thought. Then a fleeting tremolo of intuition: petals inviting, provoking the male seed in order to grow and bloom ever and again—ever to become, ever to be, as if at the behest of some transcendent, some divine force or will.

It was then he told me what I have recounted earlier of Ruskin and Wornum's desecration of offending material in Turner's bequest, with, apparently, the knowledge of a few Gallery trustees.

I wondered at the time what an account from Ruskin's own mouth would amount to, and whether such an account might ameliorate the outrage I felt. But as I sat before William Rossetti, the feeling that he was withholding something about the whole affair kept nettling me.

"You viewed them?" I finally asked Rossetti. "These scurrilous pictures?"

"Only when I protested the violence I suspected he was about to do. He showed me several, so that I would want them burned myself, I assume."

"And? Did you?"

"Want to burn them? No, of course not. They'd be illegal, possibly. They would be, I believe, more offensive than those obscene prints so readily available in Holywell Street, before Chancellor Campbell's reforms. But they might've been sealed away somewhere. Out of public view for years, or forever for that matter. I speak of the general public."

"But you did nothing to try to save them?"

His large, gentle southern eyes gave me a look I had not seen from him before, as if I had accused him of some horrific violation. I let the thrust of my question strike home.

"There were, he told me, scores of them," he finally said. "I was a mere assistant. Ruskin was Hell-bent."

"I appreciate your position, William, believe me. But could nothing be done?"

I saw that I had wounded him and uttered some words of apology.

What would I have done in Rossetti's place? I asked myself, as we sat there staring at the fire. I think we were both stunned, he all over again in recounting the incident. Could Rossetti, whom I had come to know and trust as a friend, have really done nothing? This man of the greatest sensibility for art and a most wonderful understanding and humanity? This man whom Pauline Lady Trevelyan had called "one of the best informed and balanced minds I have had the luck to know"? Would I have had the courage to challenge Ruskin or to try by any means to save some representative portion of the condemned folio?

I looked at my friend, bald at an early age, in his moustache and muttonchops, his impeccable civil servant's coat, collar, and tie with pin, and I thought that it was entirely possible he *had* done nothing. From his youth William had been a radical idealist and student of art and literature, but now his whole family depended on his income at the

Excise Office. Like Mr. Trollope, he was a man whom necessity sentenced to years of clerkship, but unlike Trollope, William had subjugated his talents to the financial security of others. He was the solid core of his frayed family, and his brother Gabriel above all had used his selfless toil as the rock upon which to found his own self-indulgent, bohemian life.

When I asked whether he, William, at the time had private access to the work, he answered indirectly. "I was only one of several assisting Ruskin then. But some other depictions were later found, very few, that Ruskin simply consigned to a particular tin box of waste materials marked **'Valueless. Two or three grotesque figures left in it.'** "

* * *

"You mean to say there were... *scores* of specimens of this material?" Mrs. Fullerton asked as soon as I completed the story Rossetti had told me. She understood immediately the enormity of the holocaust. She was not a woman one had to explain things to.

"Ruskin said scores, first, and later hundreds; he may have been exaggerating, I don't know."

She seemed to peer right into me, then gathered her speech again, almost breathless. "A man such as he, an artist himself, would have to be mad to destroy Turner's work. Were they really so terrible?"

"Rossetti assured me most would find them utterly obscene."

"Twaddle!" Her voice sounded as if she had tasted something disgusting.

"Madness," I said. "Rossetti tells me he had seen Ruskin suffer severe episodes of melancholia."

She kept her gaze on me. "Only those few in the tin box survived? You're sure? And you've seen nothing of them?"

I hesitated. Immediately I knew that she understood what my hesitation meant. I would not be able to fool her, nor did I really want to lie as if to protect her conscience or sensibility. So I said, "I've seen them, those very few. The only ones, I was given to understand."

"According to Rossetti?" She kept looking at me as if testing my veracity, or his.

"Yes. But ever since I've been wondering if there might be something to these sketches—"

"Some profundity?" she interrupted me.

"And some *clue*, perhaps. To the public work."

She nodded.

"Well then," she said, "Ruskin and Wornum inflicted an irrecoverable wound, but if one doesn't laugh at the picture conjured in one's mind of such punctilious gentlemen discovering the Turner sketches to their mutual horror, one surely must scream or weep instead."

I felt heartened that she neither counted my tale against me, nor misinterpreted my intent.

We finished our dessert in silence, as if we understood that each of us wished now to consider what I had just revealed. As we prepared to leave, she said, "Rossetti. He's the one you should approach, don't you think?"

I hesitated, not sure I took her meaning. Then it became clear to me. "About any other surviving studies? Perhaps absconded?"

She nodded yes.

"I had secretly wondered the same thing myself," I said, smiling confidently. "I know there's something he's not telling me, and I've been convincing myself he never would've let them all be destroyed had he caught slightest wind of what they were about to do."

"There you are, then," she said, rising from her chair. As I escorted her toward the restaurant door, she added, "Precisely my own thoughts. Rossetti's our man."

* * *

Emboldened by Mrs. Fullerton's encouragement, I still could not during the following week make up my mind quite how to approach Rossetti. How to question his veracity? How to get this fine man to "confess," after all, to lying to me, and to a violation of John Ruskin's trust—no small thing among his circle. While I vacillated and divagated, Mrs. Fullerton swept into my rooms one day wearing an audacious purple walking costume—rather the color of French lilacs—and a sunset-colored wool shawl, both of which complemented her complexion.

"And the issue of this Rossetti business?" she asked peremptorily, after a brief exchange of pleasantries.

I looked away. "I haven't seen him yet, I'm sorry to say." She stood there as if awaiting an explanation from a wayward schoolboy. "Government matters have absorbed my attention."

"Government matters! My dear Stillman, such shilly-shallying only diverts your attention from any last chance to discover or even secure some rare portion of the master's work. You've given me to believe you're an artist."

"So I once was. But as I've explained, that's not my purpose in being here."

She removed her hat and threw it on a chair.

"I assure you, Mrs. Fullerton, I intend to see him very soon."

"You intend." She shook her hair and stood there looking at me, but I could not hold my eyes to hers. Finally she added, "I should hope it's very soon, indeed!"

"It is."

"You're sure? Would you like me to accompany you? I know the Rossettis."

She was one of those women whose disconcerting sensual magnetism, even in mid-life, seemed to breathe from every pore through no conscious effort on her part. But I was learning she could be irritating nonetheless. I looked right at her now and said, "Wouldn't your presence rather make him all the more reticent?"

"You're no doubt right," she acknowledged after a moment's thought. She looked at me a bit longer, and then added, "I take it your courage has failed you."

I was beginning to feel humiliated. I stared like a bumpkin at the russet ribbon and pendant around her lovely throat.

"It's not a matter of courage," I said. "Anyway, I shall go soon, alone, and sound him."

She took a step closer and put her hand on my right arm near the shoulder. The softness of her touch weakened me. Her eyes again plumbed me. Again, I felt no longer in control of my own will. "See that you do," she said. "I'll take you to supper this time."

I looked right back at her. "You see right through people, don't you?"

"When I was young I took it as a gift. But as I grow older it feels more like a curse."

"Curse?"

"It's not always pleasant seeing through people you like."

"Tests the friendship?"

"I've learned to live with it," she said and turned. She picked her hat off the chair, sat, balanced the hat on her lap, and smiled. "Have you a glass of Sherry, Stillman?"

While I poured two glasses, she added: "Just send your card around with a date, please. So you can tell me what Rossetti said."

Chapter 5

What I had not yet explained to Mrs. Fullerton was how my position as Consul to Rome arose out of my much-delayed reunion with Laura.

Following my travels in Switzerland with Ruskin, my eyes had gradually improved while I rested at St. Martin. So I returned to Paris to winter over before sailing home to America. I began to receive old and new letters from my fiancée. She knew from my letters that I had suffered an illness. Laura's letters asked after my plans, but stoically withheld her deepest apprehensions.

I knew that there was a side of her—call it a tenderness of sensibility—that seemed fitting to her petite stature. And although through her family she had cast off the religious fervors of her more rampant Baptist relatives, there remained some gloomy wisps of glory trailing Laura's person as she made her way in this world. The other side of her, which attracted me from our first meeting, was her core of strength and free-thinking. She had been born at Brook Farm, the experimental community outside Boston, and her advanced Unitarianism felt like ballast to my upbringing in a veritable stew of Calvinistic zeal. It was perhaps her independent mind that withheld her doubting of me, but her mother Maria Barstow Mack and her father Dr. David Mack—a prominent lawyer, with whom I had boarded while painting scenes of picturesque Cambridge—had no such reticence.

"Mr. Stillman," Dr. Mack wrote, "you know our eldest daughter Laura well enough to understand that she hesitates to play the distraught girl pining for her adventurous love. But I take this opportunity to tell you that she is profoundly perplexed by your prolonged absence. I do not say she doubts or disbelieves your constancy. But she has, you must admit, sufficient grounds, and we fear for her reason if you do not return."

I hadn't doubted my love for Laura, but I now understood that my affections from a distance were insufficient and selfishly, if unintentionally, cruel. *We fear for her reason....* I had been distracted by my self-indulgent fascination with Ruskin and my convalescence.

So I sailed at once for America, and Laura and I were married. Before long, we returned to France. Our plan was to honeymoon in Paris and then travel down into Normandy with the spring of 1861. We wanted quiet living so that I might, as I finally did, recover my vision sufficiently to continue nature study and regain some measure of power in my drawing. But our intentions were thwarted. The American Civil War rousted me from my quiet, happy life in Normandy, and Laura and I returned home.

The frailty of my vision being still apparent, however, I was not accepted into the Union Army as a combatant, despite several efforts. Seeking some means by which to earn our living and serve the Northern cause, I was finally, through various associates (including my old mentor Dr. Eliphalet Nott, president of Union College) able to obtain a post as Consul at Rome.

By then Laura's pregnancy with our firstborn was advanced, and her family insisted she stay behind during her confinement.

Laura wanted to rebel, to thwart their wishes; but upon considering the inconveniences of ocean travel and settling in a foreign city without friends or family, she acquiesced. I shall never forget Laura standing before me on the Boston docks as I was about to depart. The tears in her eyes as she looked up in the full bloom of her pregnancy caused me a great sense of loneliness already.

"We shall be together again, my dear," I said, "as soon as you and the child are strong enough to make the long journey. It shan't be long."

"The heart disdains the head," she said. "Time will pass slowly for me until the baby is born. For you, who are to be so busy, time will pass quickly." She looked down. "But we've been all over this; my staying behind is the only responsible thing to do."

"Still, I understand that it feels all too soon, after we've finally come together."

"Much too soon," she agreed, "but it'll be good to have our independence—and to contribute to our government's cause." I worried about her occasional propensity for dejection, and I felt that dejection as we stood there so close to one another. When she looked up at me again, however, her face was determined, her gaze steady. "You must stay true to me, darling," she said.

"Of course, my dear." She said nothing. "I promise," I added. "We shall remain true to one another."

She reached up and embraced me awkwardly—our heights so disparate, her stomach so large. I felt a tremor of sorrow ripple through her body. We stepped back and held hands a moment longer, looking in silence at one another. Then I turned to board ship.

* * *

En route to Rome that November of 1861, I traveled alone by way of England to deliver U.S. government correspondence and to report back on the temper of the English, who were throwing their support to the South. I looked to my old friend William Rossetti to give me a realistic sense of how the British government was leaning. So I invited him to dine at the Wellington on Piccadilly one evening.

"What can they possibly be thinking?" I asked Rossetti. "This British ruling class!"

His face turned serious. "I'm afraid your Confederate politicians know our rulers see benefits—as to trade, to our political and industrial dominance—from a separate, reactionary government in your South."

"And revenge?"

"Well, Will, no healing some old, old wounds." He laughed quietly. "But when your Union warship forcibly removed those two Confederate commissioners sailing for London, you rather played into the opposition's hands."

"But we contest their very right to establish separate diplomatic relations—we contest it with our own blood."

"If your President will respond to our leaders' ultimatum," he said, "disaster will be averted, and you may travel on to Rome."

"Our minister, Charles Adams, tells me war with England is entirely possible—flaring into an American-European war, a disaster indeed for our civilization," I said. "And I must say, I'm tired of hearing American merchants insulted in the streets and, from what our Consul at Liverpool told me, in the Exchange."

"Mr. Lincoln's response will defuse the bomb," he said, completely serious again. "The Queen herself has resisted all measures that might precipitate hostilities. And her closest advisor, the Prince Consort, wishes to avoid war. He's a moderating influence against powerful war mongers."

That December when the Prince died of typhoid fever, I would recall Rossetti's words and come to believe Albert's death sealed his influence in the Queen's grieving heart.

We debated the possibilities of war between our countries until we finished the meal. By then, as we settled over our cognacs, we felt so oppressed by the looming danger that I diverted the conversation.

"I've thought a great deal during the last two years, William, about the destruction of those Turner sketches."

He smiled as if he understood how, even for one who had not seen them, the pictures gathered curiosity. "As have I," he said, snifter in hand. "But there's no turning back the clock."

"I must confess that my imagination was overactive during a long and lonely convalescence," I told him, "but I confess as well to something more. Perhaps a vain hope that there was some clue in the secret work to the grand public works we know."

"Some Rosetta Stone?" He chuckled.

"Or Rossetti Stone?" I laughed with him. "It's not an utterly wild speculation, is it, my friend? Can't one hope that some survived?"

"Some? Well, as I said when, I believe, we last took up this subject, a few remained. And the fire had already burned. I think the heart had gone out of Ruskin for further immolations."

"No one tried to save any before the fire?"

"Remember, those of us assisting were not in a position to." He swirled his cognac slowly and gave me a quizzical look.

"But surely if there were scores as Ruskin has said, he would not have missed a dozen spirited away to some safe corner. He had not catalogued them, after all, had he?"

It was then I saw something in my friend's eyes that convinced me I had touched a nerve. "No," he said, and contemplated his snifter. I didn't wish to press him hard at the time, but he must have felt the growing awkwardness, for he added, finally, "I'm prepared to try one avenue to slake your curiosity, which I must say threatens to drive you to monomania, Will." As we shared the same first name, he had early in our acquaintance taken to calling me Will. "Why don't you come with me to the South Kensington Museum, where the Turners are for now being stored, Saturday next. I'll try to arrange something through Ralph Wornum. Perhaps we can steal a look at those few remains."

"Perfect," I said. I knew he was using this offer as a ploy to change the tack of my questioning.

Nonetheless, that Saturday I met him as arranged at Hyde Park Corner and we had a pleasant noon-hour walk of a mile to the South Kensington Museum of the National Gallery at Brompton. Admission being free on Saturdays, we took a moment in the Glazed Court to examine current objects on loan—a Flemish group, as I recall—before meeting Wornum as scheduled in nearby administrative offices. Rossetti introduced me to Mr. Wornum, a rather daunting man, as a young American artist and friend of Ruskin's who had made a study of Turner. My interrogation was brief. Satisfied that I was knowledgeable and legitimate, Wornum opened the lower storage room for us where much of the vast Turner collection remained. For some reason, perhaps his trust of Rossetti and my Ruskin connection, he allowed us an hour in the room, so long as we left all implements, notebooks, and satchels of any kind upstairs. With little delay, Rossetti found two of the drawings I had come to see. It was then I realized just how familiar with the bequest he was.

The first he showed me was a watercolor of two women in bed together, done in Turner's "Swiss Figures" sketchbook, he told me, but it had been quickly and awkwardly executed, as if one of his mere notations for something more ambitious and compelling. The women in the sketch were nude, with light falling upon the torso of the nearer figure, and shadow obscuring the partially hidden body of the farther. They appeared disengaged, as if in some post-coital repose, perhaps in some degree of disillusionment. It was a disappointing work, both from its awkwardness of execution and for its serenity, its lack of joy or pleasure.

"This looks rather innocent," I said, "compared to what I've been hearing."

"Yes. Not equal in approach to the destroyed studies."

He rummaged some more and turned up a pencil, pen, and ink drawing that, unfolded and placed on the worktable before us, was far more striking and salacious once. On either side of the sheet fold were two nude figures in sexual embrace. On the left side, a man squatted on his knees while a woman lay supine beneath him. Both her knees were drawn up, one against the man, the other spread against the bedding. The male figure's face was turned away from the viewer, the woman's hidden by the back of the male figure's head, which made his ears curiously reminiscent of a faun's, or perhaps those of a Silenus, as if for a classical theme. The woman, in her appetency, reached up with both arms to hold the back of the man's head and shoulders. The man's right arm reached down between the woman's legs to stimulate her sex, his thumb teasing into her vagina and, barely noticeable, her tumescent bijou exposed. On the opposite leaf of the fold, two figures were sketched very partially. The clearest elements of the pen and ink drawing were the male figure's testicles, his penis inserted into the woman's vagina, her legs seemingly wrapped over his shoulders.

"Yes, I can see how this would inflame Ruskin's ire," I said. "More typical of the offending material?"

"Where there are two figures involved, yes. Some were drawn with more detail."

He turned the sheet over for me. Here among a vast number of faint pencil lines was the figure of a woman performing fellatio on a man. Rossetti fumbled a bit longer and turned up another sketch much obscured by rough lines. This one the obverse: a man performing simultaneous osculatory and digital stimulation on a woman's vulva.

Rossetti then managed to locate a final sample. It was an exceptionally obscure watercolor of two figures in the most common posture of recumbent copulation, perhaps in homage of Rembrandt's *The Bedstead*. But in Turner's painting, the watercolor had been washed to leave the figures barely discernible, as if the couple had been espied in the darkness of their candlelit bedroom by the stealthy painter. The darkness swirled around them in whorls or torrents reminiscent of the engulfing storms and seas of his paintings in the 1830s and '40s. It seemed to me to be the least offensive of the three. "What do you make of the obscurity?" I asked.

"It's of a piece of most of his nature studies at this time, is it not?" Rossetti said. "That search for sublimity through obscurity, or as Burke would have it, through 'uncertainty'."

"Is this an accurate character, these few you've shown me, of the whole?"

"Accurate of those that I happened to see," he said, beginning to put away the materials. "But not similar to his solitary female figures, especially in postures of display."

"And only these remain," I said.

"I don't have free access to the collection. There may be others yet undiscovered or merely hidden in the mass."

"I see. And there remains the possibility, I assume, that others were removed to save them from destruction."

"The possibility? There's always the possibility of anything. But who would have had the courage to risk it?" He carefully restored each picture to its former place.

We returned the key to Mr. Wornum, I offered our profuse thanks for the general illuminations a mere hour had brought me, and we left unhurried, stopping on our way out to see what hung of the Vernon and Sheepshanks collection from the modern British school: Wilkie, Leslie, Mulready, Creswick, and Cooke among them, and a very fine Reynolds, *The Age of Innocence*, which Rossetti told me cost the museum over £1500. We spoke little before walking out to catch separate hansoms. The silence that enveloped us was unusual for our friendship, each of us absorbed in contemplating the implications of what we had just observed in Turner's legacy.

* * *

In my hansom, I kept returning to what I had witnessed. What in the name of God had been the old man's intentions in the first place? Were the lubricious illustrations merely obscene graffiti, left behind on purpose to poke the eye of a hypocritical public: a sort of parting shot from a disturbed and disillusioned old man? Or, were they the private, natural channel of that stream of erotic stimulations Turner, both young and old, had experienced while observing the models in his life classes, the bodies of his lovers, and the private parts of his "sailors' women"? In short, were they a personal record of one man's erotic life—both lived and imagined—as recorded by a compulsive artist who, quite literally, sketched nearly every natural form he had ever encountered?

Or, were they Turner's typically literal observations and specifications—the merest data collected from reality—to be used in his construction of the greater, and far more respectable, emblems of the deeper energies flowing through humanity and nature?

Chapter 6

Now encouraged and maneuvered by Mrs. Fullerton's recent visit to my rooms and her convincing admixture of boldness, tenderness, and admonition, I finally called upon William Rossetti at home to confront him boldly. He kept a study and quarters in the house at 45 Upper Albany Street into which, upon his promotion at Inland Revenue, he had some years ago re-installed his mother, father, and sisters in London, after their period of self-exile in Frome, Somersetshire. "It is still the most congenial habitat for my labors," he previously explained, "out of long practice and the mutual interests of my family."

Rossetti came down immediately after I sent my card up to him.

We ensconced in his study and talked for some time of our current projects. Finally I came to the deeper point of my visit. "I've something I feel I must ask you, William," I said. "I ask it on the rock of our mutual respect and friendship. Our past collaborations and understandings. If I ask it, however difficult, will you tell me the whole truth of the matter?"

"Have I ever done otherwise?" he said, an eyebrow twitching upwards.

"All the more reason I rely on your integrity and our mutual affection."

"You look distraught, Will," he said. "You had better ask away." He laughed lightly to encourage me.

"Please take no offense, my friend. I understand why you've had to remain silent, if my suppositions are correct. But I've come to the point where I have to unburden myself, if nothing more. Did not you or someone else—you said others assisted Ruskin—preserve some small or greater portion of those disturbing drawings that were about to be destroyed?" He looked at me as if unable to speak. "There," I said, "I've put our friendship in your hands."

He looked away, then stood up and moved to the window. He bent over and opened the window wide, letting in a gust of air that billowed the curtains. Had I lost forever my friend and colleague? He turned toward me with a grave countenance.

"You are perhaps clairvoyant?" he said. His expression did not change.

I motioned him back to his chair. He sat down across from me, hesitating to speak still.

"Thank you, William," I said. "How many?"

"A comparatively small packet," he said. "A dozen or so."

"It took great courage on your part, my friend."

"It was confused desperation rather than courage, at the time."

"I admire you for it, William. Please, believe me."

"It was not so admirable a thing. There wasn't time to think about it once I realized their intentions."

"A dozen or so," I said, letting out a deep breath. I was comfortable again in his company for the first time since I had entered this house. "That's something. That's something, William. Thank God you did it."

"God had nothing to do with it. Had there been more time, I'd have talked myself out of it."

"But your quick action is laudable in any case. Can you tell me one more thing?"

"They are hidden in the room of a prostitute," he said.

"A prostitute."

"Yes. A friend of my brother's. She serves sometimes as his model. And, why not admit it, his mistress."

"How did your brother—Gabriel—come to posses them?"

"I knew no one who would be less prejudiced against them, no one who would be more capable of appreciating them, no one who would find a better way to keep them hidden from those who might ever be in search of them. I was one of the few, after all, who had access to them. Had they been missed, I'd have been suspected, immediately."

I recalled a remark of Gabriel Rossetti's to the effect that art and morality have nothing to do with one another. "I think you are quite right," I said. "A brilliant move, to go to your brother. But this prostitute, are you quite sure she's the best possible…curator? Has she even heard of Turner?"

"He didn't tell her about their being Turner's. But she's no four-penny knee-trembler, you understand. Anyway, she believes they're his own productions, given to her safekeeping as a trusted companion. Who else can hold such items? Who better to scorn the laws?"

"Yes. But they're of enormous value, are they not? Or some day shall be."

"Indeed, Will, but she doesn't know that, only that my brother places the highest value on them as his own. For that reason, he's assured me, they're as safe—safer—than anywhere else."

I must have looked incredulous.

"Look, Will," he finally said. "My brother trusts very few people and trusts institutions less. In our family it is he, despite the aspirations of the rest of us, who captured the Muse's breath. He's a man of genius and like so many of the type not known for his logic or practicality. Even what money he has, he never puts in the bank. And he would never consider a deposit box for his valuables. His money he keeps in a locked drawer. His idea of security is not like the ideas of more sober-minded men, like us. But considering the nature of these studies, I can't say that even I think he's made a fallacious choice. Had you seen them—and so many at once—you would understand his choice immediately."

"As you say, had I seen them," I said. "Is that not possible?"

"My brother's much indisposed. His wife's very ill; her life appears in danger. He's very troubled these days."

"Still, might you intercede? Wouldn't this other woman allow you to show them to me?"

"I suppose she might, but it wouldn't please Gabriel. He knows you; he'd want to take you there himself, I'm sure. And until his Lizzie is beyond utter loss, I think we'd better not trouble him. It's simply not the appropriate time, you see."

"But I leave for Rome soon, on my government's business, as you know." Images of the pictures' vulnerability flashed through my mind—fire, theft, water damage, violence, the harlot's death or expulsion: anything might be possible in the woman's chambers crowded into, I assumed, the most ragged neighborhood of the city. These were perhaps indeed brilliant temporary quarters, but temporary quarters were grossly insufficient. I was desperate to see them before it was too late, before they were inadvertently lost or destroyed forever. I imagined myself grabbing the contraband objects, clutching them to my chest, and fleeing London, the Rossetti brothers at my heels, while Mrs. Fullerton cheered me on.

"Surely," I said, "you can take me to them just once."

"Let me think about it, Will. Please don't press me at the moment. I'll do what I can." His voice trailed off, almost as if he were talking to himself. "Maybe my brother won't oppose it." He rose to usher me out. His handshake was firm and his smile genuine. I had hope. But I knew the longer he thought it over, the more arguments he would be likely to develop against my request.

Chapter 7

Back at my rooms, I could no longer dismiss a memory crowding my mind: my isolation and recuperation after my eyes failed me in Switzerland. I recalled how I had mused a great deal over Laura and my behavior toward her. And I suspected that it was my long separation from the woman I loved that had stimulated my fancy. That kept returning me to the sexual subterfuges that complicated the mysterious life of "William" Turner (as his friends called him). My imagination probed again and again his secret life at Wapping—the investment properties he had inherited from his uncle and turned into a tavern in 1827. Many a time, as I lay with eyes closed, breathing deep draughts of Switzerland's autumn air, my mind—with unbidden energy—created floods of images and questions. What compelled him at Wapping? How did J. M. W. Turner, distinguished member of the Royal Academy, and once a young genius patronized by the aristocracy, come to consort with navvies and whores? Was there some outbreak of nostalgia for his roots in the humbler orders—his father a barber—of the mercantile classes? If so, wouldn't he have stopped far short of "wallowing," as Ruskin had put it, in unseemly public houses and outright bagnios? And Pyne, in those endless London conversations, had said something to me once about Turner's youth. There had been some rumor of wantonness associated with his extensive journeys through English villages and countryside. Maybe the old rumors were true.

That such questions could no longer be answered, nor such rumors settled, did not deter my imagination from prying open a door to his hidden life. I would envision Turner, of a Friday evening, or perhaps Saturday afternoon, arriving in New Crane, Wapping. What? Seven miles from his 47 Queen Anne Street abode, where he cohabitates with Sarah Danby, or nearly twice that distance from Chelsea, where he later lives with the lusty Margate landlady, Mrs. Booth. His destination is the Ship and Bladebone Inn, on the waterfront but 200 yards from the great commercial and engineering enterprise in London of the time—the digging of Sir Marc Isambard Brunel's pedestrian tunnel under the river. A place of boatmen and laborers, the likes of which will appear in Turner's *Dido Directing the Equipment of the Fleet* and *East Cowes Castle—The Regatta Starting for the Moorings.* But Wapping is also the very center of his subterranean yearnings and obsessions. Even by the late 1820s, he is becoming ever more eccentric and duplicitous: he slips in and out of the Academy on Varnishing Days, gives (some would claim) incoherent lectures on perspective, and becomes shabbier in dress and appearance. Furthermore, he relates false stories about his identity to strangers he meets or employs, and later calls himself Mr. Booth or sometimes Admiral Booth. London Society has come to accept rumors of his madness. But some of the erotic drawings, Ruskin had estimated, predate this period of "public madness" by more than ten years when, even then, there had to be long lucid intervals when he accomplished brilliant and original work.

Indeed, while recuperating, lying on my couch with eyes closed and invention unleashed, I would one moment visualize with extraordinary detail and clarity sublime crags and eminences, as when Ruskin and I at St. Martin had left our Hotel de Mont Blanc one evening at sunset to stand on the elliptic curve of the single-arched bridge over the Arve and saw the huge dome of Mont Blanc come out. What is obscured by clouds, even in fine weather, emerges at that time of day, glowing in sunlight while the observer stands in shadow—this great rosy orb, appearing like a second, massive moon rising above the clouds. Gradually, the lower remaining clouds melt away and the entire mountain rises before you, the upper reaches still shining like a divinity. Then, but a moment later, I would see Turner the ambitious young painter, not yet an eminence, climbing among such heavenly prominences or suddenly earthbound, walking London's streets on his way to Sarah Danby, his sometimes figure model and mother of his two or three illegitimate children. And I would be reminded that even during these fruitful cohabitations, the inn was his place of assignation. Convalescence is an especially hard taskmaster of the imagination. With so much leisure, one has little control over the wanderings of fancy.

* * *

Imagine with me then as we, invisible companions, step off the omnibus or hired cab with Turner. Carrying his portmanteau filled with sketchbook, pencils, chalk, watercolors and equipment, and perhaps a change of stockings and linen, he is a short man, an egoist—not handsome, yet magnetic—with shaggy hair and a clean-shaven sailor's weather-beaten face that reveals dazzling, gray Ancient Mariner's eyes. He is by turns bold, shy, audacious, and confident. Among those aware of the art world, he is enormously famous—to some infamous—and by now a man of substantial wealth. The taverns, inns, and chop houses among which his property sits are not ramshackle; rather they look comfortably seedy as they slouch toward the waterfront, toward riverbank stairways and wooden balconies on piers arising out of river mud or water, depending on the tides. Many windows look out onto the river: its shipping and boating, its waterside laborers and lumber.

He has made his reputation largely on his marine paintings—this boat-man who handles paint with spectacular daring.

As landlord he would likely have a private room awaiting him; he looks forward to his dram and, later, his supper. His clothes frowsy, he enters the smoky bar parlor and is acknowledged by and speaking to a few of those who refresh themselves at bar and table. He loves to amuse himself with controversies of the day. Some customers he knows as regulars, certain others he greets as strangers. These are men who work on the water and at the waterside, and these are the blousy women who serve them. I do not imagine he needs the amatory serv-ices of the prostitutes who inhabit the waterfront. Perhaps he exercises an occasional peccadillo. But that is not his primary purpose on such weekend excursions. Instead, they are rather like his endless travels around the British Isles and Europe, when travel becomes feasible be-tween European wars and revolutions. These weekends are in fact sketching journeys, note-takings of the painterly sort. If he does not have to unearth and sunder corpses surreptitiously as Leonardo or Mi-chelangelo did, he in his own way makes clandestine studies of the human body and of the sexual postures of the species bent by the re-lentless storm of self-propagating lust.

Let us not fool ourselves. The student of anatomy and copulations is a man not only of high sensibility and discipline, but also a man of in-tense desires. His cold techniques of life studies are warmed by his life's blood. We would misrepresent the man if we view him as a mere observer, the disinterested anatomist, the man of heartless science. Let us say, therefore, that in his private room, chosen for its light, on this late afternoon or early evening when we have followed him, he affably converses with a woman on subjects that will not challenge her at-tainments. For all his reputed arrogance as a prodigy in the world of art, he is an able companion, like an old seaman full of boating lore, to the laboring men and women of Wapping. He has no need for arrogance here; in fact, it would not serve his art or himself. He has left his arrogance behind at the Royal Academy and the more respectable, competitive neighborhoods of the great smoky city.

The artist and woman are sharing a bottle of favored Sherry he has brought along. The wine, let us say, is Domecq, imported by none other than Ruskin's father. It gives the artist and his model a measure of delight in their undertaking. She is being paid for her time and considers his hiring her rather a lark, an intermission from coarser labors. She is perhaps Irish or German—sailors' women being seldom English. He retrieves his pen and handsome, leather-bound sketchbook from his portmanteau. On this afternoon, the fog does not encase the river and neighborhood; he pulls back the window curtains to increase the light to his advantage. He opens the window slightly, letting in a whiff of river mud with the brackish air. All the while they sip Sherry and talk of unimportant things, sharing a joke or two. His voice is deep and husky; his sentences hesitant, but full of wit and humor.

When his preparations have ceased, he adjusts his chair to face the bed. The woman rises, still chattering at her ease like an old friend (indeed, one suspects they are acquainted), and moves toward the bed. She sits, tests the comfort of the mattress, begins to disrobe unhurriedly. He opens the double polished latches of his sketchbook and makes himself ready to draw, testing with his eyes the indirect fall of light on his subject.

Naked now, the woman lies sidewise on the bed, her legs toward him, her head farthest away. He rises, asks her a question about the postures of her calling, and adjusts her. They agree on a position for comfort. He resumes his seat, peers studiously at the woman's raised knees, and begins to sketch. Their conversation dwindles as he concentrates on his work, and as the woman lying before him feels restful at her labors, within range of sleep. In his sketchbook a beautiful, accurate, technically adept drawing of her pudendum begins to unfold like the redolent whorls of a dark blossom.

Nearly an hour later, the good light somewhat obscured now, he thinks she might have fallen asleep, but he does nothing to rouse her. Her sleep, if anything, lends her humanity and increases his affection for this hard-working woman. He continues his sketch at his convenience, the legs and feet are completed, and now the stomach and breasts of a supine woman are appearing, sketched in roughly compared to the rest of the drawing. Does he rise to awaken her? Would he wish her to assume another pose, perhaps lying prone this time? Or might he touch her tenderly and sketch arousal?

Only the actual drawings and paintings would answer such questions. But at that time I believed, by all accounts, they had been destroyed.

Chapter 8

Before the week was out I sent a note to William Rossetti; his card returned immediately with a time and an address to meet him. It was a beer shop near a boarding house in Dean Street, Soho, the very epicenter of accommodation for London's whoredom, where women rent their seven-shilling furnished rooms by the week.

I sent a two-sentence note round to Mrs. Fullerton intimating my success thus far. It was not difficult to find one's way into such neighborhoods of London, although I doubt I would have ventured here after dark and alone. I passed all manner of street stalls and costermongers' barrows selling fruits and vegetables, toys, jewelry, combs and brushes, cutlery, stationery, baskets of firewood, and nearly everything else one might imagine. Many of the women—of all ages—appeared to be Irish, sitting on upturned bushels or three-legged stools and smoking their pipes. The men and boys were mostly working people and more than a few raggedly down on their luck. And there were children—regular street Arabs—in all their motley show of tattered dresses, trousers, and coats, often barefoot, but quick of eye and gesture.

Finally, I spotted the sign of the Dancing Pig and found my beer shop nearby. I was relieved to discover William there before me, for this was a mixed but rough looking crowd in London's den of thieves and mollies.

We sat at a dirty table with our pints of beer. The few about us were sharing a pail and looked to be the middle order of prostitutes—the dress not so high as some, but the powder and rouge and other make-up worthy of actresses at the Victoria Theatre.

A man I took for the landlord was a squat, thick fellow who must have been once a fighting man, given his massive neck and broken nose. He was having a joke with three other brutal-looking fellows loafing about the bar. One of the women started singing in her beer, her perhaps once-lovely voice crowing out the lyrics and tune of "The Dark-Eyed Sailor." When this was met with a round of bravos and applause, she immediately proceeded into "The Dandy Husband," followed by "The Week's Matrimony." In the middle of this last ditty, Fanny Cornforth, the woman William had arranged for us to meet, came in.

* * *

Over our beer, William had explained to me that Gabriel had moved the woman over to Tennyson Street in Battersea, to arrange for her a less scandalous address more proximate to his own lodgings at Chatham Place. "After all," he said, "Gabriel is married now and devotes much of his time to Lizzie." I took him to mean that this other inamorata filled her free time in these, her former haunts. "Fanny's bringing the sketches with her," he added.

He also told me that Fanny Cornforth was the nom de guerre she had given herself upon moving to London from a village in Sussex where her father was a blacksmith. Gabriel, he said, had grown obsessed with her. "If Lizzie is his Beatrice, Fanny is his Helen, his beauty-of-the-flesh. His Guinevere, his Lilith."

His face became grim. "She understands that Gabriel is not to know of our inspection of the drawings, so as to avoid upsetting him, to avoid giving him anything to distract his thoughts from the care of his wife."

"And she, this Fanny, has agreed to this?"

"She's always agreeable, as you shall see."

* * *

Now, before us stood Fanny herself. He introduced me as "the artist fellow I told you about who has an interest in Gabriel's drawings." She was a woman who, despite her profession, seemed to accept happily whatever the world sent her way, perhaps because, whatever the limits of her birth, the world had always served her well enough due to her stunning appeal. She was large and full-figured, handsome of face, sexual in the most open and unself-conscious way, with a head of wavy golden hair that must have reached the floor when fully loosed. I could see why Dante Gabriel Rossetti had chosen her for his model. She gave one the feeling that if sex was no mystery to her, neither was it entirely a matter of business, but rather a fine and mundane pleasure to be taken simply as nature's offering.

We spoke for a few minutes about brother Gabriel and then about the pictures. She rattled on in her engaging cockney talk, and finally said, "Well, it's for 'ese pictures, right?" She rose and headed toward the door. We finished our pints without hurry and went out.

We followed her at some distance, even though men following a woman up to her room caused no notice here. She did everything simply "by the way," even as she sat us on her bed, telling us to make room for the material to be placed between us. "I rent 'iss room by the week, some o' weeks I mean," she said. "Dependin' on whether I need a bit a' extry change. 'Appens I'm 'ere 'iss week." She laughed. Then, drawing a key out from her ample bosom, she went to a small bureau with a locked drawer and turned the key. She cautiously drew open the drawer and removed a packet wrapped in oilcloth, rather a large packet. As she unwrapped it, I discovered part of a broken sketchbook, several larger folded sheets, and a group of studies on small sheets.

"Go ahead," Rossetti said, "I've seen them before."

Mouth dry, hands shaking slightly in anticipation, I first picked the sketchbook off the mattress and opened it. Here I found pen and pencil studies of female genitalia—some almost medical in their detached precision; others warmer, engorged, treated tenderly like a rare lotus; some attached to legs and torsos quickly sketched in; still others alone like pulsing stars isolated through a telescope in the night sky. The more tenderly depicted gave the impression of having been lovingly drawn, as if with more than passing familiarity, as if the painter were seeking some profound, some ineffable, mystery in these women: their connection, it might have been, between their pleasure and their fertility; a connection to birth and life that men can only imagine. There was considerable variety in the vulvar folds: obviously not the depictions of one woman.

"'E's rather a good 'un," Fanny said and laughed lightly. "'E knows 'ow to draw 'em."

"Quite astonishing," I said.

"'E ought a let me sell the lookings at 'em," she said. "They's plenty who'd pay."

"I expect so," I said, putting down the sketchbook and opening some of the folded sheets. These were studies of male-female copulations, much more fully drawn as to the human figures, some washed in with watercolors, some quite sketchy and much less clear of line, as if to obscure the activities of the worshippers. The viewer was seldom presented with the men's and women's faces, but the bodies— enthralled, some ecstatic—were drawn with more attention to limning the attitudes of human anatomy. Male musculature, female calves and feet and hands—all and more were accurately and carefully delineated as they functioned in the service of Eros, with solemn joy, with attentive fervor.

I wondered about the convolved effect of the pudenda and of the swirling atmospheric energies that sometimes had been brushed in to surround the engaged couples. Were these effects of a piece with Turner's depictions of nature's vortices, of those energies, all the massive forces of nature, that overwhelm human beings and the world they construct? He had written in his long poem *The Fallacies of Hope*:

Extinction follows

And the toil, the hope of man—o'erwhelms.

These lines he had appended to his painting *The Fall of an Avalanche in the Grissons*. Here, now, I witnessed Turner's studied depictions of the instinctual gale of animal generative impulse within and beyond the flesh. I recalled that Ruskin had said Turner composed *Fallacies* to create lines to attach to his paintings because he did not find lines in the work of other poets equal to his view of humanity and history.

Another thought occurred to me. The male figure here and there seemed to be a short man. Were these few self-portraits? Could not some be a kind of memento from the artist's weekend in a brothel or a country house, say, Petworth, the house of that patron-rake Lord Egremont? Or on the road during the long painting trips of his youth? But I was being granted only a matter of minutes, rather than hours or days, of inspection and analysis. Still, at long last here they were. What had survived the flames of outraged decency was all anyone would ever have to speculate as to their purpose and importance (or their private, incidental lack of purpose and importance).

I was overwhelmed by the candor and specificity. It was a glimpse into another, previous era—strange yet familiar—all in opposition to the world William Rossetti and John Ruskin and I and my friends in Schenectady and Cambridge and Boston were bred to—the half-century-ago world of laboring men and women and children. Turner frequently depicted rough, coarse people who were, nonetheless, never vulgar, never presented with the unsympathetic eye of the condescending satirist. These were perhaps "portraits" from that same world: that world of carefree pleasure, not unlike Turner's public depictions of sailors and their women cavorting in drunken abandon. His renderings of such people contained the same coarse dignity as the drawings I now held in my hand. It was the dignity, perhaps, of the earth and her creatures. Their lives without hypocrisy or pretense; lives without the ambitions of fools.

And of course Fanny was right: there would be many who wished to step aside momentarily from the respectable world and were willing to pay for an intoxicating glimpse of another.

"So, what think ye, sir?" Fanny's voice was saying to me.

"Think? Why, Fanny, I think these are remarkable. They rather overmaster one's ability to quite make sense of them, however, taken altogether like this."

"Sense?" she said. "'Ere's sense enough in 'em." She laughed easily. She bent down and began to put the specimens together to be wrapped back into the oilcloth.

"Thank you," I said. "I hope we didn't disturb you from other business." I reached into my waistcoat pocket and withdrew a few shillings.

"Not necessary, sir," she said. "It's a favor to 'im." She prepared to replace the package in the locked drawer.

I left the coins on her dresser nonetheless as we took our leave and thanked her again.

* * *

Once we regained the street Rossetti asked, "So what do you really make of them?"

"I'm not sure," I said, "but they seem a small part of a much larger plan."

"In what way, do you think?"

"He made thousands of studies during his life. These are a mere fragment of the whole."

"I'm more given to believe they're some product of a certain eccentric monomania," he said, "a certain sensuous madness, which grew upon him as he aged. I think Ruskin may be closer to the truth of the matter on that score. If the old master felt trapped at times by his own madness, perhaps these sketches were a sort of freedom, the freedom of a mind closing in on, imprisoning, itself."

"He was incontinent—maybe a sort of erotic volcano—but nothing else suggests he was an addicted sensualist, like the Prince Regent's friend the Marquis of Hertford," I said. Rossetti said nothing. "And what would give one man the right to destroy another's work? Well, thanks to you they have not all been demolished."

"Not quite all."

"All the more reason to properly curate these. This," I waved my arm back toward Fanny's room, "is hardly worthy of them. And I expect it is little better at her newer, permanent residence."

"Don't forget, Will. There's no way to bring their survival into the open without implicating both me and my brother in a crime."

"You're right, of course." I stopped in the street and turned toward him. "But there must be some other way, some other device, for their security."

He hesitated a moment, looking directly at me. "I don't know what that might be, Will. Gabriel will no doubt find some means." We began to walk again. "But be sure to tell me if you hatch any brilliant ideas," he continued. "I think by now, anyway, my brother may never simply give them over to anyone."

"Surely he would return them to you."

"I'm not even sure of that. He's rather possessively bent on his own plan—their secret survival."

Chapter 9

Late one evening, Mrs. Fullerton took me, as promised, not to one of those notorious supper rooms well off Haymarket, but the better sort of Regent Street place where, nonetheless, a man and a woman could meet and talk privately against the din of other conversations and culinary clatter. She had hired a cab and gathered me at my rooms for a ride into that region of architectural distinction mixed with the gaudy illuminations of shops, cafes, Turkish divans, and concert rooms, where courtesans in their silks and satins promenade among the fashionable throngs and West End swells.

I was proud to report the success of my investigations.

"You say there were perhaps a dozen?" she asked.

"Easily. Using different mediums, but mostly pen and ink drawings."

"Well, Mr. Stillman," she said, having digested my tale, "what do you think we should do about these endangered illustrations?" Her keen, bewitching eyes never wavered from my face.

"I've been wondering what, if anything, could be done for the past two days and nights!" I said. "But reflecting on the design of the Rossetti brothers to keep them under their own protection, I don't know what, if anything, we can do."

"But surely *something* must be done. You can't allow them to remain bundled in a harlot's cabinet. One can understand choosing such an initial hiding place, but—"

"There would also be the problem of my betraying William's trust," I said. "And to steal them outright would be to add a crime to the previous crimes of their theft and mere possession."

"True, but remember that for a long time William Rossetti was being dishonest with you about his saving any of these sketches. No one seems to have been able to discuss these studies honestly."

"But more to the point, what possible plan could there be for such theft? Even if I wanted to?"

"Let's step back a moment." She paused and folded her hands slowly. "We agree they are unsafe where they are."

"Of course."

"We agree they must be preserved."

"We've said as much."

"Then the question surely is not whether but *how* to ensure their preservation."

"Logically, yes. But you're forgetting all the practical matters and the violation of trust. We always return to that. William—out of friendship—went against his better judgment for me."

"You're certain William can't be persuaded to see the same necessity?"

"William would never go against his beloved brother's wishes. And Gabriel would never give them over to me. Or anyone else for that matter."

"And to broach the topic again might raise suspicions that would make our ever obtaining them all the more difficult. And in the case of your absconding with them, all the easier to trace the missing portfolio to your door."

"Indeed. But as I say, I see no means of absconding."

"Still."

I could not outlast her gaze. "What would you have me do, Mrs. Fullerton?" I finally asked.

"That's the question we have to answer," she said. "It's only a matter of *what*. On that we seem to agree. How could we possibly give up the field to an unlettered prostitute and the man who uses her? We simply can't wallow endlessly in this paralysis you yourself describe."

"You wish to concoct a ploy."

"You were made aware of this collection of stolen drawings for a reason, don't you think?" She continued to search my eyes, as if testing my potential for resolve. "It's true you, and then I, once hearing this story of Turner's secret sketches and Ruskin's terrible lapse of judgment, sought knowledge of any that might have somehow survived. But now you must see this as a duty, don't you think? You were given knowledge. You are no longer innocent. And you pursued this knowledge to the point of everything you just described to me today. Irrevocable damage has been done, by the very people Turner trusted. The betrayal is theirs, not ours. We're speaking of salvaging some mere portion of the work, back from the larger conflagration of stupidity and misguided conscience."

"You make a convincing case, Mrs. Fullerton. But still I have no idea how our goal is to be effected."

"Our goal is to be effected by not giving up the goal in the first place. Strategy takes time."

"I take your point."

"It is a point very easy to see." She smiled warmly, as if relieved finally to reach me. But I wondered if there were not something more in her smile—in that coy language of looks and glances women employ so effectively—to secure my resolution.

Nonetheless, I was married now to the former Miss Mack, whom I had left home in Cambridge to deliver our child. Despite the more disturbing longings of my separation from her, I pushed all thought of making any detectable response to Mrs. Fullerton's blandishments, if that they were, down into the nether reaches of my mind. Had she not been a woman of such charm and accomplishment, of such sensual magnetism, my resistance to her would have been far easier, my sense of—what? guilt?—far less. But the heart of the problem before me was that she was simply right. Her cause was my cause. And it was a just cause by any measure of justice larger than that of petty courts. Was I to turn coward now, full of compunctions and self- justifications?

"You recall I must leave next week for my consulship," I said. "President Lincoln has replied by the last steamer to the message from the English government, which the Queen ameliorated from the language of Palmerston, Gladstone, and Russell. The President, being given a degree of flexibility by her intervention, has made a peace offering over the Mason and Slidell affair. I'm expected at my proper post in Rome immediately."

"Then there's all the more urgency." She had not withdrawn her smile.

I looked at my pocket watch. "Let me try Rossetti once more."

"If you do, he'll grow suspicious, just as you said, and all the more protective of the packet. Believe me. This week, prior to your departure, we have to find a way to get it out of Fanny's and into safekeeping, before she leaves again for Battersea, and into safekeeping. Sending it out of country, I think, will be best."

"You mean for me to rush off to Italy with it?"

"That would be better than the current circumstances. But Italy is in disarray again. I recently returned there—after having left in the worst of times back in 'forty- eight—hoping for a little more freedom of movement. But it's still all wrong. You're going to a dangerous post. Did they tell you?"

"Somewhat of the difficulties."

"Political and social life has been crushed. Rome especially. Only the English and Americans mingle now to any extent. The theocratic government considers itself beyond all reproach. It defies diplomacy as much as insurrection. The only industries are jewelry, art, and the apparatus of the Church. There is no rule of law, only of incompetence enforced by the arms of a foreign army despised by the population. But then the Pope himself despises the French protectorate. Yet he fears Garibaldi's return to Rome more! He doesn't believe the French garrison at Rome offers sufficient protection against his foe. Brigands operate freely everywhere. They rob and abuse travelers and even residents at night locked inside their apartments and villas. Husbands lend their wives as mistresses for compensation. And the only law the church upholds against all this disarray and violence is the law against heresy—to the point of persecutions. No," she added, "you mustn't think of removing Turner's works to Rome."

"As I've explained, I hadn't thought of a means or a place for their removal. But again, Mrs. Fullerton, what would you have me do?"

She remained quiet for a minute. Finally, as if her mind was made up, she said, "Laudanum."

"Laudanum?"

"Here's a plan to consider," she continued. "You return to Fanny's room before this week's rent is up, as if a customer this time." She stopped a moment to watch what must have been my reddening face. "You know where the materials are stored. You know where she keeps the key. You play upon her expectations. As you describe her, surely, such behavior wouldn't be exceptional to her. I'm certain men who've viewed her but once return to her all the time for something more, men from all stations of life. It would be an effective ruse precisely for its seeming predictability. A common enough event in her— Is 'sordid' too strong a word?—life." She stopped to judge my reaction.

"She doesn't for a minute think of it as sordid," I said. "She's quite jolly on duty and off, so far as I could see."

"Beside the point. I'm not judging her here; it was but an expression. More to the point, you would engage with her just enough to convince her of your intentions, lead her along to get her to imbibe a dose of laudanum sufficient to put her into a deep sleep."

"A sufficient dose. Isn't that rather a dangerous game?"

"Not without risks, but we shall take care. From what you tell me of her, and if she's not an habitual user, I'd say 40 minims ought to do it. It has a stimulating effect at first, but then soporific. You could slip the opiate into her drink—say, some brandy you bring along for your mutual pleasure. Brandy's often used to disguise the taste."

"And how do you know?"

"I take laudanum myself, on occasion. When I cannot sleep. I have for some years."

"You can't sleep?"

"Sometimes. As you get older you'll see what I mean." She smiled. "I've used it since I broke my ankle nearly ten years ago on a sketching trip to the White Mountains in New Hampshire with fellow artists. Laudanum was my physician's recommendation. Until I healed and the pain left me."

"It would be a great risk. It might very well not work, for any of several reasons a moment's reflection will reveal."

"Of course. But I defy you to delineate a plan that would be otherwise. The point is, again, to make every effort we can imagine that would allow you to seize the Turners."

She had rendered me speechless.

"You have another idea?" she asked.

"You know very well I don't. Not yet."

"We are nearly out of time, as you said yourself."

"Indeed."

"And returning to Rossetti in any way to plead for their removal would be futile; you've said as much yourself."

"Very true."

"Well then?"

Finally, I said, "I can't agree to such a dangerous masquerade and betrayal."

"Not yet," she said. She appeared to enjoy my discomfort. She reached across the table and patted my hand, now like an older sister awaiting the arrival of her brother's reason.

"Not yet," I said.

Chapter 10

I was unable to resist Mrs. Fullerton's view of necessity. And besides, what other options had we? On the very eve of my departure for the continent and Rome, I set out for Fanny's Soho room.

The thought of enacting the ruse tormented me. I found the courage only by recalling an old instinct—some power within that I had used, indeed developed, over years of wilderness painting and fishing and hunting in the Adirondacks, the Berkshires, and the White Mountains. Although now lost, like so many other innate faculties, through centuries of civilization, this guiding faculty I now believe to be something human beings can recover, something that is inherent in all healthy minds.

One instance of this faculty occurred when I had made arrangements with H. K. Brown, the sculptor, to rendezvous at a lake near Hancock, Massachusetts, on the border with New York, where the fishing was wild and exceptional. But I had missed my train on the New York side and had to take a parallel track to Pittsfield, Massachusetts. On leaving that station I was told that the distance to Hancock was about a dozen miles straight over the mountain, but for lack of a footpath I would have to travel twenty miles around. I knew going around would never allow me at that late hour to arrive in the morning at our agreed upon time and place. So, determined to keep my appointment rather than abandoning my friend in the wild, I struck out over the pathless mountain, heading in the direction I was certain I needed to follow. I relied upon the guidance of this inner sense, without calculation, following that direction as darkness, rain, and fog began to hamper my progress through dense woodland. I do not exaggerate to say that I could not see the trees at arm's length by the time I was well into this journey. Yet I kept on, following my inner sense of the way, even though I had to descend, finally, through forest and declivity where sometimes my very foot extended over an abyss as, hanging on to trees, I felt my way. After a long time, I recognized only from the sound of frogs that I had reached a marsh and the end of my descent.

I ultimately came to a road and then to a cottage with a light on, some farmer no doubt up for his chores. I now spied outlines of a few other houses shrouded still in darkness. As soaked as if I had been swimming in my clothes, I knocked on the door of the lighted cottage. A man holding a lamp appeared.

"Can you please tell me the way to Hancock," I inquired.

"Why you are *in* Hancock!" he said.

"Thank God!" I said and shook his hand. "I've just come over the mountain from Pittsfield."

He gave me a strange look. "No white man could've made it over that pathless forest on such a night!"

But I had, I explained, and I was soon at a small inn drying my clothes before the fire and catching a short sleep. I had walked to my destination with the precision of an animal whom nature had not abandoned. And that is but one example of the inner guide I now turned to in that other wilderness of the very streets of Soho, London, with a vial of tincture of opium in my pocket, and a bottle of brandy in my waistcoat, in search of Fanny.

The landlady declared her room unoccupied at the moment. I dawdled in the street until I saw Fanny coming toward me with shop parcels. When I greeted her she remembered me. I asked if she would agree to entertain me. She smiled invitingly and told me to return to her room that evening at half past eight.

I bided my time in an unremarkable coffee room and returned to her temporary abode at that hour. She was pleased to let me in, laughing when I showed her a bottle of good brandy. She sat me in the only chair in the room—a stuffed, uneven wingback from a previous generation, covered now in cheap green chintz, the same material that curtained her four- poster bed. The room seemed larger than I remembered, with a fireplace whose mantelpiece held lackluster crockery surmounted by an ancient, gilt-framed looking-glass.

Her abundant golden hair was held up loosely by pins and a black ribbon, and the front of her violet dress unbuttoned to reveal a white lace undergarment barely containing her breasts.

"So ye've come to view the pictures again, have ye?" she said and gave me a mischievous look.

"No, Fanny, I've come to view you this time, instead."

She threw her head back and laughed fully, her bust shaking against her white garment.

"Well, then, sir, you just open that bottle and pour us both a glass while I undo this lot. Glasses over there." She began slowly unbuttoning her dress, and then the lacy undergarment, to her waist.

I got up, turned away toward the dresser, and uncorked the brandy. I removed the small vial of Mrs. Fullerton's exact dose of tincture from the inner pocket of my coat and added it to her glass. When I turned around, her dishabille revealed the full heft of her breasts, keeping only the nipples just hidden. I handed her a glass, toasted her, and returned to the chair with my own glass. She immediately sat on my lap. The scent she had rubbed on —a not unappealing lilac odor— enticed me. She began delicately to sip her drink.

"Oh, that's a good 'un," she said and tussled my hair. "Ye've good taste, Mr. Stillman."

It unnerved me that she recalled my name, but why shouldn't she? She would have no trouble describing me to William Rossetti anyway.

"Nothing's too good for a beauty like you," I said. I think, because of my desire to do nothing more than have this whole business behind me, I was not aroused. But when she pushed back the little fabric covering her large nipples, I began to lose what self-possession I had retained. She pushed the slender chain holding the key out of the way and gave each nipple a slow and careless tug, causing them to swell. She took another sip of my concoction from her glass and threw her head back, forcing her breasts even closer to my face.

"Uhm," she said, smacking her lips. "Tasty good!"

I wondered if the laudanum were taking hold already. I supposed it might well be, but then I was reminded of something Mrs. Fullerton had said: if she were habituated to the potion it would take much more to put her under than we had anticipated. I had no more with me, for fear of serving her a too strong or even lethal dose by mistake.

She put her glass on a little table beside us. "Do ye like 'ese, sir?" she said, cupping her breasts toward my lips.

"Luscious, indeed, Fanny," I said. I don't suppose I had much composure or dignity left by that point, and my second sip of the brandy was having its effect on my own state of mind. I put my glass down beside hers, determined not to have another sip.

I would of course have to act as a real customer would, but it was getting more difficult all the time to tread the line between my act and my natural responses to such a voluptuous and utterly available woman. I teased her nipples a little with my tongue and lips. Her hands reached up and held my head. I thought with a part of my mind that her breathing might indicate the onset of deep lassitude or sleep. But she was, as well, clearly responding to my attentions. I pulled my face away and reached for my drink again, pretended to take another sip, and reached over for her glass. Laughing, she took her glass from me and nearly drained it this time.

How long would it be before the opiate took effect? She smacked her lips and slowly shook her breasts. "Don't stop now, sir," she cooed, and gave another little laugh.

I continued my tentative acts of worship, holding back from going any further as long as she would allow, and as long as self-control didn't desert me.

Finally she got up, quaffed the dregs of that first fortified glass of brandy, and pushed her dress and underclothes to the floor. I couldn't take my eyes off her, and she would have wondered what sort of man I was if I had, but I was beginning to sweat. The dose of laudanum must not be sufficient, I thought. I recalled Mrs. Fullerton's saying that it usually had an initial stimulating effect before inducing sleep. Fanny went to her bed and lay down on her stomach, raised her backside, and turned her face over her shoulder toward me. Her eyes did look a little dazed. But her voice was clear. "Come now, sir, everything's yours as 'ye likes it."

I got up, removed my coat and waistcoat, untied my necktie, moved slowly toward her, prayed for her sudden somnolence. She kept looking at me in that glassy way, beckoning me to get on with her, shifting her backside back and forth. I stood over her and caressed her full lovely bottom, tickling two fingers along the groove, which only increased her shifting back and forth. I knelt down and kissed each globe, savoring the bouquet of still more lilac mingling with her own musky flesh, while she emitted little murmurs of pleasure. I then turned her over, whereupon the mass of golden hair covering her pudendum confronted me, and I was recalled to my true mission, despite by then the painful state of my own arousal.

Never had I experienced a woman so comfortable in her body, so nonchalant in opening herself to a man, a stranger really, with such unabashed pleasure. She was by now obviously aroused and no doubt—the thought flashed through my mind—the very sort of woman old Turner had inspected and drawn with such bold attention of his own. I stood to buy myself a little more time, still hoping the concoction would take hold of her, and continuing my act by running my fingers gently around her now slippery sex. But she did not seem to be falling asleep. My heart was beating in a torrent of anxiety and desire.

"Come now, sir," she said. She took my caressing fingers in one hand and pushed them firmly around her swollen labia. She began to move her hips quickly to increase the pressure and stimulation of my fingers, all the while making those same little murmurs. I did not think that she was acting her part. It occurred to me that a woman of such fulsome beauty, who could manage a degree of selectivity in her clients, might have been enjoying our encounter. William had told me that she was not a hypocrite about the pleasure she often took in her labors with a better class of men. She was by now thrusting harder and harder, and I was about to abandon all pretense of control, when suddenly she let up and sighed deeply. I didn't know whether she had managed to spend her passion or whether the laudanum finally was having its effect, but she closed her eyes, relaxed her arched back, and appeared to fall asleep. I remained as I was. I continued gently touching her still a while longer to determine if this was truly sleep.

Convinced it was, I lay on the bed beside her and lifted the chain off her throat and chest. Her recumbent head and abundant hair made all possibility of sliding the chain off her head doubtful, so I pulled the chain slowly round and round on her neck, examining every inch of it for some kind of clasp. If there wasn't one, I feared, I might be thwarted yet. But there finally appeared a barely noticeable twist mechanism that blended well with the slim chain. In another minute I determined how it worked and had the key in my hands. I was at her bureau drawer in a moment more, and soon the oilcloth packet was mine. I uncovered it carefully and saw that indeed the Turners were still within.

I glanced over at Fanny's sprawled and naked form. She was snoring now; her regular breathing reassured me. I removed from my overcoat a new oilcloth, a small book, and some newsprint to insert into the original oilcloth. I sacrificed the Turner sketch on top to the cause, leaving it on top, and placed the dummy packet in the drawer. I closed and locked the drawer, replaced the key and chain around her neck, and dressed quickly. In spite of my overwrought condition, on my way out the door I remembered to put a half guinea on the dresser and to tuck the brandy back under my coat with the packet.

Chapter 11

When I arrived at Mrs. Fullerton's painting rooms about ten o'clock, she answered her door in a satin floral dressing gown, looking sleepy but not surprised to see me. I pulled out the oilcloth.

She brought me immediately before her fireplace, bid me sit on the couch, took my offered bottle of brandy, and poured us each a celebratory glass. Then she sat opposite me on a chair, and said simply, "Now, my dear Stillman, tell me all about it!"

All about it! "I'll spare you the prurient details, Mrs. Fullerton," I said, "but everything went according to our plan, with only two dicey moments."

"Only two?" She was eying the oilcloth package on my lap.

"The laudanum took forever to work. And I had considerable difficulty figuring out how to unclasp the key chain around her neck to retrieve the key."

She chuckled. "Forever?" She looked at the clock on her mantelpiece.

"Perhaps an hour. That, I assure you, was forever."

"Goodness. You said she is a large woman?"

I decided to match her inconvenient banter. "But in a most appealing way."

She smiled, rather coyly, I thought. "I had adjusted the dose accordingly."

"Yes, but I wondered if, as you once mentioned, Fanny might be inured to it, from habit."

"A possibility, of course. But it does take some time to reach full effect." She considered a moment and then added, "And what did you do while you waited to see if it were ever to work?"

She did not speak into my silence, letting me stew. "Do?" I finally said. "Why I acted as a client would. How else could I carry out our plan?"

"As a lingering client," she said rather merrily. "And you consummated the transaction?"

I was taken aback by her boldness—nay, by her inquiry in the first place. Was she toying with me or truly curious about the sexual play of my encounter? I realized that comfortable as I had grown in her company through our conspiring and mutual sympathies, I didn't really know this woman. I had thought that the questionable reputation she bore in the eyes of the conventional world as a widowed and much traveled artist was nine-tenths gossip and envy, but now I wondered if she might deserve her reputation.

"You mock me?" I finally said. "I restrained myself. But played my role only so far as necessary. Our dalliance required more than a little dithering on my part."

"Was it so painful as all that, Mr. Stillman?" She was enjoying herself at my expense, at her leisure now that we had the Turner portfolio in our possession. I refused to answer. "I'm sorry it cost you such discomfort."

She had found me out, but I didn't begrudge what a woman of her apparent experience of the world surmised. I merely wanted to stop feeling as if I were the butt of some jest.

"You want to see them?" I asked, holding the package up. "As I've warned you, these are no images to put before a lady."

"I thought we had gone beyond such cant, you and I." She reached out her hand.

I looked to see how much humor remained in her eyes, but before I could rise she got up and took the package from my extended hand. "Well, Mrs. Fullerton, you can't say I didn't warn you."

She said nothing, sat down again, and opened the package. As she turned the leaves of the partial sketchbook she registered no shock or pleasure, merely the quiet appraisal of one artist for another's labors. Taking her time, she kept the same demeanor as she opened the larger and smaller leaves of the watercolors. All the while I sipped my brandy and contemplated sleep. It was nearly eleven o'clock before she spoke.

"Utterly original," she said. "In approach, I mean. And in a few cases in precision. But you can also see his signature method in the watercolors—that most delicate application of washes and the minute hatch work and stippled color."

"And the variety of media as well, don't you think? I believe I detected pen, graphite, watercolor, chalk, and so on."

"Yes," she said. "And now I understand as well why you and Mr. Rossetti were convinced that whoever possesses these, whether by right or theft, is likely to breach the law."

"But of course at this moment that's our very selves."

"Indeed," she said, "by theft and possession." She studied a few in the sketchbook once more, and then added, "And I think there may be something to your theory, Mr. Stillman, of how these too may be seen as notations to some broader philosophy, so to speak."

"And something of Brueghel or Rembrandt?"

"In the copulatory images," she said, looking through several again. "That same brutal honesty. But it's a humane realism, even so."

"I quite agree," I said. "Part of that same sympathy with ordinary men and women."

"That's always been my impression of Turner," she said, as if musing. "If his figures appear clumsy or disfigured, it is the disfigurement and clumsiness of heavy toil. Of real toil." She continued her examination. "And even in these reside the same sorrow and joy of humanity, the same vulnerability and nobility—an organic and immutable human drama."

"Ruskin once told me Turner had continued as a *student* in Life Academy classes into his late sixties. And he was fond, apparently, in his own life classes of posing real women beside classical representations of the ideal, that his students might see more clearly the differences between idealized beauty and the beauty of living flesh."

"Really? Isn't that admirable of the old man. And you can see the influence of his long study of the human body in some of these."

"Then is there any other course but to hie away with them to Rome tomorrow?"

She thought a moment, looked up again. "That would be dangerous for other reasons, which we've already discussed."

"Which you've discussed, Mrs. Fullerton."

She flashed me an unsympathetic look and got up, still holding the sketches. "I see two other alternatives," she said.

"Two?"

"First, there is a friend, recently returned from America, in fact, who has the experience to secrete and preserve these, against all investigators and interlopers. Were he to take these for safekeeping, no one would be able to find and wrest them away."

"A friend?"

"I don't wish to implicate him without asking him first."

"You say there are two alternatives. I trust your second one is less fantastical."

"Well, Stillman, you've come to know me. So I offer myself." She smiled. "I think it would be much better for their preservation if I were to change my plans and set off for Boston with them, on the first steamer for America." She spoke with a new firmness in her voice. "You may very well be suspected at some point, whereas I will not."

"Do you really believe they would invoke the police?" I asked. "Wouldn't that implicate them in possession of this…pilfered contraband rather more even than ourselves?"

"Once the Rossettis discover the theft, sooner or later, they'll devise a plan for recovery," she said. "There'll be an investigation, whether policial or private. We can't say just now whether they'll be able to trace the purloined art to you; the later they make the discovery the less likely, I should say."

"If Fanny for some reason unwraps and examines the lot, she'll see the ruse. Not likely soon, I'd say, but it is a possibility."

"You believe not so likely?"

"I flatter myself that my decoy is sufficient to keep her from examining the contents immediately. Opening it, after all, she will see only an original Turner sketch."

"Nonetheless, eventually it shall become all too clear that someone has stolen the originals at some point—from Fanny's room, during their transport, or from her Battersea apartment."

"But the later the better. I'll be far removed."

"In any case you're far more likely a suspect than I. Than anyone. And they'll never trace these to America. They know nothing of my knowledge of them. Unless you told Rossetti."

"I have not."

"Well, then," she said with more than a little satisfaction. "I rest my case, Mr. Stillman."

I had to admit she made a far more cogent argument for her plan than I could make for mine. And I knew I would be consumed with responsibilities and uncertainties once I arrived in Rome. And finally there would also be the later arrival of my wife and infant son.

"And what, pray tell, will you do with them back in America?" I asked.

"Do? Why I shall conceal them securely and without anyone else's knowledge in the whole wide world! And when you return, look me up in Boston, and I shall offer them to your safe keeping and disposition. Once in America, they'll never leave my possession."

I had the disquieting sense of being overmastered by her. Had the hour been earlier and my fatigue less, I might have jousted to better effect.

"You had said something before of retaining them in your estate," she went on. "With the explicit exception that they will be returned to the National Gallery upon such time as you or your heirs receive documentary assurances that they shall be preserved forever for the study of future generations of artists and scholars. Why isn't that still a good plan?"

"It's my only plan, Mrs. Fullerton, but I hadn't thought of relinquishing them to you—or anyone—as an intermediary, however temporary or lasting."

"You don't trust me, William?" She calmly resumed her seat across from me. The sudden use of my name and the new warmth and note of sympathy in her voice and face unsettled me. I had barely recovered from my disconcerting adventures with Fanny when I was being thrown back into a mire of confusion by this most skilled woman, whose appeal was something quite other than Fanny's, but not without a disarming dose of carnality. I felt by now at once enervated and incontinent. I struggled to keep my wits about me.

I sat there looking, I fear, rather dumbfounded. She looked at me in silence. She then rose to return the package, standing over me for a time, as if waiting for me to speak. But I was engulfed by a strange lassitude, running to helplessness and indecision, which I believe, looking back now, she must have divined completely.

Her hand ruffled my hair, sending a shock of strange, delicate pleasure all through me. "You will be ill if you don't get some sleep, William," she said. "You seem utterly discomposed. Would a dose of Salvolatile help?"

I looked up at her, my eyelids straining. "No. Thank you," I said.

"You've had a rather terrifying adventure, for one of your constitution," she said. "And you're no doubt suffering the biliousness of one whose passions have gone unquenched. It's understandable. You need time to think and consider my proposal. But then you leave in the morning and are not yet packed."

"I'm packed," I murmured. "Ready for guilt-ridden flight, a man who betrays his friends."

"For a higher cause," she said.

"Of course," I said. "Betrayal's always for a higher cause."

"You may sleep here, if you like, on the davenport. It may be safer and far less anxious if you hold off returning to your rooms till the last moment before your departure."

"My bags have been sent to the steamer."

"Then you shall remain here." She knelt before me and affectionately, attentively took my hand. "And I trust by morning you'll approve my plan."

"By morning," I said.

She leaned forward and kissed my forehead. "Poor William," she said. "I only want to help."

I don't know, even today looking back on this period of my life, whether it was the result of her own magnetic appeal, to which I had become so deeply attuned, or whether it was the incompleteness of my ministrations to Fanny, but I held her face and kissed her gently on the mouth. Her tongue darted against my own, accepting the challenge. But she did nothing more at that precise moment. I pulled her close to me in our awkward positions, tugging the bow loose that bound her dressing gown so that it fell open to expose her nightdress to my hands. I recall trying to convince myself that I wanted then just to feel the reassuring embrace of the woman I had temporarily come to trust with the most devastating secrets of my life. We had become, after all, criminals together. For a higher cause. But it was that embrace which emboldened or signaled her, and I was from that moment completely under her command.

She pushed me back on the davenport and began to unbutton my waistcoat and trousers. My arousal was instantaneous, and despite my exhaustion desire returned, painful and raging all the more, I suspect, for the incompleteness of its course in Fanny's room. I was the ripe victim of my own folly, as I lay there gasping under the ministration of her knowing fingers, the efflux of which attendance she caught in a large, silken handkerchief pulled suddenly from the sleeve of her dressing gown. The entire episode of my seduction, or hers—I wasn't in that crisis sure which—couldn't have lasted more than three minutes. Afterwards, she helped me finish removing my clothes and then went into the other room to retrieve a counterpane and pillow.

"Sleep well now, dear William," she said as she arranged the bedclothes comfortably for me. "You've earned it. You'll feel much better in the morning."

Chapter 12

The next morning I was awakened by the same voice that had ushered me into sleep. "You have a steamer to catch, Mr. Stillman!"

I turned on my couch, felt her standing there observing me, and fumbled for my waistcoat and watch fob. Opening one eye, I saw that I had an hour to arrive at the gate and present my passage.

"Good thing your baggage has already been sent aboard," she said. I heard her pouring water into a wash basin. "Here's a cup of tea," she added a moment later.

I forced myself to rise. She left the room while I washed my hands and face. She had placed a comb and washcloth by the washstand. I gulped the tea.

As I began to comb my hair, my face started to blur in the cheval glass she had turned toward the washstand, as if my sight were once again failing me. I strained to see my face and suddenly recalled a vision—or dream—sometime in the night. It was Turner, standing over me, looking very much as he did when I first met him as an old man, a rather Punch-like figure, at Griffith's gallery. He fixed me again with his eagle eye, standing straight, then bending at the waist only to come closer to my face, the same restless energy coming off him like an aura of light, the same teasing expression of malicious good humor, but mixed with something more this time. What was it? Disapproval? A curse? I had the lingering feeling that somehow he thought me unworthy of the task I had undertaken. I knew I was certainly no longer worthy of Laura.

A shadow appeared in the reflection of the full-length glass. Adjusting my vision, I saw Mrs. Fullerton standing behind me, partially visible in the mirror. "I have the portfolio safe now, well hidden away here."

I turned to her. "I haven't made up my mind—"

"You haven't the time to think a moment more about it, William. You can't take the package with you; we've been over all that."

"But what assurances do I have of their safekeeping? It's not that I don't trust you, Allegra. But you must admit, after the risks I've run and the value of the materials, I'm not being unreasonable about leaving them behind—what? A year? Two years?" She stood there looking at me, perhaps a little amused by my disarray.

"You could bring them to me," I suggested, "later, after I'm safely ensconced in Rome."

She came forward and handed me my waistcoat and jacket. As I was putting them on, she said, "They'll be much safer in Boston. I'll ensure their safe passage and hiding. No one will expect me of complicity. The Rossettis, however, will most assuredly wonder about you."

I hadn't a rational rejoinder. And the thought of her showing up in Rome after Laura joined me shot a sudden charge of nausea through my gut.

"When you return to Boston," she went on, "just look me up. The Turners will be with me. We'll determine their final disposition then."

"I'm not sure—"

"Don't worry a moment more over them. Go to Rome and fulfill your duties. Return to me and the portfolio shall be returned to you. It's very simple, and the safest plan."

She moved me out the door before I could protest further or gather my wits. A cab awaited me. She had thought of everything.

In twenty minutes more I was on a steamer for France, awaiting momentary departure for my consular post at Rome.

* * *

I fled—at that moment it felt entirely like fleeing—to Rome, by way of Paris to Marseilles, and thence by sea to Citivavecchia, in late December of 1861. The journey from Paris to Marseilles took twenty-six hours in a third-class carriage. Traveling was tedious, the odiferous exhalations of the male and female coach passengers growing more ghastly by the hour, even as the cold exacerbated my discomforts. I was, moreover, unsettled in mind, in the first place from my inability to fathom Turner's true purpose with these sketches, and in the second, from my recent adventures and errors in relation to them.

As I deliberated endlessly over the first matter, I kept returning to a portion of my early conversation with Mrs. Fullerton that I had not written down because I was unsure of its usefulness. But as the coach rattled along, I began on this journey to think differently.

I had mentioned to Mrs. Fullerton at the Sabloniere restaurant that in my early studies in Paris, I had met Delacroix, Gerome, Delaroche, Ingres, and Rousseau, who was perhaps most important to me. When she asked how I had come to know such men, I explained that I had enlisted my services under Kossuth, the Hungarian patriot, whom I met during his travels in America. It was he who had set me the task of helping Mazzini's attempts to free Italy of their Austrian occupiers.

"Mazzini?" she said, surprised. "I met him, through Margaret Fuller, in 'forty-eight, I think it was." Her face took on a dreamy look. "A noble but continually frustrating cause."

"Well, it was those frustrations that kept me in Paris through '52 and '53," I said, "studying at the Ecole des Beaux Arts, awaiting the revolution that failed to come. That's when I met these painters. But I returned home in the spring of '53 for painting and sketching excursions in the Connecticut and Housatonic River valleys. Months on end tramping and camping, especially in the Berkshire Hills."

"Still, you learned from these men?"

I began to speak with passion of that time and was soon confessing what, on reflection, had impressed me about similarities between Turner and my mentor Theodore Rousseau.

"Although after his travels in Italy in the 1820s Turner became a Bacchanalian colorist; Rousseau was a vestal tonalist," I continued. "Turner was a lover of mountains and Rousseau, who had no feeling for mountains, a lover of trees. Both men in the essential features are to my mind the same."

"Essential features?" she asked.

"I mean their impressions of the world depicted on their canvasses are based on an intimate knowledge of nature, but *without* copying nature."

"Without any thoughtless replication of natural detail."

"Precisely. Techniques are fitted to the ends—not theories but effects."

She smiled and raised her glass of wine. "And what techniques do you see in particular that yoke two such different sensibilities?"

"Neither man, for example, painted from life or nature directly— onto the finished canvas."

"They observed and studied first."

"They took—what to call them— memoranda, endless sketch studies, endless natural detail, recording just sufficient information to allow for maximum imaginative development of the composition, working from visual memory."

"Where their contemporaries are fragmentary, they are harmonious?"

"And more lyric, and one might almost say rhythmic. Look at the passion of line and tint, for example."

"And the revolt against precedent," she added.

"I see you understand my point." I raised my glass to her.

As we spoke, her eyes didn't waver from my face, as an interlocutor's eyes often do, and I found the intensity of her gaze rather unsettling. But her eyes and her face were of such intriguing character that the sensation of her scrutiny was to a younger man strangely pleasurable as well.

"And yet," she said, "in both there is likewise passion for subtlety of gradation and for infinite space, air, and light."

"Don't you think that's the foundation of their originality? Their greatness?"

"I wouldn't disagree," she said, smiling again, "but as to their ultimate stature, isn't that for posterity to judge?" Her smile had a trace of indulgence in it, as if she were allowing a younger enthusiast to vent ideas that seemed to her rather unremarkable.

So I tried to impress her by telling a story about Theodore Rousseau demonstrating to me how to make a painting whole, growing, as he said, in all its parts: *pari passu*. That is going over, developing and revising the whole each time you worked on it. Her eyes grew more curious.

"He took his palette and flipped it over," I explained, "turning from the painting he had on his easel. He pointed to his window and began to paint a little scheme of a picture on the back side of the palette suggested by what we saw as we looked out his window. He told me that one should have the whole conception of the painting in the first five lines of such a sketch, or one would never have it. And he showed me many such sketch studies, these mere notations on his larger conceptions, from his huge collection. Notations, some nearly illegible and some remarkably detailed, from which his fully realized paintings emerged."

"And Turner likewise."

"Ruskin tells me Turner left nearly 20,000 sketch studies behind in his bequest." All the time I was talking to her I still couldn't forget what William Rossetti had revealed to me regarding the studies and their destruction.

"And you take this now as your own method?"

"I first had to discard my niggling faithfulness to natural fact, but by the time I might have made progress, I was exhausted in my studies and diseased in my eyes, and other matters came to the fore in my life."

Now, reliving this part of our conversation in my mind in the coach toward Rome, as I say, some sense, still dimly seen, began to dawn on me of the key to the technical purpose of the salacious Turner sketches. I was unable to keep myself from puzzling the matter, hoping for enlightenment. Or I should say, the one thing that distracted me from such puzzling was the second matter that plagued me during these travels. I realized that although I had succeeded in stealing the oil-cloth packet from Fanny, I was thereby confronted with the fact that I had become a schemer and a thief. And the persistent memories of my activity in Fanny's room troubled my conscience as not only a liar and a thief, but as a betrayer and a fool, as well. Was I to live the rest of my life despicable in my own eyes? I had turned a corner I could never now retract—all merely to take wholly upon myself the security of a batch of explicit sketches from the hand of a painter I admired. Could the cost to my self-respect justify that result? Justify that these same studies were in the hands of another? Of one who had been all too wise in maneuvering me like a child into believing I controlled my own destiny through acts of my own volition?

I wished I had never heard of the infernal sketches, nor had ever seen them; better that old Turner had destroyed them properly himself.

And now it occurred to me that I might well have failed to salvage even some lesser tracings of Turner's bold, unblinking, and dangerous explorations. The old master was perhaps mad, as many have said, but his was a finer madness than that of his greatest apologist. For I was coming to believe that Ruskin's madness was all time-bound, weighty, encrusted with the detritus and bric-a-brac of his momentary culture and, worse, of his familial inhibitions and mannerisms. Able to rise above the Empire's slavish philistinism and worship of Mammon, he was nonetheless a slave to his country's fears, to his country's infatuation with its parochial manners, and to the priggish Christianity of schoolmaster and clergyman. His fine intelligence was, in the end, hardly able to rise above those desiccated, dogmatic ladies swimming breathlessly in their black crinoline. This hero of my own youth, whose principles had informed and braced me, was, I now saw, not even sufficiently "unconverted," for all his travels and protests, to rise above the limiting admonitions of his education, his father, and his mother. He had been better off an orphan, a voice in the wilderness, a pagan in a creed outworn, than a prophet in a frock coat and a filial mansion.

Having come to view Ruskin in this disillusioning light, I was further disheartened by my folly in agreeing with Laura to name our first born, if a son, John Ruskin Stillman, affectionately "Russie." I worried that such a name might portend some ill Fate. But it was too late, and Laura too distant, to become possessed by such misgivings. As I approached Rome, I shook off all these speculations that had consumed my days and nights en route, and prepared myself to assume my new post and succeed in it.

Chapter 13

I arrived in Rome shortly before Christmas, when the city was all astir with preparations for the celebration. The unseasonable heat, combined no doubt with my recent period of anxiety, caused a relapse into my eye troubles. From the start, the activities of ecclesiastical authorities and their police disturbed me. The police operated as petty tyrants over the least murmur of heresy, while brigands ran freely and sexual license flourished among "celibate" priests and their married flocks. I soon discovered also that I was locked in a contest with Miss Charlotte Cushman, the famous actress. Her brilliance, venality, and self-importance instigated the "Artist Wars" once she assumed leadership of a clique of women sculptors (notably Misses Stebbins and Hosmer) in order to make war on all sculptors of the opposite sex that her chosen protégés might reap the golden harvest. I had battles enough with Confederate Americans abroad who, by order of the government in Washington, were required in my presence to take an oath of allegiance prior to renewing their American passports. But whenever I thwarted Miss Cushman's tendentious ambitions, within the lines of my official duty, I found that battle invigorating.

Although by then I had no sympathy with any creed, given my position as American Consul before the arrival of our American minister to Rome, I was granted audience with Pope Pius IX, a devout man who never questioned his divine authority, but who was not of a persecuting or bigoted disposition. I liked him, and he me, so far as I could tell. But he had the failing of reposing his faith on the ability and integrity of rigid clerics who knew nothing of human nature or practical politics; they understood only, rather, a sort of paternal and absolute control over wayward humanity. He seemed to me a more or less benevolent father caught in an immense and intricate machine, over the movements of which neither he nor any other Pope could exercise much control.

On the other hand, it was men like Cardinal Antonelli who might have stood for a portrait of Mephistopheles, the very type of the unscrupulous and malignant intellect who, under this system, manipulated faithful persons and laws to sate their appetites.

My principal recreation amidst such circumstances was to spend every Sunday on the Campagna. Once my eyes improved, I began to try my hand again at landscape painting. Whether taking up my brush was in reaction to my contest with Miss Cushman, or a response to the fact that the consulate was traditionally given to an artist, or both, I cannot say for sure. But ultimately I managed to sell several landscapes to the amount of six hundred dollars. That additional income allowed me to go home to retrieve my wife, Laura, and our newborn son, Russie. While briefly in America, I at first tried to locate Allegra Fullerton. However, not finding a soul in Boston who might suggest her whereabouts, I soon had to return with Laura and the baby to my post in Rome. Some time later, I received my first letter from Mrs. Fullerton, in the summer of 1862, addressed to my consulate.

> My Dear Stillman,
> I trust that you are well and your consulship full of interest and challenge. I hope by now Mrs. Stillman and your new child—whom you would have yet to see—have joined you, and that all loneliness has abated. I write to assure you that all is well with the T——s. I

did not leave London immediately for fear of the dissolution of our country in civil war and for business to hand that required my attention for some months. Nonetheless, I have returned and taken up work and residence in Boston, as I told you I would.

I will add just now that I finally think the Union cause may win after all, despite looking quite otherwise for a long demoralizing period, which turn of circumstance should weaken any British fancies (and those of France and Spain) of entering the fray. You may recall my saying that someone was in America back in 1860, ostensibly on an adventure across the continent to study the natives and the Mormons. I can tell you now that it was Richard Burton. His book on that journey, City of the Saints, says nothing about it, but I feel certain, given what he has intimated later in conversation, that he also traveled deep into the incipient Confederacy on a secret mission for the British government. His covert—and I can only assume extensive—report on the capacity of the Confederacy to prosecute war, I am given to infer, had something to do as well with Old Mother England's ultimate decision to stay aloof from the conflict. I think now it is only a matter of time—and much, much more bloodshed—before our cause is won.

It may be of interest if I mention William Rossetti, who told me in private one day after we had met at a gallery and stopped for a cup of tea that he and Gabriel have hired a private investigator "to find some potentially scandalous sketch studies from Gabriel's hands," and that he had left temporarily in the Soho rooms of one of his models. It seems the chief suspect, though still unknown and at large, is a certain desperado witnesses glimpsed once or twice as he broke into and wrecked several apartments in the neighborhood in his search for booty—anything of possible value. The man apparently did purloin certain "sketches" wrapped in oilcloth, such as they were! Rossetti gave no indication that anyone else was under suspicion.

I enclose here for you my Boston address. Please make it your business to visit me whenever you find yourself back in New England. We have much to discuss.

Yours faithfully,

Allegra Fullerton

In the envelope I found her card.

Mrs. Allegra Fullerton, Portraits
9 Tremont, 3rd floor
Boston in Massachusetts
Painting and Exhibition Rooms

It was our fate, I presumed, to have just missed one another. Nor was I able to shake growing doubts about her constancy.

And what of this Burton? Yes she had once spoken to me of him as an old friend, an admirer. But I had the unsettling feeling she was intimating something about him she dared not speak outright, and I couldn't put my finger on it. I had met the man once, but what did I know of him? I knew only what anyone might know—through his prolific books and the sensational legends that surrounded him—of his fame and infamy; his fearless global explorations; his penchant for disguises and penetrating secret societies; his mastery of something like thirty languages and more dialects; his gargantuan appetites for exotic sexuality, cannabis, opium, and alcohol. Was not he (like Turner himself) the very opposite of Ruskin: the Englishman who rose above his nation's infatuation with propriety? Whose travels and education had led, rather, to largeness of mind and adventurousness of spirit, to the open pursuit of the darker obsessions of heterogeneous human culture? Yes, Burton and Ruskin were opposite poles of "the sophisticated Englishman at mid-century"—that was plain enough. But instinct kept suggesting that Burton now had something to do with Mrs. Fullerton and the Turners.

Knowing full well that I would not be able to leave Rome and Italy for years perhaps, I put this letter and card from far America aside and, after months of painful separation, I threw myself into enjoying the presence of Laura and my son Russie. Laura's own joy in our reunion seemed to have removed all traces of that dejection from which she at times suffered, those gloomy wisps of glory I have mentioned. We took a few opportunities to travel when it was determined we might do so safely. We were, in fact, once held up by brigands. But soon that seemed the least of my difficulties.

* * *

Some months after I received Mrs. Fullerton's letter, a somber little Englishman sporting a light grey suit and great black mustaches appeared at the door of our apartment one morning just as I was leaving for the consulate. "Winslow. Mortimer Winslow," he introduced himself. "May I have a word with you, sir?

"I'm in the employ of Messrs. William and Gabriel Rossetti," he added as he came in.

I led him into the dining room where Laura and I had just finished breakfast, closed the door, and seated him at the table with a cup of coffee. "What can I do for you, Mr. Winslow?"

"Much obliged, sir," he said. "Do you know a certain Miss Cornforth, from London?"

"Fanny Cornforth? Why yes; it was William himself introduced me to her."

"Indeed."

"Has something happened to her?"

"No, nothing of that sort. I've spoken to her at length, however. She finally told me you were among several people to enter her room during the week when it was broken into and, to be candid, sacked."

"Sacked! I'm sorry to hear it. Yet you say she is fine?"

"Yes." He didn't smile but his eyes flashed slightly. "So you know her. Well?"

"Not well. William had introduced her to me as one of Gabriel's models. I'm a painter myself, you see."

"So I'm given to understand, sir."

"I never did use her as a model. Consular business drew me here right after our introduction."

"I see. So you only saw her once, then?"

"Once? No, I believe we met on...two occasions."

"And what was the nature of those occasions?"

"As I say, an introduction to her, as a painters' model."

"But you said two meetings, sir, and I'm wondering about the second if it was not to use her services as a model."

"Look here, Mr. Mortimer. I don't appreciate being made to feel like some kind of criminal suspect. I certainly never broke into her apartment. Would you pay me the courtesy of explaining what this is about, please."

"But you did enter her room twice, as I understand you, sir. You know of certain studies of Mr. of Gabriel Rossetti's?"

"Yes. I repeat: What is this about, sir?"

"I believe you know that these drawings, or whatever they were, technically speaking, were held temporarily in Miss Cornforth's room.

We are simply trying to assess every possible person who had access to her room during the week in question. We're looking for any lead, any knowledge of the artifacts, by anyone."

"The Rossettis asked you to speak to anyone who had access? Surely that might truly be anyone. Did they describe to you the nature of these studies?"

"Not precisely, but their value as life studies, mostly of women. And of course anything of the artist's has considerable value in some quarters, and potentially greater value as time passes."

"Isn't it possible then that the theft was quite intentional: I mean to say the life studies had been targeted?"

"Perhaps. But it seems only four people knew of them, and the sacking of several apartments in the neighborhood has all the earmarks of a random and desperate act. Such matters, of course, are what I'm being paid to determine. Would you please describe for me now the nature of your second visit to Miss Cornforth, after you'd been properly introduced, that is."

I hesitated, perhaps too long. "Well, it was business of a sort. I wanted to view the life studies one last time before leaving, within twenty-four hours, for what might well be years in Rome."

"There was no other purpose?"

"Has Miss Cornforth made up some story about me?"

"She has said only that subsequent to your viewing, along with Mr. Rossetti, the materials in question, you returned for a more commonplace visit."

"And you're willing to take the word of a harlot over mine."

"I'm not taking anyone's word over another's at this point, sir. But surely you understand it wouldn't be the first time a gentleman might have denied a secret life or his true intentions with a lady."

"A lady?"

"With a woman, let us say then."

"Well, this woman had materials from an artist I had been studying and appreciating, as John Ruskin can tell you, for years. That's why I returned to her to see them."

"Did you pay her?"

"Pay her? Why yes I did, in fact. She's the kind of woman whose time one must pay for, in any capacity. Surely that's clear to you by now."

"Indeed."

"I don't begrudge her payment for her time. If she tells the truth at all, she'll tell you that the package of drawings was there when I came to her room the second time and still there after I left."

"So, to be clear, sir, you are saying that your second visit was merely to view the drawings, that there was no other motive, and that you left the country within twenty-four hours to come to Rome."

"Absolutely."

"Well, then, now I have your statement, I must be traveling again in pursuit of my clients' interest. I thank you for your time and forthrightness. And for the excellent coffee. Should I need any further information, may I call on you again, sir?"

I hesitated once more, though I had not meant to. "Of course. But I don't know what else I can possibly tell you about the matter."

Part II, 1863–1872

The whole system of modern society, politics, and religion seems to me so exquisitely absurd that I know not where to begin about it—or to end. My father keeps me in order, or I should be continually getting into scrapes.

— John Ruskin, letter to Rev. W. L. Brown,
November 8, 1853

In a community regulated only by laws of demand and supply, but protected from open violence, the persons who become rich are, generally speaking, industrious, resolute, proud, covetous, prompt, methodical, sensible, unimaginative, insensitive, and ignorant. The persons who remain poor are the entirely foolish, the entirely wise, the idle, the reckless, the humble, the thoughtful, the dull, the imaginative, the sensitive, the well-informed, the improvident, the irregularly and impulsively wicked, the clumsy knave, the open thief, and the entirely merciful, just, and godly person.

— John Ruskin, *Unto This Last*

Chapter 14

I didn't know whether Winslow went away convinced of my veracity. I know only that I didn't hear from him again while I resided in Italy. Other matters pressed me, and as the end of my second year approached, my post was complicated due to the arrival of other ministers to Rome. Therefore, Laura and I decided to return to America, by way of Florence and Turin that I might see George Marsh, our minister to Italy. Here was an admirable diplomat and scholar: to my mind the one bright presence of our diplomatic service on the continent.

I arrived with my family in New York July 4, 1863, right after the bloody victory of Gettysburg. For the first time during this troubled American epoch I felt certain of the end. My own purpose was twofold: to gain employment with my elder brother Thomas in his office as head of the Construction Department of the Revenue Service, under his friend and Secretary of the Treasury, Salmon Chase, and at long last to locate Mrs. Fullerton, whose Boston address I knew.

That summer, while we were visiting Laura's family in Cambridge, one day I took the opportunity to slip over to Boston. The New England heat was infernal. I climbed to Mrs. Fullerton's rooms and knocked. I expected she would observe the common practice and affix her painter's card to the door. But there was nothing to indicate her presence. I tried the doorknob, which was locked. Something like panic flared across my chest.

Perspiring heavily now, I hurried downstairs. An old man in a shabby black suit, a pipe clenched between his teeth, was sweeping the front steps.

"Excuse me," I said. "Does the landlord live nearby?"

He stopped and looked up at me, eyes slowly focusing. There was not a drop of sweat on his face, as if he had simply dried up years ago and stifling summer mattered not a bit to him.

"Mrs. Bellerrhino," he said. "Manages for the landlord. First floor there, number two." He returned to his task, finishing the broom stroke he had begun, as if I had never appeared to interrupt him.

"Thank you." I reentered the foyer, found number two, and knocked. I heard a heavy-footed stirring. The door finally opened. An enormous old woman in a summer dressing gown with a wet cloth pressed to her forehead opened the door.

She glanced me over. "Yes, sir? Rooms?"

"No, thank you, Mrs. Bellerrhino. I've only come to call on one of your tenants, an old friend, but despite her assurances, she seems not to be in her rooms. A Mrs. Allegra Fullerton?" I held up her card.

"Oh, Mrs. Fullerton! The artist. Lovely woman." She looked me over once more. "I'm afraid you're too late, sir. She's gone, nearly a month now."

"Gone?"

"Yes, sir. Some painting expedition, I expect."

"She left no forwarding address or hint of intention?"

"No, sir. Paid up and left. All her traps off in a pony cart." She smiled for the first time and wiped the entire expanse of her forehead with the cloth. "I'm not one to pry. I can only say she told me of her growing conviction that desperate Confederate forces were targeting Boston for attack. Part of that larger invasion people talking about, sir.

All we hear is the rebels are more bloodthirsty than ever." She sighed. "And to escape the summer heat."

She reeked of sweat, garlic, and too much lavender water. I lingered long enough to be sure she truly knew nothing of my friend. But the old lady was ignorant, or adept at feigning ignorance. Could Mrs. Fullerton have betrayed me?

I returned to Cambridge in a melancholic state. I said nothing to anyone about my disappointment, excepting my old friend Eliot Norton. The next day I walked over to his capacious residence Shady Hill, overlooking marshes and huckleberry pastures. The avenue led from Professor's Row to the white clapboard house. The weather had cooled somewhat. We sat on the columned piazza, with a pitcher of lemonade, looking east over azaleas and clethras down to the tidal flats of the Charles River, and beyond the river to the gilded dome of the statehouse on Beacon Hill.

His wife Susan had recently given birth to their son, Eliot, and Norton seemed to bask in his new role of *pater familias*, a relief from his grinding lecture and literary work on behalf of the Union cause. He had been convinced of the Union's success even before Gettysburg, believing a protracted war for all its carnage—and he had lost friends and relations himself—had the benefit at least of "knocking a good deal of shallowness and nonsense" out of the nation and pushing the rebels into "unconditional surrender."

"Subjugating or even exterminating the slave-holding class could never be a quick process," he said. "If only Lord Palmerston's government will avoid its temptation to support the rebels. It'll be bad enough as it is when it's all over, Will, that our resentment of the British governing classes will smolder for decades."

We spoke of our mutual friend George Marsh at Florence, whom Norton had enlisted to find him a copyist for Benvenuto da Imola's

"Comment" on the *Divina Commedia*. I then brought up our other mutual friend, Ruskin.

"He introduced me to the American painter Allegra Fullerton." I told him. "You know her?"

"Yes, I know Mrs. Fullerton," he said. "We've met at one or two gallery openings and a fundraiser, or something like, if I recall rightly."

"Have you seen or heard of her lately?" I handed him her card. "She's departed this Boston address with no forwarding information. She holds some sketches for me, some Turners to be exact."

"Turners, indeed!" His face brightened.

"Have you heard anything of her?"

"No, sorry to say. I recall my initial viewing of Turners with Julia Sturgis in Tottenham, the Windus collection—about the same time you were first in London, I believe. Eighteen-fifty? Anyway, I've been a true believer ever since." He laughed.

"Yes, but I got to Denmark Hill five years before you ever did."

"Be that as it may," he said, "I purchased my first Turner then."

"I recall. His vignette of Scott's house in Edinburgh."

"Yes! This Mrs. Fullerton—you say she holds Turners for you?"

"Just so."

"Well then, find her we must! I'll ask about. Someone might know something."

I did not tell him the nature of the sketches; it would have deflated his enthusiasm. We spent the remainder of our hour together talking of Turner. Norton said he had in mind to write about this "finest of landscape painters" some day. In fact, years later he would organize an exhibition of Turners in Boston to "display the range of his genius." I would save the exhibition catalogue and guide he had prepared, as well as his copy of the lecture introducing the exhibit. Turner, he wrote, is a force still useful "to undo the prevalent taste and prevalent modes of artistic study and discipline."

It was such a pleasure to see my old friend that I was able to hide from Norton my utter disconsolation at Allegra's disappearance.

* * *

I was by now ready to try anything. I had very little time left in Cambridge, and for all I knew in America. When Laura and I had visited my brother Thomas in Washington, I recalled for him our days when brother Jacob and I experimented in spiritualism. What I told Thomas, I later told Ruskin during our sojourn in Switzerland, during those long conversations about art and religion. I explained to Ruskin my experience of meeting a young American named Adele who had convinced me of her unique powers

Could she help me in my desperation now?

"She was a girl of fourteen," I remember telling Ruskin at the time, "of timid and nervous organization, who had suffered loud rappings that followed her about, breaking out on any occasion whatever."

I could see Ruskin's interest focused.

"She was being driven from her position of assistant teacher in a primary school for the noise scaring the wits out of her students during recitations," I went on. "My brother and I got permission from her father, a well-to-do man for whom one of my other brothers worked, for a séance. By that time the rapping had evolved into involuntary motions of her right hand, which she finally determined was an effort of this 'influence,' as she called it, to express itself in writing."

"And you saw no opportunity for fraud in this?" Ruskin asked.

"Not after we determined that she could write equally well whether looking at what she wrote or whether we had bandaged her eyes."

"I see. There has always been a great deal of charlatanism about, but it has long been my belief that there are depths in some few but certain persons that are beyond the rest of us," he said. "Even my own mother has had a bit of second sight in her time—"

"Mine as well," I said.

"But I too have sat with mediums, including one who sounds very like this young woman, as you describe her."

"In our experiment, and under these circumstances described," I continued, "Miss A. produced a better written imitation of three of our deceased relatives than I could have done myself, knowing their penmanship well—the wife of this very brother Jacob, my brother Alfred, and my childhood friend and cousin Harvey. All dead. She had known none of these people.

"As we were ending the session," I went on, "I asked my dead cousin Harvey, who had been communicating by written answers to my queries, if he had seen old Turner, whose death had happened not long ago. The answer was yes. I asked what Turner was doing, and Miss A. made a pantomime of painting." At this point Ruskin's face changed from surprise at first to a frown of doubt. "I asked Harvey if he could fetch Turner for us. He replied that he would see. Miss A. said 'the influence is going away," and then shortly added, 'There is another influence coming in that direction,' pointing over her left shoulder, 'and I don't like it.' Upon which she shuddered and then sat up in her chair and began to appear as if the influence had indeed entered her, or become her. In the look from under her brow, the pose of her head, it was as if the ghost of Turner had come back quite as I had seen him at Griffith's. My entire flesh, to the tips of my fingers began to creep, I can tell you!"

"As well it might," Ruskin said. "Are you certain of all this you are telling me, William?"

"I swear by my own dear mother's saintly life."

"Then continue, please."

"I asked Adele if Turner could write his name for me, to which she replied with a sharp negative sign. I then asked if the old master could give me some advice as to my own painting. Again she gave a decided negative response, with the fixed and sardonic stare the girl had put on at the coming of this new influence. I said then that since the influence that purported to be Turner had refused me my requests, there was nothing more to be done.

"Yet the young woman sat still and helpless. We waited. She finally got up and moved across the room with the feeble step of an old man. She took down from the wall a colored French lithograph, laid it on the table before me, gesturing to it. She then did a pantomime of stretching a sheet of paper on a drawing-board, sharpening a pencil, and tracing the outlines of the subject in the lithograph. Then she seemed to choose a water-color pencil, noting carefully the fineness of the point. And finally she performed the broad washing-in of a drawing. Miss A., we later determined, knew nothing of drawing or painting. Next, she took out a pocket handkerchief and with it and her pencil began taking out the lights. I mean in the technical sense, my dear Ruskin, *rubbing-out*."

"My goodness! And she was completely without any training or experience of such things? You're sure?"

"Absolutely. We made certain. I asked whether she meant to say that Turner rubbed out his lights, and she gave an affirmative sign. I then recalled one of the master's drawings, *Llanthony Abbey*, where the passage of sunlight and shadow through rain could not have, to my mind, been done such-wise. I inquired whether it had been done so, and she said yes. Now I began to believe there was some simulation of personality or fraudulence afoot, for I was convinced otherwise as to the drawing's execution."

At that moment, Ruskin rose from his chair. "The contrariness Miss A. manifested is just like old Turner," he said, moving quickly to fetch the very drawing in question.

"I had once seen a bit of it myself," I said.

Ruskin returned and laid the drawing before us. We examined it with the greatest scrutiny, and he demonstrated convincingly that rubbing-out was indeed precisely the manner of its execution. We stood looking at one another. A chilling tremble ran up and down my spine and over the muscles of my face and scalp. It was like being vouchsafed a momentary view into the other world—frightening and fascinating and horrifyingly convincing.

"You must send an account of this whole business to *Cornhill*," he said.

"If you say so," I responded. "I'll try."

I wrote it up, showed it to Ruskin, made one or two alterations on his advice, and sent it off. I took special care to demonstrate how this instance of rubbing out was, on Ruskin's instruction, but one of many techniques the master used to manipulate pigment, along with scratching out with a fingernail and with the handle tip of a paint brush, covering with gum mastic base, lively impasting with a palette knife, and even painting with finger tips. But Mr. Thackeray rejected my essay, and I imagined him tossing into the wastebasket what he believed to be a fraud I had hoped to perpetrate upon him.

When I next visited Ruskin, he immediately returned us to my story of Miss A. "What do you make of such things, finally, William?" he had asked. "And of the skeptics?"

"I don't know what to make of it," I said. "And I don't expect to convert the skeptics. They have not shared my experiences. Moreover, perhaps they were defrauded. Who can say? But if they were to make their own observations and investigations, as I have, at the sacrifice of great patience and time, and approach these phenomena with an open mind, who can say but that they might not begin to doubt their own skepticism?"

* * *

When, as I say, I reminded my brother Thomas of this story, he recalled my and my brother Jacob's experiment with Adele.

"I've heard something of her," Thomas said, looking toward the ceiling. "Let's see. She married and moved across the border to Massachusetts. Pittsfield? No. No, it was Hancock. That's it. She married into the Wholemate family. A farmer. Elijah Wholemate. I believe her days as a medium are over, however."

Hancock! I thought. The very town of my former "impossible" nighttime trek to rendezvous with Henry Kirke Brown at our fish camp.

But now in Cambridge, with Allegra Fullerton missing and no other plan to find her, I posted a letter to Hancock saying I was on my way by the railcars to Pittsfield on business and would be stopping by the Wholemate's farm. I then saw Laura and Russie off back to Washington, where I was to follow immediately after my visit to Adele.

I hired a gig from the railway station to the Wholemate farm, not far from the Shaker community, I discovered. Adele was no longer the teenage waif I had once consulted. She was a full-grown woman and mother of four children, who looked as solid as any prosperous farmer's wife one might meet on her daily rounds. She recalled my family and my brother and me. And she thanked me for my polite letter.

I wasted little time explaining that I was pursuing a certain missing female artist who had left Boston with some precious art work that belonged to me. We sat on her porch in two chairs facing her fields and the green Berkshire Hills.

"I was given to understand," I said, "that on rare occasions you still practice the spiritualist arts."

She looked at me, grasping now the whole purpose of my visit. "On occasion," Mr. Stillman," she replied. "Only when there is opportunity to do by them some good in the world. Which is rarely."

When I told her that the valuable works in question were the product of Turner's pen and brush, she frowned, as if she remembered the consuming abrasiveness of his spirit during our sessions shortly after the old painter died.

"Let me assure you, Mrs. Wholemate," I said, "I wouldn't ask you to call upon Mr. Turner again. I'm seeking only Mrs. Fullerton. Some clue to her whereabouts." With that I handed her Allegra's card. "She has, it seems, disappeared from her painting rooms."

"I see," she said, looking at the card and then delicately turning it over and over in her hand. "No. She is no longer there."

"Can you tell me where?"

She looked up toward the lush hills. "They'll be wanting their supper," she said.

"Your husband and children."

"I should get started." Her left hand began to pick at her right sleeve. "I don't think I can help you, Mr. Stillman."

"I didn't mean to rush you into anything. Only I have to meet my wife and child in Washington within a day or two. I hope you'll forgive my feelings of desperation."

"I understand you want to recover your loss—"

"But I'm importuning, arriving suddenly like this, asking after all these years for you to indulge me. You're being perfectly reasonable."

She finally turned her head toward me. "I'm unaccustomed to using my gifts," she said and paused. "They have grown weak, and they have brought me more trouble than benefit."

"Still, you've done some good, as well."

"At rare intervals." She rose from her chair and turned fully toward me. "You've come a long way to ask for my help. I'm sorry. I'm afraid it is you who shall have to forgive me." She extended her hand. "It's going to be too late to return," she said. "Will you stop the night in Pittsfield?"

"Is there no where in town here? I seem to recall an inn on a certain long-ago adventure in these parts."

She directed me toward the inn. I thanked her for hearing me out and promised to say a final good-bye on my way to the railway station in the morning. I walked to my gig, reached into my bag, and removed a little package of English teas. I returned to her and handed her the packet. "For my troubling you, Mrs. Wholemate. Please accept this."

"You've been no trouble. Sorry I can't be more helpful."

* * *

I spent the night in a state of disquiet. I arose in the gray light, break-fasted at the inn, and rode out to the Wholemate farm shortly after seven o'clock. The air was growing oppressive already, the clouds thicker. The Wholemate family was out and about their chores, at-tempting to stay ahead of the looming storm. Mrs. Wholemate came from her kitchen to greet me at the door and asked if I had time for coffee.

"It was a night of unsettling dreams," I said in good humor.

She turned from the stove, coffee pot in hand. "You, too?"

"I saw you, Mrs. Wholemate, just once, near a mountaintop—as if you were about to fly off from us." I laughed lightly. She handed me a filled cup, not smiling, but impassive, her look expressing neither approval nor disapproval.

"Let's go into the parlor," she said.

She drew the curtains, and we sat down at a small card table. "We shall see," she said. "Now, Mr. Stillman, when you finish your coffee, just breathe deeply and relax your entire body."

"I'll do my best," I said, wondering at her change of heart, wondering about the power of my dreams.

"Good. Yes, just deep even breaths," she said.

The room was not dark, but the early morning light, dusky from the approaching storm, felt more like evening coming on. I heard two or three birds, one a thrush, off in the woodlot. The thrush song added to the sense of looming nightfall. The house was remarkably quiet with her husband and children off in the barns and fields. Nothing happened for perhaps ten or fifteen minutes. My breathing into myself, so to speak, obscured my perception of time passing.

"I am not seeing her," she finally said. "But I see mountains. There are many clouds among the summer mountaintops, and wind." She paused. "And an eagle."

The Catskills? I wondered. The Adirondacks? Or the White Mountains, perhaps? Or the Alps? Did it really matter? I had to return directly to Washington and a last ditch effort to find employment. I soon would have to make decisions that would affect my family for years.

"Mountains? Can you say which?"

"No," she replied immediately. "But there is someone else, not she and not among mountains. A man. Tall and fierce looking. With great mustachios, a broad-brimmed hat to keep off the sun. I see his shadow—a strong jaw. Now a little light on his face, not much. I don't know him. He's rather an evil looking sort, like an actor playing the Devil. He's swarthy, like some sort of...with eyes like a gypsy."

"What can he have to do with her, with Mrs. Fullerton?"

"Unclear." She searched her vision a moment longer. "He's very tall, broad-shouldered. Heavy chest. A proud man." She paused once more. "I can only tell you the images I see, Mr. Stillman."

"That she's in the mountains. Somewhere."

"That's what I see."

I recalled that Mrs. Fullerton had told me of painting trips in the White Mountains, after the manner of her now deceased mentor, George Spooner. Might that be it, the "White Hills"? They were spectacular, rising at times above 6,000 feet some seventy or eighty miles from tideland New Hampshire. There was no way I could find her there on this slight evidence, if she were even there, and if I had time. It would be difficult enough if I had the name of a town or mountain, or a resort even. The whole idea was of course fantastic, insuperable. For all I knew, Adele Wholemate was leading me astray, unwittingly, in the first place.

When it was over, I thanked her. I had been shown something, but I had also been shown how useless such fleeting visions were to me now.

* * *

On the train for Washington, I became convinced I had lost Mrs. Fullerton, or that for reasons of her own she had escaped me. Unless I could find a suitable post with the Treasury Department of the Union government, there wasn't much possibility that I could prosecute my quest in America for the "purloined Turners," as I now thought of them, with any hope of success. Nor would I be able to support my son and wife. As had happened so often in the course of my life, financial necessity drove my destiny.

Chapter 15

Laura! Laura is a difficult, painful subject for me. In due course I shall find the strength to describe something of the awful tragedy that befell us. But I must return to our story as it happened.

After I joined Laura in Washington (where she had been staying at my brother and sister-in-law's residence) she turned to me and said, "Now, William, I know you're troubled over finding a post in Washington, but I'm sure there's something more that's disturbed you. A wife knows these things. And because I'm your wife you must tell me the truth, as soon as we have a private hour."

I looked into the eyes of this woman I loved, this woman who had indulged my studies and travels abroad more than many other women would have, this woman who was the mother of our dear boy. There were many things I had not told her. There were two or three things I could not possibly tell her. But I promised her that once we were entirely alone I would reveal the cause of my morose demeanor.

"That's a promise, then," she said, and reached to take my hand.

As we lay in bed that evening I told her what I have written here regarding my adventures with John Ruskin, the illicit Turners, and Mortimer Winslow's arrival in Rome—everything that would not offend her or undermine our marriage.

It was becoming ever clearer that we would be returning to Rome to resume my consulship. My brother Thomas had hopes of giving me a position to assist him in the Revenue Service, but his wife must have seen such an association with "poor relations" as inevitably leading to a reduction in her, or their, status, and bitterly opposed our staying on to take the job my brother had in mind. Moreover, she was perhaps understandably quite out of patience from our living with them.

Leaving little Russie with a nurse, we left my brother's house for a light supper in private the next evening.

"It's a good thing you have an adventurous spirit, my dear," I said to Laura. "And that I didn't trick you into believing you were marrying a man of means."

She laughed. "I knew exactly whom I was marrying."

"Well, my inability to focus my attentions on our material well-being is a trial, I realize. I've been blown about, and no doubt will continue to be blown about, by the winds of necessity."

"We married for better or worse. And so far we've managed," she said in a tone of voice that put an end to such talk. Indeed, we had managed. And I believed in spite of all that our marriage was better than most. I had come gradually to understand that we shared love, and mutual respect, if not a grand passion. But my pursuit of Turner's secret life, and my consequent associations with women like Fanny and Mrs. Fullerton, had lodged a question in me that would, I was coming to believe, have disturbing endurance. Could not marriage, or love, or both, be still something more fervid? Could I, or could Laura, awaken some transforming passion in one another?

When she finished her soup, she looked up. "I understand you believe these sketches are a sort of key to Turner's art."

"That his fascination with Eros is in some way at the center of his work—"

"His muse, perhaps? Well, maybe so. And who knows anyway? But don't you think, William, that it's just possible their loss, to have them off your hands, is a stroke of good fortune?"

I looked at her a moment. "Do you mean, dear, for their illegality?"

"Of course. But also were they to be stuck in America till you might venture to sneak them through customs to their proper home? As you've said, they belong to England, whether the British people want them or not. Surely someone could be found to curate them properly—out of the public eye."

"But they're already in America."

"From what you told me you have no evidence of it. They need not be, I really mean to say, your responsibility any longer. They can no longer be a future source of embarrassment."

"I'd as soon have kept them hidden, even among my heirs, for a hundred years."

"What is there to guarantee that?" She looked at me without speaking. I didn't have an answer. "Like it or not, you're a public official," she continued. "Our entire livelihood depends on your appearance of probity. You haven't sufficient political connections to weather any storm. Look what that woman has been able to deny us." She was speaking of my sister-in-law.

"You're perhaps right, darling, but I'm afraid the Turners may be lost *forever.* That's what concerns me."

"I think not. This Allegra Fullerton, as you describe her, would never destroy them or be careless of their survival. Would she? The difficulty for you, rather, is simply your loss of control over them. For good enough reasons you did what you could and then had to abandon that precarious responsibility."

"It's not a responsibility I wished to abandon. I had assurances that I hadn't."

"I understand. As you've hinted, you put yourself at risk to obtain them. And then this hired investigator—Winslow's his name?—has his suspicions, whether the Rossettis do or not. But it's also becoming clear that we're to be traveling again. We're not wanted here. I'll wager that woman will find a way to cut you out of Thomas's will."

"Darling, don't be overly harsh."

"Mark my words, William. She'll impede any further benefit coming to you from her husband's generosity."

"In any event, we have to move on anyway for me to work."

"We do now. Besides, I don't hesitate to leave the despoiled Union behind us once more."

"You were always adventuresome, Laura."

"So long as I was capable of adventure. And able to convince you to allow me to accompany you on yours!"

I laughed. "Well, my dear, I'm glad you are, for here we go again."

"So it appears," she said. "Let's have our adventures, then, all of us together, and forget these dubious Turners. You could hardly drag them about with us. And with whom would you leave them? Norton? Hardly, I think!" She stopped to test my agreement. "In any event, we have our own lives to make."

"What other position do we have? I'll tell them at the State Department tomorrow that I'm prepared to return with my family to Rome."

Chapter 16

And so we did return to Rome. By then Laura was pregnant with our second child. But I soon found that troubles were about to begin, for I found in Rome that General Rufus King (the new minister appointed by his friend Secretary of State William Seward) had appointed in turn a minion, a certain "Copperhead" American banker. This appointee, without governmental authority, had removed the source of revenue for my position—the visa on the passports of all Americans that also ensured we would keep track of Confederate residents abroad. I made several appeals concerning the illegality of this decision to General King, the Department of State, and others. But Seward backed his old crony King. My appeals had no effect. Friendship was more important to Seward than legality and diplomatic scandal.

I therefore managed to release myself from all obligations of my consulate and took once again to sketching and writing in hope of supporting my family. The Campagna di Roma became my favorite haunt. We managed, barely, for a time in this way until the assassination of President Lincoln and the attempt on Seward's life. Everyone in the American community abroad felt horror and grief. But we also felt that the President's work was done and his fame secure before any political blunder could tarnish it. My immediate interests were affected, however. Mr. Lincoln had somehow (perhaps from my brother) discovered the injustice of Seward's treatment of my case and appeals, and as one of his final acts of American minor diplomacy, he had me appointed to the consulate in Crete, an appointment that changed my life—my family—forever.

This consulship would alleviate our immediate financial straits, but due to the cholera rampaging through the Levant and the quarantine on all ships passing through any Turkish port, we decided that Laura, Russie, and our new baby, Lisa, barely three months old, would stay in Rome while I set out for Crete. When I arrived at my post, the consulate was deserted, the consulate archives missing. I found my vice consul, a Smyrniote Greek and an honest man who had been awaiting my arrival. I also met the man who was to become my enemy, the pasha, a renegade Greek named Ishmael, whose policy it was to buy or break every new consul who came his way. I always liked a good fight for a good cause, so we engaged in our struggle. It came as a joy of many inhabitants of the island every time I bested this petty tyrant, whose power came from his Turkish overlords and paymasters.

I missed my family terribly in those first months, and the lost sketch studies still haunted me. One day, tormented by my losses, I had been making a visit to the provincial *mudir*. When riding my horse out of his courtyard, I glimpsed the flutter of a woman's robes in the nearby garden. The garden was protected by a hedge of cacti, but I leaned into one of the openings and saw the young woman's face. Her sudden, unadorned splendor distracted my judgment. We stared at each other for some moments before she remembered that a Muslim female must not be seen. Regaining her composure, she quickly wrapped her veil about her head as she fled into the house.

I had never seen such grace, such exquisite proportion, color, and delicacy of modeling, nor such eyes of lustrous brown—like a creature not really of this world. It was, however, the vacuous beauty of one untroubled by mental activity, which activity I speculated (even at that impossible moment) must leave its traces upon the face of man or woman. She had a dignity, that supreme animal repose and serenity, which was no small part of her transcendent charm. I could compare her presence to nothing so much as a morning in the wilderness of the Adirondacks, on one of my fishing and painting expeditions, when in the fired mists of sunrise over the lake, a deer, glowing like some supernal creature, gracefully appears and arrests the viewer in a species of ecstatic vision.

It was no doubt that this vision of the woman, combined with my long separation, I say, that blinded me to the brutal facts. I made the fatal error of returning to Rome to fetch Laura and the children to Crete.

Our passage was the roughest I ever endured. Laura, Russie, and Lisa sank into the lowest depths of seasickness. I was fast approaching the troughs myself. I staggered up the companionway steps toward the sea air, some dim part of me wondering how the world would look in such frenzied paroxysms of squall.

On deck, I clung with both hands to a lanyard that was wildly flapping against the cabin wall. I lost my hat to the blast, and looked into the spume and spew—one vast maelstrom of dark sky-sea. With my life—all our lives—in danger, I nonetheless thought of Turner, his perilous study of storms and seas. His creation of vortices of water and unearthly light, foundering ships and overwhelmed humanity caught in avalanches, in deluges, in the convulsions of oceanic apocalypse. Nature's wrath and God's. The very face of our own deaths, now. Or someday, soon enough. *The Wreck of a Transport Ship, The Wreck of the Amphitrite, Slavers Throwing Overboard the Dead and Dying—Typhoon Coming On, Snowstorm—Steamboat off a Harbour's Mouth*: all these and more passed before my inner eye, even as my outer beheld cataclysms of water and air in the immediate cyclone.

After coming as close to shipwreck as it is possible to come and yet survive, Laura, the children, and I arrived in Crete on the very eve of the Cretan insurrection against the Turks, Egyptians, and their Muslim collaborators.

The Cretan people's petition to Constantinople had been futile, and then there were endless months of maneuvers, feints, betrayals, and provocative violence on all sides. I always knew that although Laura's body was small and in some ways fragile, her will was strong. She had an unshakable sense of justice and duty, which now was to be tested.

Even before the worst hostilities broke out, when she and women of the other European consulates were out walking between Canea and Kalepa, the Muslim soldiers amused themselves by shooting as close to their heads as possible without hitting them.

"You must leave for Syra with the children," I said when she told me about the near misses. "I'll begin making the arrangements tomorrow."

"No, William," she insisted. "I can't abandon the Cretan women. They look to us for protection. If they see me panic and run, they'll flee to the mountains where they'll surely die, either through exposure or attack."

"Then I'll give up this post. And we shall all leave on the first boat."

"William, we can abandon neither your post nor these people."

"We could return to Rome, or go on to Athens, where I can paint again, just until I can find other employment, or the means to return to America."

She looked at me, her eyes expressing both exasperation and love. "You know we can't afford to strike out with no expectations of income." She hesitated. "We have nothing in reserve. But it's not only that. As you've said yourself, your hand and your eye have grown stale." She halted again. "How can we think of throwing ourselves at the mercy of tourists seeking romantic views?"

"It's a frightening thought, I agree. But I've had some little success before."

"Do you remember telling me one night, 'Laura, I'm no Turner and thankful for it'?"

"Yes."

"Well, genius has its own burdens, and mercifully given to few enough. But, my dear, you're not even a John Ruskin, himself a mere moon among the planets of Turner's sun. You've said as much yourself." She paused to see how I was taking it. "I'm telling you nothing you don't know. The children and I love you no less."

" 'The man who examining his own mind finds nothing of inspiration ought not to dare to be an artist'," I said.

"I did not say you lost your inspiration."

"That's the least of it, I fear," I said. "But I was quoting William Blake, the eccentric poet and artist few know and fewer care for these days. William Rossetti told me of a curious little manuscript book filled with verse and drawings and epigrammatic prose that his brother had purchased of an attendant at the British Museum. It was Blake's working manuscript that Gabriel found inspiring, so he and William took on the task of copying out whatever they could make of the tangled lines of cancellations and interlinear markings and false starts. But what's stuck with me, along with some of the epigrams like that one, is William Rossetti's account of Blake's jabs at the artists we now hold in highest esteem. I mean not only Reynolds and Gainsborough, but Titian, Rubens, and Rembrandt, among others, for their 'fulsomely florid, or lax, style,' as Rossetti put it to me, 'or for swamping ideas in mere manipulation'."

"Mr. Blake seems to have given no one quarter," she said. "But as Ruskin always says: 'The faults of a work of art are the faults of the workman, and its virtues his virtues.'"

"Yes. Blake would've admired Turner." I returned her look. "'What has reasoning to do with the art of painting?'"

"Blake again?" she asked. "The test of originality and inspiration?"

"And only guarded obeisance to one's predecessors." I thought a moment. "Something of the outlaw seems, to Blake's mind, a first requirement."

She smiled, finally. "Turner," she said. Neither of us spoke for some moments. Then she added, "You've breached the law, William, with the theft of those sketches. But an original genius is by nature beyond the law: He is, I mean to say, a transgressor of a wholly different sort."

"But you really mean to say I'm a government official and should aspire to nothing more."

She smiled again. "Don't be histrionic. You're a good father and husband. You have a need to capture images, a need to write your thoughts and experiences, and of course you may paint away to your heart's content. But we must see this through. Then if you can find work from your writing, or some other pleasurable pursuit, we can make changes in our lives, with caution."

"I was speaking only of working in temporary circumstances—"

"Our circumstances *here* are temporary, compared to the circumstances of these people, of the havoc being wreaked on them and their generations to come. I'm saying only this—we have a duty here, an obligation for which you're being modestly compensated."

"Modest is too generous a word."

"You once spoke of photographing ancient ruins here and elsewhere," she said. "In peaceful intervals. Wouldn't that be a more worthy, and perhaps eventually more remunerative, project? Don't you believe in your deepest heart that the idea of painting for our living, however temporary, is untenable? You're a representative of our government and we have work to do. Work of the most serious kind, involving the lives of thousands."

I knew all this, of course. And she knew I knew it; she was only speaking my own thoughts. But I truly feared for her and my children's lives by then, and had begun to see my folly in bringing them here. Moreover, she was right: I knew my youthful dream of becoming a painter—living by my art—was nothing more. But it was nonetheless a dream I found painful to abandon, as if I were an unmarried youth ordered to abandon his infatuating mistress.

* * *

Our circumstances did not improve. My brother, concerned for my safety, sent me two new pistols and insisted I arm myself henceforth. His concerns proved prescient. By August of 1866 our security grew more tenuous by the day: I discovered that the Turks had decided to kill me. Three Muslim men waylaid me as I rode down to the yacht we used to travel to Greece and to help refugees escape the island. Only one spoke English. He told me to throw down the rifle in my saddle and dismount. He said they were under orders to question and search all Christians and foreigners.

When they remained astride their horses, I knew I had met my assassins. One man dismounted and came towards me.

"Turn around," the English speaker said from his horse. His voice was calm. "Toward that field," he corrected me when I had turned to face my horse. The man pushed his rifle in my back and reached out to pull my coat waist high for any concealed weapons.

"Walk into the field," the leader said. "We will search you off the road." He told the other mounted man to bring my horse to him. I had seen enough bodies—some of them terribly mutilated—in ditches and fields beside the roads to know what they were about.

My hands were clasped behind my head as ordered. I started for the field. But just as I stepped into the drainage ditch I pretended to stumble and dropped to one knee, throwing one hand out to break my fall. While the men laughed at my fear-stricken clumsiness, I let myself roll into the ditch. As I stood, I reached into my open coat where I had concealed one of my revolvers. It was strapped against the hollow between my chest and left armpit. With a single motion, I withdrew the gun as I turned to face them and shot the dismounted man twice in the chest. As he collapsed onto the road, I continued firing and hit the English-speaking man in the thigh near the height of his groin. His rifle went off and dropped as he grabbed at the wound. His horse reared, nearly throwing him. The third man had already turned and galloped away.

"Leave my horse," I shouted at the leader as he was righting himself.

He let go the reins and turned his horse to flee. I almost pulled the trigger again, for I had a fair shot at him, but instantly thought better of it. Anything more the Turkish government or Ishmael could use against me through their own construction of the incident would increase my vulnerability to both official censure and local revenge. I rolled the body of the dead man into the ditch, mounted my horse, and sped on my way to the yacht *Kestrel*.

I now took even greater precautions. I traveled little beyond the consulate and went heavily armed when I did. I made such an ostentatious display of my skill with the new revolvers, that my enemies attempted nothing in daylight when they might have waylaid me. I remained with-indoors most of the time, constantly at my balcony, looking out to sea through a spyglass for the arrival of a British warship we had requested to quell the hostilities and preserve the European consulates.

The house we had taken in Kalepa—a suburb of Canea where many of the consuls lived—became our fortress. Laura and I barricaded our windows with mattresses. I hired an assistant, Hadj Houssein, as a sort of bodyguard, and the three of us placed a rifle and cartridges by each window. If a battle broke out, we feared all the consulates seen by the Muslim rabble as friendly to the Cretans would be attacked and whole families slaughtered. We dared not let the children out.

Laura, more than I, refused to be intimidated and occasionally walked out on necessary errands. On one occasion, it was necessary for me to be away at a crisis meeting of the European consuls in Crete. I had taken two other body guards along with me. While I was away, a man in the street yelled "Death to the Christian Dogs!" That evening, the entire Christian population of Kalepa was at our doors beating to be admitted. However, Houssein refused to open the doors without orders from me. Laura later told me that she awoke immediately to the clamor, leapt out of bed, ran to the foyer in only her nightdress, and, pushing poor loyal Houssein out of the way, flung the doors wide.

"Man the window!" she commanded Houssein. Seeing she was right, now that the crowd had been let in, he obeyed.

Laura then locked and barricaded the door. That accomplished, she held out a rifle and asked "Who? Who?" Three or four men stepped forward from their frightened families. She handed each man a rifle, made sure he knew how to handle it, and sent a man to each barricaded window.

The rest of the families spent the night huddled on the main room floor. From upstairs, Laura held watch the remainder of the night for any sign of impending attack. But fortunately nothing happened. Our enemies must have seen how we had fortified and armed ourselves and determined a strike not worth the cost. After all, they had only to wait for the people massed inside to return to their homes.

That was the kind of woman Laura was through the long months and finally years of horror: the Christians murdered in the streets of Canea; others fleeing to (and later driven to) the mountains only to be massacred; the dead bodies in the roadsides and ravines, to become the feasts of boisterous ravens; the attacking and burning of villages; and the retaliatory forays of the Cretan insurgents. Anarchy and devastation ruled, with civilian refugees taking the brunt of the violence.

We were able to help in the escape of refugees, particularly women and children. But for every life we saved hundreds perished. When Mustapha Kiritly Pasha, the Turkish Imperial Commissioner, arrived and raised his armies from Crete and abroad, his campaign of repression and cruelty only amplified the violence. As a result, the insurgency grew, Hellenic volunteers in support of the Cretans poured in, and what turned out to be years of struggle began. Mustapha was of that school who believed in military victory by devastation. He was in that regard a fool, of course. But the tale of his atrocities, as one Egyptian officer later told me, was a tale "of things too horrible to be repeated." Meanwhile, the Sultan back in Constantinople had gone mad over the resistance. He would not listen to any offered concessions, but rather vented his fury by bombarding a scale model of the island with a little cannon.

I finally insisted that Laura and the children leave Crete for the safety of Syra. She saw that it was futile to protest now and it was impossible to believe in safety for our children. She agreed to leave, however, only so long as things remained at such a horrific pitch. She insisted that she would not abandon the Cretan women and children for fear of her own life.

For a time I remained active in Crete, doing whatever I could. I boarded the *Kestrel* and helped run refugees to Greece, no longer with the support of my government. Whole villages had been plundered. The women, by order of the officers, were violated even unto death. Any Cretans who had escaped hid in caves along the shore. It was these suffering people that I and the crew of the renegade yacht carried to safety.

Laura remained away for some weeks because, though I would not have believed it possible, the situation further deteriorated. Mustapha Kiritly was recalled for his failure to suppress the insurrection; and Omar Pasha, a conceited and bombastic old warrior, was sent in his place. The savage excesses of his military campaign surpassed anything we had seen before. I firmly believe that nothing more savage and needlessly cruel has taken place in the history of the Ottoman Empire. But brutality seldom defeats insurgency; it has rather the opposite effect. The international community finally stepped in when the slaughter on all sides reached insupportable proportions.

I recalled that Turner, like Byron, had enormous sympathy for the Greeks in their long oppression at the hands of the Ottoman Turks. Turner's painting *The Temple of Jupiter* was but one expression of his political sympathies that I now understood more deeply.

Laura returned in October, 1867, as A'ali Pasha, the grand vizier of the empire, came out to negotiate for conciliation. But his failure to reconcile the opponents led us back into the third year of the Cretan insurrection.

We had been living a life of deprivations for over two years in a state of siege, when Laura went into confinement with our third child, Bella. The doctor ordered us all off the island as soon as she was fit to travel. We took a tiny house in Athens, simply furnished by the local Cretan committee. We were by that point effectively destitute. My consular salary of $1000 a year, without expenses for any travel, had left us in a difficult position. Moreover, since I was unable to return to my post in Crete, my salary was soon suspended. We hadn't even the money to return home. Our position was further aggravated by the mental depression Laura had slipped into following Bella's birth.

In odd quiet moments in Crete I had begun photographing ruins; now I turned my camera to the ancient sites of Athens. I found this employment a relief from my duties and dangers as consul. But there was a moment of foreboding one day—a short energetic young man in black dodging among the ancient ruins caught in my peripheral view. When I turned directly toward him he disappeared around a column, as if he could exist only at the edge of my vision. I had a sense of his movements and posture reminding me of nothing so much as a faun or a young satyr. I turned away as if to ignore him. Shortly, I glimpsed him again out of the corner of my eye as he leaned against a column to look at me. I swung toward him, and again he vanished behind a column. Had I recognized the face from a self-portrait, slightly faunlike, from his early years—William Turner? If his clothes had dropped from him I would not have been surprised to see furry goat legs. I pursued him as best I could with the impediment of my photographic apparatus, but soon had to give up. Whether there was something within me in these difficult times to cause a trick of vision, or whether there was some haunting, so to speak, I cannot say. I know only what I glimpsed.

And dark omen it was. Although my photographic occupation served for a time to bring in a small income, it was not enough. The accumulated burden of our lives over more than two years, Laura's harrowing sorrow over the suffering Cretans, and the weaning of her baby sent my poor Laura into the profoundest of delusional melancholies. I could do nothing for her, try as I might.

There came a day when I heard two gunshots. I told Russie to watch the children and went to our bedroom. I found her, one of my revolvers in hand, with severe wounds to her chest and head and her blood pooling on the floor where she lay. I lifted her onto the bed and pulled the coverlet over her lifeless body. Though I was now myself in a state of shock, I again saw Laura during those past instances, infrequent but telling, when her dejection caused her pain and came between us. I recalled her father's long-ago admonition: "We fear for her reason." And I recalled how despite her courageous actions in Crete that when action was not required or possible Laura brooded over the terrible suffering of the women and children. All those memories consumed me no longer than a matter of seconds as I stood over her, stunned and debilitated. Then, somehow, I summoned briefly the presence of mind to leave her and go out to tell the children there had been an accident, and to stay where they were while I went to the home of another consul for help. From that moment I moved about in a complete daze while others took care of the body and the children until I regained my senses.

One never quite knows how one survives such loss. But my three children needed my care. In light of this you will perhaps understand how difficult it has been for me to write every word I have about Laura, from our courtship to her self-inflicted mortal wounds.

The Cretan community in Athens—many of them refugees—insisted on taking charge of her funeral. The Cretan women canonized her after their fashion of always referring to her as "the Blessed." We buried Laura there in Athens' First Cemetery beneath a memorial reading in Greek:

Laura Mack,
Wife of W. J. Stillman, American Consul in Crete.
To the eternal memory of her love and good deeds
unhappy Crete in grateful mourning dedicates this pillar.

They were honoring her quiet but indomitable courage, her refusal to take any credit for the work of salvation she had accomplished, and for her sense of duty to the oppressed in horrifying circumstances. These were the qualities she drew upon when she kept my consulate functioning whenever I was away, when she navigated the yacht to meet me on my return from Greece, and when, though physically diminutive, she cowed the most brutal of the barbarians who gathered around us at Kalepa. After her death, I became a physical and financial wreck upon a foreign strand.

Chapter 17

Looking back, I now see that those Cretan years were the turning point of my life, shaping all that happened to my family, to me, and—yes—to the Turner studies. I began to think about returning to America where Laura's family could help with the children while I sought employment. Of course I also thought of searching for the elusive Mrs. Fullerton again. Mrs. Dickson, our friend and the wife of my old colleague, the English consul Charles Dickson, proposed that she look after my children and that we move in with them while I tried to put my affairs in order. I was first called as a guest of the government at Constantinople, no longer as an agent of my own government, to help in the solution to the Cretan problem. Though the Turkish officials ultimately were unable to accept certain technicalities of my proposed solution, I was later sent a hundred Turkish pounds for my efforts; that money would be our ticket home. There was no possibility of lingering in Greece, for our lives were about to take another fateful turn.

Upon my return to Greece from Constantinople, I found my seven-year-old son Russie limping from a heavy fall. He had been knocked unconscious briefly and couldn't recall just what had happened. His playmate could add little, other than to say the poor boy had been playing upon some sort of wall or parapet. His condition had not been accurately diagnosed or treated; in fact, quite the opposite, aggravating the injury and instigating tubercular disease. En route to America at Paris, I had the disease diagnosed through a specialist. The hip had begun to fuse. I placed Russie in a sort of wire envelope constructed to make his transfer from one vehicle to another during our travels relatively convenient. But the poor boy was in incessant and wasting pain.

He would look at me from his recumbent position, eyes full of despair and hope. "Papa," he said on our way to London, "I'm getting well now, aren't' I?"

"Of course, son," I told him, feeling like a hypocrite. "And once in Boston again we'll continue your treatment with the best doctors in America."

To see him now grieved me, for he had always been a child of precocious strength, activity, and intelligence. His bright eyes, even now, reminded me of his pleasure when one day we stole an hour to slip away to go fishing just offshore in the Mediterranean Sea. I deeply regretted not having had opportunities to teach him to hunt and fish and was now determined to make a beginning. Everything we did together gave the boy pure delight and energy, an energy that shone in his face and bouncing bright locks as he ran back and forth to the boat with our equipment and later, as he followed my instructions to bait and cast his line. Even seated he seemed in constant motion. He seldom stopped talking due to his enormous curiosity and delight in learning anything. He had a fine and extraordinarily retentive mind. I had to teach him to be careful around certain rather dull adults who could not keep up with the rapidity of his conversation and the extent of his knowledge, and who resented, it seemed, their own comparative slowness. I recall our minister to Italy, George Marsh, saying he had never seen a more beautiful and intelligent lad.

In London that September of 1869, awaiting our passage to America, we met with much kindness and sympathy. One of my first acts was to see Michael Spartali, Greek Consul General and chairman of the Committee for Relief of the Greek Community of Crete, and his wife Euphrosyne, at their country house at 2 Lavender Gardens, Clapham, known as The Shrubbery. My purpose was to report that Crete's Greek and Christian communities still required substantial help.

His daughters Marie and Christina joined our conversations regarding the suffering on Crete. Marie, the older sister in her mid-twenties, seemed to take an interest in these details and in my own story. In answer to their queries I told them of my wife, mother of my three children, being driven to despair and self-destruction.

I soon came to see Marie as an artist particularly accomplished in watercolors. She was, in fact, known for her floral pieces and decorative female heads. Yet I now understood why she was even better known for her beauty. Only Jane Morris was considered her equal. Marie had that faultless dark loveliness that one rarely encounters in life or on canvas. Her knee-length auburn hair—which she wore plaited and piled on her lovely head—her classically straight nose and impish pouting mouth, and the accomplishment and charm of her singing voice all arrested me. I saw immediately why Gabriel Rossetti and Madox Brown took her as another of their models.

Marie had been raised within the genius of the international cosmopolitan circle her parents had gathered. Her private education at home and her immersion from childhood in the world of art, music, politics, and lively debate kept her curiosity alive and inspired this sophisticated woman with a girlish vivacity. Her grace recalled for me the Muslim woman I had espied in Crete, but Marie's face was filled with the light of her intelligence and education. She seemed to me a creature of no particular culture—British or Greek—but of many.

One afternoon at the Spartalis', while I was speaking privately to her tutor Madox Brown, I heard the rustle of a dress as someone came into the parlor. Before I turned around, I knew it was she.

"It's such a pleasure to see you again, Mr. Stillman," she said, extending her hand. "How is dear little Russie?"

I told her of my son's unimproved condition and thanked her for the tenderness of her concern. Once again her comeliness struck such a deep chord that I suddenly found it difficult to make conversation.

"And how is your work going?" Nothing else occurred to me.

"Well enough." She looked at Brown and smiled. "But I have much to learn."

"Indeed," he offered. "Marie has her own way, you know—that jewel-like finish and flat perspective. A delightfully naïve touch." He made a little humorous bow. "She shows at the Dudley."

"But all too few are purchased, wherever they show," she said. "It's a good thing father allows me to live on here studying and painting, for if I had to depend on myself," she said, pausing to laugh, "I'm afraid I'd be wearing rags!" She stepped back as if to display her charming bronze-colored dress, enticing us to imagine it substituted by rags.

Brown winked at me. "Her father would, I think, see her married. But by now he would not see her stop painting, either. The courtier would have to be an extraordinary man indeed."

"And one of some means, I fear," she said, pretending to frown, "to make father happy."

"But a creature of means who would have his wife painting away her days is rather hard to come by," I suggested.

She laughed, tilting her head back. She was remarkable, among other things, for her lack of self-consciousness, for her absence of studied English mannerisms. I did not think Brown's influence on her especially salutary, for he was too much the academician. Neither a colorist nor a great draughtsman, he was too literary, didactic, and un-poetic.

I said nothing of all that to Marie. Her capacity for empathy beguiled me. Meeting her was a stern reminder of how unsettling a beautiful woman can be, even to a man still mourning his wife and burdened with loving children he is determined to care for. It all felt for my part like a harmless, incongruous flirtation. I could hardly expect my growing feelings for this young woman nearly sixteen years my junior to be reciprocated. She was independent, and her family wealthy. I was ill and in despair with three motherless children in tow, one of whom was suffering severely from illness himself. I had no pecuniary prospects at all.

Nonetheless, we began to meet in that circle of mutual friends, most of whom I knew through William Rossetti. I had worried about how the Rossettis would react to my return to London. Had they, through the researches of Mr. Winslow, come to suspect my role in the stolen Turners?

"No," William Rossetti told me, when I asked whether the man who had burgled Fanny's neighborhood had been caught. "Obviously the trail is rather cold by now. We are, I take it, an open case while Winslow pursues the needs of more recent clients. So whoever he is, he remains at large."

"And one begins to believe he shall ever remain so."

"That becomes a greater possibility with every passing year." He looked at me not with suspicion but with, it seemed, strained comradeship.

I decided a frontal approach the wisest. "Mr. Winslow came to visit me, in Rome, back in '62," I said. "I must say, he made me feel rather like a suspect myself. But my understanding was that he went away satisfied otherwise."

"No doubt your second visit to Fanny interested him," Rossetti said.

"Oh, well yes, I returned on the very eve of my departure to request one final look at the Turners, that's all. I assumed I would not see them again for years, if ever. It wasn't, I realized right away, a very smart thing to do, but my impulsive nature got the better of me under the circumstances."

"Winslow mentioned something of the sort."

"Fanny, perhaps out of female vanity, apparently told him another story."

"So I was also given to understand."

"But she must have told him the Turners remained in her drawer after I left."

"I believe so."

I had the feeling that my approach, on one hand, had given me the appearance of innocence, yet, on the other, Rossetti seemed to be considering the whole matter again in his mind. I had no choice now but to deceive my old friend, and it sickened me.

"We've tried not to think too much about it," he said after a few moments of hesitation. "Gabriel and I were of course devastated when we heard. Gabriel blamed himself at first. Then when Lizzie died he was consumed with grief—and guilt, I might add. Anyway, now Gabriel is in delicate health and morbidly consumed by his work, as you'll see."

"I'm sorry to hear it. I know the sufferings of the bereaved."

"You've borne a great deal, Will. And now Russie's illness too."

"Doing my best to manage. I have some hope for better medical advice in Boston."

"I'll put you in touch with our physician here in London. For a start, see what he thinks."

"Thank you."

"You wouldn't object if I told Mr. Winslow you're in London?"

"Of course not," I said as evenly as I could. "But I can't tell him anything more than I've told him already."

"I expect so, Will. Nevertheless, he was asking for you during your Cretan sojourn, so if you indeed don't mind, I'll mention your return on the chance he still has another question or two to clear up in his mind. You never know where a minor detail suddenly recalled might lead."

Chapter 18

Despite my trepidation over this Winslow business, I was drawn to enlarge my acquaintance with Marie. We began to meet beyond her father's house. On those occasions, I left the children with Christina Rossetti, among other trusted friends. Christina had known Laura and Russie when the boy was two, and she went out of her way to help us indulge Russie's well-know passion for seeing things. I had wheels put on his "cage," as he called it, and Miss Rossetti took him to the Zoological Gardens and other sites of interest. Russie had also begun treatments under the care of William's recommended physician.

Marie and I attended a dinner at Gabriel's with Ruskin and Charles Fairfax Murray, and another at the Madox Browns', during which Marie importuned Gabriel to read his "Lilith." And there were times when we met after Marie had been sitting for some hours to one of the Brotherly painters or another, or again, met at the home of Jeannie Hughes Senior.

"These days my father and I seem to cross swords at every meeting," Marie told me.

"He'll no doubt prevail," I said.

"I told him I could not at this point in my education suddenly lose my freedom to move in the circle of my friends and mentors."

"It'll do us no good to cross him," I said. But I had no idea how Marie and I could terminate our deepening friendship.

"Perhaps if you called on me at home for a time," she suggested, "it would help alleviate their concern."

On one of my visits to The Shrubbery, Marie had asked if I would sit for her. "I haven't sufficiently studied the male head and figure," she explained. "And you have such a fine face and noble head, Mr. Stillman."

She drew my head from several views, and then my torso. She made a number of full length sketch studies of different positions, standing and sitting. And before she was done she asked me to remove my shirt "so as to study properly the male musculature and body in movement." These life studies were, to my mind, among her best. She had never had unfettered access to a male model to study the stretches and turns of the masculine torso. Obliging her gave me pleasure in turn. Her parents seemed calmed by our meeting at their residence, seeing us as two artists working through technical problems, and unaware I had removed my shirt.

I cannot say whether Michael Spartali discovered then how far things had developed over the course of those two months, but given his temporary silence regarding his daughter's movements I doubt he learned about the aftermath of Gabriel's costume party.

At times, like Marie, I attended Gabriel's gatherings, including this particular party, at his grand and gloomy residence in nearby Cheyne Walk, where he had lived since Lizzie took her life. I preferred, however, to spend time with the man alone when he was not so much the center of display and his conversation was far better. The usual coterie of friends and admirers always would be there, including the young, wiry, fire-haired poet Swinburne, whom I did not care for but who interested me. Swinburne had embarked on his dangerous project to thrust Eros from the shadowy alleys and mews and out into the thoroughfares of town and country.

Swinburne, like George Meredith and William Rossetti, had agreed to pay a portion of the rent. But it was always seen as Gabriel's house, as the others were less frequently in evidence.

Often, as on the occasion of this masquerade gathering, I would take the opportunity of a visit to walk in the nearby gardens: the Garden of Chelsea Hospital, like the garden of some old French palace, with its pleasant avenue leading to open spaces by the river and its statue erected in memory of the casualties at Chilianwallah; or the "Apothecaries" Garden, the oldest of its kind in England, facing the wide river. And in fine weather I would extend my tour by walking in Turner's footsteps the length of Cheyne Walk: the prettiest waterside terrace with its brick houses and rows of trees, its rather stately dwellings on the lower stretch of the Walk, with their bow windows, balconies, old iron gates and pillars and pineapples, and on the upper part of the Walk, the line of ancient shops that end at the old church.

One could see the open fields of Battersea across the river, and recognize the four acres of its beautiful subtropical garden. Along the route I would pass Number 6 Davis Place, Cremorne New Road, Turner's waterside brick cottage, nestled between more substantial buildings. Whenever I passed, I thought of the rheumatic old man living and dying there with Mrs. Booth after he had abandoned Queen Anne Street for the soft effects of light and air upon the still reaches of the Thames. Beyond the scrutiny of his old comrades and colleagues, Turner had ended his reclusive days here on the waters he loved: the London docks where the far-flung places of the world from America to Canton meet the city deep inland from the sea; the tangle of masts and rigging and steam spider-webbing the horizon; the jutting of enormous warehouse cranes and chimneys reaching upwards and still while the moving forest of masts and rope makes its ceaseless procession up river and down with the tides. From his window and the roof terrace he built, Turner had drunk in the river's atmospherics of water and sunlight: the play of light amidst smoke and fog—irradiating, engoldening, gleaming and glittering over the river and shooting all man-made surfaces through with yellow and purple and green; the ever-shifting tidal waters entrapping all manner of diffused lights, luminous vapors transforming the gigantic works of the greatest industrial port into a vision less monstrous, more numinous. Like the aging painter, many notable personages had chosen this neighborhood in the past, as Mr. Carlyle and Rossetti, among others, did now.

Part of Rossetti's house's dreary feeling came from Rossetti's habit of collecting and decorating his residence with junk and antiques he bargained and scavenged for over the whole of London. Carved Renaissance furniture seemed to brood in every corner, and his enthusiasm for thick velvet and mohair curtains did nothing to lighten the mood.

Gabriel's garden—or urban jungle—was the most delightful space of the entire property, for its trees, jasmine, roses, marigolds, thistles, Solomon's seal, daisies, irises, and even its weeds had rather a refreshing effect on the visitor after the gloom of the house's interior.

The large, wild garden of nearly an acre contained plane, lime, fig, cherry, and mulberry trees, with one gargantuan specimen shedding its purple berries over nearly everything else, including Gabriel's collection of animals. He was infamous for harboring a private zoo of peacocks, deer, kangaroos, armadillos, pigeons, rabbits, a parakeet, an owl, and a woodchuck. A Pomeranian named Punch, companion to his Irish Wolfhound, was left over from his honeymoon with his now deceased wife. I had heard that his favorite had been a pet wombat that he used to fondle and allow to sleep beside him at dinner. This par-

147

ticular companion, however, had long ago died and now, stuffed and preserved, greeted visitors as they entered the house.

For pleasure, whenever the weather permitted, he held his gatherings in this back garden, sparing no expense. In this instance Marie arrived as Athena, entering the garden wearing a satin bed sheet for a robe, a thin yet provocative silk mask over her eyes, a diadem on her lovely head, and so far as I could tell, very little else. She was the epicenter of manly attentions, an incarnate Muse. Two or three of the men, Gabriel among them, swore he would paint her as she was. But she laughed them off. I, on the other hand, approached her at some point after we had dined and said, "Now, Marie, I don't care about these others, but since I subjected my 'noble head' to the scratching of your pen, I insist you allow me to photograph you sometime, just as you are this evening, removing only your mask."

"Well, William," she said without hesitation, "we shouldn't try that at The Shrubbery."

I knew from our previous conversations that she had by now rebelled, with a degree of success, against the strictures upon which her father had long insisted. The opening wedge, it seemed, had come some time ago after she and her younger sister Christina had been allowed, sans chaperone, to sit for Mr. Whistler in his studio twice a week. Now twenty-one, she had convinced her father that she was determined to become a true artist, not some mere Sunday-afternoon dilettante dauber, and had begun formal training at Madox Brown's studio. Under Brown's tutelage, she also attended the Browns' parties. In short, she was by now well launched into a freedom beyond her private education and the familial confines of The Shrubbery.

She turned away from me with a little laugh. Burne-Jones or some other one of the guests—I no longer recall just who—immediately offered to refill the golden cup she held out. Even the married men whose wives were present were buzzing around her.

It was another twenty minutes before I was able to interrupt her. I approached her from behind, as she was moving across the room toward another knot of guests. "Not The Shrubbery? Even though their daughter grows beyond marriageable age?" I whispered as I gently took her arm.

She turned quickly to me. "Stillman! I see you've been listening too much to Papa," she said. "But Gabriel set him straight once when he made that claim. 'Would you have her, Mr. Spartali,' he told him, 'like poor Mrs. Wells, who died in childbirth? A great artist sacrificed to bringing more children into the world, as if there were not other women fit just for that?'" She looked at me with a smile of triumph. "What Papa doesn't seem to understand is that I've been working too hard to think much of marriage, even though he and mother are the ones who provide the enclosure allowing me to work to heart's content."

"But that doesn't mean you might not sit for me, in turn, someplace outside your father's house."

"I see you've no intention of giving up. You insist on holding me to a bargain I didn't even know I'd made."

"That is precisely what I intend to do. Where then?"

She looked around the room. "Well, why not here?" she said. "Mother and father know I come here, and they see my association with Gabriel and his friends as necessary my to education and advancement."

"And they know you model in costume? Here? Elsewhere?"

"Yes, of course."

"It's settled then," I insisted. "At your earliest convenience."

"Tomorrow morning?"

I hesitated, thinking over what obligations the day required of me. "Why not?" I said. "With Gabriel's permission—and if you ask I'm sure he'll grant it—we could work during the hours when he sleeps."

I knew that her reference to Mrs. Wells was for the sake of riposte only, for I had heard her say once that she considered herself only to be delaying marriage and children until she came into her own as an artist. Gabriel had been referring to the wife of a Royal Academician whom he took to be a painter of great, even greater, talent in her own right. Marie's father had said little about Marie's prospects for marriage. When I reminded him of the example of Mrs. Fullerton, who had, after her husband's early death, eschewed all efforts to bring her back into the domestic fold, he replied with a smile, "And she is the better artist for all that!"

Still, I couldn't help wondering whether his words were merely a cover for his deeper feelings, for I felt sure, based on other innuendos, that he and his wife would prefer to see their daughter happily—and well—married, if only someone worthy of her and with the patience of a Job would come along to win her away from them. I think they relied on her beauty to salvage her for the "marriage market," as it was then called, however late she decided to enter it. Once when she and her father were joking about her lack of interest in marriage, I heard Marie rejoin with a smile that she was merely holding out for an older man with children to save her the debilitations of parturition.

Marie and I met the next morning at Rossetti's and set to. Gabriel had a large sitting room for his studio. Wonderfully flooded with north light, the studio was lined with bookshelves and many tempting sofas. It was here he had discovered the formula to make his future—paintings of a large erotic female figure nonetheless suitable to his irreproachable, well-heeled patrons. Fanny, of course, Annie Miller, and

Jane Morris all had sat for him, and Marie on occasion. Now that the house was quiet, Gabriel was asleep in the great cave of his darkened bedroom, (probably with Fanny or Jane Morris), and one of the finest studios in London was ours.

We worked, but whatever I tried, I later discovered that I had not been able to make the camera do Marie justice. She had, I decided, the kind of beauty no photograph could quite capture. Still, when Rossetti and Burne-Jones used her as a model in their narrative pieces, their depictions, though superior to my paltry photographs, were too idealized—too subservient to their themes—to represent the real woman.

I called on her the following day, having given up hope of a sufficiently appealing photograph.

"Why don't I try to get you on canvas," I said.

By her look it was plain she understood my frustration. "Tomorrow?" she asked.

"I've got my hands full."

"You have a day or two in mind?"

"I'll check with Gabriel. May I send my card around?"

"Just give me a day's notice."

"I'll start with a mere sketch," I said. "See how it goes."

My idea, like Turner's in his life classes, was to avoid idealizing the face or form, despite the goddess robe, and present the actual woman before me, a woman of loveliness and proportion enough. It was as if all former doubts about my ability to paint again were melting under the influence of her youthful spirit and beauty—the enchantment, or the tender yearnings, of a troubled man.

Chapter 19

On the appointed day, Maria returned in costume to Gabriel's studio.

"Just recline, please, on that sofa," I suggested.

She took a little time adjusting the satin sheet and finding the posture that would allow her to be comfortable for as long as the first layer might require.

"There," she finally said. "Is this suitable?"

"Suit your comfort," I said. I left my easel to adjust her wrap. The slippery cloth was difficult to keep elegantly fitted, but I wanted to hold to my original idea. I tugged at the satin and rearranged it for several minutes, causing her to giggle with a coyness I hadn't seen before. I exposed one of her lower calves, one shoulder nearly to a breast, her slender neck, and of course both her graceful arms. She looked serene as she tilted her head back to rest it on the crook of the sofa. Her composure set me at ease. I don't know that there has ever been a woman in whose company from the very first I felt so much myself, so unguarded.

I thought of Turner: his academy models and his harlots. I fought to contain the ardor thickening my throat and loins. The scent of her flesh, so much exposed and just graced with a hint of some Grecian perfume, nearly unhinged me. It would seem a rude trick, however, to use the occasion as a ruse to unleash my passions. Would she ever forgive me? I did not want to breach the affection and trust we had built between us. I did not want to act the cad or fool.

Could the depth of Marie's feelings begin to match my own? Perhaps my lack of certainty in our relations restrained me. And there were the memories of Laura, for years the only woman whose body I had known completely. Would Laura want me to find happiness with another woman? I wanted to believe so. She had always been generous and empathic, before the stupidity and violence of others began to drive her deep into self-destructive melancholy.

Still, I kept my passions in check as Marie lay before me. Over the course of an hour, I sketched in the essential features of her face and the lines of her lithe, partially draped body. When we finally stopped for her to regain circulation and for me to mix my colors, we didn't speak much. She walked about the room and stretched while I concentrated on formulating the precise hues I wanted to lay out as my base. She eventually came around to look at what I had sketched.

"Oh," she said. "No one's ever drawn me like that."

"I wonder how it might be with your magnificent hair down," I said.

She smiled and began to undo her plaited auburn hair. She returned to the sofa and adjusted herself for comfort, her loose hair still in her hands. "Is this how I was?"

"The hair might flow naturally over your shoulders and breast and down the side."

"This way?"

I went over to her again and arranged her plenteous hair. "Good, let's go ahead with it," I said and began my first application of paint to canvas.

But within another hour I was already discouraged. My hand and eye, I understood once more, were no longer sufficiently supple and practiced.

"Have you had about enough for today?" I asked.

"May I see?"

"I'd rather not, just yet. I'm not happy with it, Marie. Maybe tried to do too much for one sitting."

As I cleaned up she became playful, pretending to sneak over to my easel for peek. Every time I turned she hurried back toward the sofa. I threw a cloth over the canvas, but she pretended to tiptoe over and lift the slightest corner of the cloth. I rushed over, caught her up into my arms, and carried her back to the sofa where I plumped her down. "Stay put, for the love of God, you charming devil!" I said. She laughed; the robe had fallen into disarray. I held her arms against the pillow and kissed her mouth hard. She returned my kiss with equal intensity, and then pulled away.

"You're not making it easy for me," I said.

A rather serious look crossed her face. Then she smiled again and seemed suddenly to relax. "You may kiss me just once more, if you wish. And then I shall go change out of this thing."

We kissed more tenderly this time. I remember saying her name over and over, and I began to touch her too boldly for the state of our relations so far, but she responded with little murmurs of pleasure.

Before we descended into the ultimate embrace, she pulled away once more. I followed her lead and stood up in considerable, breathless pain. Her face was deeply flushed and more disconcertingly tempting than ever; I no doubt looked like a madman tottering above her.

"You're very sweet and desirous, William," she said. "But this is not the time, not yet. Let me change." She stood up, wrapped the sheet modestly about her, and walked to the door. Just before she opened it, she turned and said, "I really don't know what to do with these feelings I have for you, and yours for me. Don't you think we had better slow down, regain our composure?" Without waiting for an answer, she opened the door and left the room.

I recalled what Gabriel had told me: That Marie had recently ended a love affair with Thomas Jones, Lord Ranelagh, a former officer in the Life Guards (who was later a member of the Hogarth Club, a Pre-Raphaelite dining circle).

"Her father put an end to it," Gabriel said. "Undoubtedly he knew Ranelagh's reputation as a notorious womanizer. Who did not?"

"How far had this affair gone?" I asked.

"Who knows?" Gabriel said. "I had most of the tale from Holman Hunt, who knew them well enough. He said—and I suppose it possible—that Marie had set her heart on marrying the rake."

"Possible? You think such a man ever intended marriage?"

"Here's one beauty might have snared him!"

Ranelagh I knew was considerably older—he in his fifties to her twenties. I fully understood now that she was a woman of more than a little experience and passion, with perhaps a penchant for older men. It occurred to me when Rossetti had spoken, furthermore, that Marie's very associations with Gabriel himself, who had made it his chief business to escape into an erotic freedom of his own—and his brotherhood of artists whose wives and lovers seemed to grow ever more interchangeable—hardly could *not* have influenced Marie's own attitudes and assumptions. She was obviously not a sexual Gnostic of Gabriel's proportions, against the dogmatic proprieties of English society. But she had witnessed, had been initiated into, the exhilarations of erotic self-determination. I began to see her as a woman of ardent desires, of carnal passions perhaps equal to her artistic. She was perhaps even a youthful version of the extraordinary Mrs. Fullerton. Or the youthful William Turner.

That night I slept little before dawn. When I finally collapsed in heavy sleep, I drifted into a frightening dream.

In the dream, Marie and I were again in Rossetti's studio, but I was not the painter before whom she posed. Instead, a youthful William Turner, about Marie's own age, stood before my easel in a posture expressing utter self-confidence and mastery over paint, brush, and canvas. But Marie had abandoned her satin robe and lay before him, hair in cascades, loins glistening, in an attitude of the most feral sensuality. I understood immediately that he had taken her away from me. That I had lost her, as surely as I had lost Laura, forever. That he had pulled her planet into the orbit of his sun, the overwhelming glare of his artistic and erotic power.

I began to call out to Marie and started awake. I awoke in a sweat to my own garbled voice struggling to call out Marie's name. Sleep fled, and my churning thoughts in the night began to throw images of Marie and Gabriel together, as well, against the imagination's tablet.

In the light of noon, I was able to put the dream and my wakeful imaginings aside as an irrational threat. But some residual terror remained throughout the following week. After all, Laura had been taken from me, and Russie's illness and slow deterioration had planted in my breast the knowledge that he too would someday be taken away. And now Marie? Was I about to lose her as well?

She had sent me a little note the day after our truncated lovemaking. "I think of you and wish to see you, William," she wrote. "Come to me Thursday next. We can consider our feelings a little more dispassionately then."

It was the beginning of another series of meetings at her father's house, for he finally had come to the point where he absolutely forbade her to see me anymore at friends' residences. "He takes it that we are beginning to 'cause remarks of scandal,' as he put it," she told me. "I then insisted that you be allowed to visit me at our residence, and that when you do so you and I shall be given the courtesy of private conversation and study."

"He saw you would settle for no alternative and relented?" I asked.

"He and mother have the widest culture and freedom of thought, as you know, but they would move heaven and earth to avoid a family scandal."

By now, I was in some degree jealous against Gabriel's attraction to her as but one more of his many "stunners." I confess that I wished to have Marie with me—and me alone—always.

I kept to myself a modest skepticism over the lingering influences of our friend Madox Brown. But Marie had innate taste, a strong imagination, and a work ethic worthy of a New England husbandman. Although mastery was some distance away, she gained technical proficiency all the time. We had been growing closer with each meeting, and her great powers of sympathy flowed out to me.

I told her I could not complete the painting. She understood my self-doubt as an artist would. But she added, a trace of humor in her voice, "And better I not provoke you further with my satin robe."

"I would abandon the painting," I said, "but not the model."

"I don't want you to abandon me."

"Would you come with me to America?"

"For how long?"

"To marry me if you will. I don't want to be alone anymore, Marie, not now. Once I get certain matters settled—Russie's health, journalistic assignments, and so on, we can return to London."

She rose off her chair and walked about. "My dear William," she said, turning to me. She looked at me with the most vulnerable warmth. "My darling, that's something I can't possibly answer at this very moment. You understand, don't you?" She turned toward the window. "My parents will not be happy. Certainly they don't want me fleeing to America. You are older, you have children, you are still mourning Laura, are you not?" She turned back to me. "They won't understand it."

"Can't we win them over, your mother and father?" I was standing now. "I can't keep on as I am. Beside my three children, I don't want to be with anybody else. Only you, Marie. If you feel anything of the same towards me—" I couldn't speak further. I was so angry at beginning to break down in front of her that my anger rose up in me sufficiently to regain control over speech. "I've learned to care for my children. I would never expect you to give up your painting. Together we can—all of us—live our lives as we would. My feelings for you, and all my instincts, tell me that for us it would be possible to live not only a stable and routine life, but a passionate life, a life that I know would reawaken me. Marriage would be an act of courage, for both of us."

She smiled. "The life of passionate intimacies, Gabriel says, is the most vivid life, the most productive of creative energies."

"You'd give me back my life, Marie. And I would do everything in my power to create together a life that would release you fully to practice your painting."

"Give me time, dear William. You understand, don't you?" She was looking right into me, and I was unable to speak again. "I must test my mother and father before you say anything to them. Your children don't dissuade me; they are lovely. And I do want to be with you, you must know that. Come to me in two days, if you can. Then we'll decide a way forward."

* * *

When I arrived at the Spartali's manse, Maria herself greeted me in the foyer. She whisked me into a side parlor.

"I've spoken to them," she said. "About us."

"You don't look happy," I said.

"To them you are a friend, a colleague. But you are an older man, a child- supporting widower whose fortunes— whose very em- ployments—fluctuate." She hesitated. "To them we are too much of a scandal already."

"You mentioned our marrying? Are you telling me there's no hope?"

"Not that there is no hope, William. I'm telling you only that they're opposed, for those reasons."

But Marie seemed to believe her parents misunderstood her true in- terests and the nature of her affections. We discussed it for some days, and by January she agreed to marry me. Her parents resisted, yet we considered ourselves engaged.

Just after Marie and I reached our agreement on January 15, I went alone to speak with her parents. Mr. And Mrs. Spartali sat on a sofa, waiting for me. Their greeting was cool and we exchanged few pleas- antries.

Mr. Spartali said, "You know our affection for you, William, for your many sacrifices in the cause of the Greeks and Christian Cretans. We know you have been a helpful companion to our daughter, who feels great affection for you as well. But is it so difficult to understand why we cannot approve this marriage?"

"No, sir, it is quite easy to understand."

"But you do not agree with that understanding?"

"I cannot, sir. Because of my love for your daughter, because of my great respect for her as a woman and artist. My feelings may blind me to the conventional skepticism regarding a union such as ours, but I find such skepticism unequal to our devotion to one another."

"Others have sought Marie for her beauty and for the advantage of a comfortable settlement," Mrs. Spartali said. "But she had no interest in them, not in that way."

"I'm happy to forgo any settlement, Mrs. Spartali," I said. "And anything else that would convince you both of my honor and my devotion."

"Neither your honor nor your devotion is in question," Mrs. Spartali said.

"I shall soon be gainfully employed once again," I said. "Marie's beauty, intelligence, talent, and love are dowry enough for me. And, yes, you know me well enough now to see clearly who I am. If I have a failing, it's perhaps that I haven't regarded my personal material gain and benefit highly enough. I've made my share of mistakes, but I've learned from them."

"I don't doubt it," Mr. Spartali said.

"You can't expect us to change our feelings and convictions about this, Mr. Stillman," Mrs. Spartali said. "We cannot give you our blessing."

"I see." There was a daunting silence. Then I added, "Thank you for speaking with me. May I speak with Marie?"

"We have not forbidden her to speak with you," Mrs. Spartali said, and they both rose as I took my leave.

I can't say I blamed them. They did not understand the depth of our love, our plans to grow in intellectual sympathy and aspiration. It is a love the world rarely sees, and perhaps still less so between a man of my age and a woman of hers. As a result, Marie and I did not so much change our plans as we hesitated in the hope that her parents might be brought around. As an added difficulty, Michael Spartali took this development as one more blow to his fatherly authority. Just the year prior, his younger daughter Christina had eloped with Comte Edmond

Cahen d'Anvers, who was of a wealthy Jewish banking family. Her father did what he could to block our hopes, asking many in Marie's circle to intercede and bring her to her senses. I too thought it better to retreat from the field for a time.

As we discussed how to proceed, Marie said something that gave me an idea.

"Gabriel's grown far too inward," she said. "He's suspicious of everyone and everything, and sickly from overwork and irregular hours."

"I've recommended chloral for his sleeplessness," I said. "It's helped me with mine."

"He needs to go away and rest."

I thought a moment. "I have an idea. Let me inquire of Barbara Leigh-Smith, who has extended an invitation to Gabriel and me that I haven't been able to accept."

"Madame Bodichon?"

"Yes. But I knew her as a landscape painter years ago in London. I'm quite sure she'd agree to allow me to bring Gabriel for a stay at Robertsbridge. She's seen his excessive morbidity and self-involvement."

"I never thought his working all night with that huge gasolier over his easel was good for him. It only feeds his weakness and his monomania of persecution."

"I'll do my best," I said. "And your parents will have time to calm down and perhaps reassess while you and I are apart."

Chapter 20

After our return to London from Robertsbridge, Gabriel Rossetti seemed much improved by my imposition of chloral, daily walks in the woodlands, and freedom from the city's nervous excitations. Because we had no gas at the manor to allow for night work, and only a slight company of friends beyond the presence of the Bodichons, who fully understood his need for quiet and regularity, Gabriel regained his health. On our walks he told me the story of his life with that frank egotism he was known for, seeing everything and everybody merely in relation to himself.

"You understand me, Stillman," he said one day on our walk. "You have remarkable powers of empathy."

"There're some who might not agree," I said and laughed.

"Perhaps it's because we are both men who lost their wives by their own hands."

I stopped and turned to him. "You can't survive blaming yourself."

"Not completely, I suppose. And I don't see any reason why you should," he said. "But I'm not entirely blameless. For hours, days even, I can escape that thought. But it always returns."

"No husband whose wife terminates her own life can escape it."

"But you have Marie now, and she'll bring you joy and new freedom." He hesitated a moment. "They tried to get me to put you off her."

"Her parents?"

"Yes."

"It would have tested our friendship if you had!"

"It was not my place, and I didn't wish to contribute to your separation."

"We can't have their blessings, but we may have one another yet."

"I'm in love with her myself," he said and laughed lightly.

"Gabriel, you're in love with every beautiful woman you see and speak to."

"True enough. The heart ever hungers to be utterly known and forgiven," he said. "But Marie—"

"I know, my friend. You don't have to explain to me. But if we marry, you shall have to give up your pursuit."

He laughed again and I joined him, two men at ease talking privately of women. I brought up the stunners he still drew to himself. He spoke about several of them, their merits and demerits as models or bedmates. I think by then he was beyond marriage, whether he knew it or not.

Following our return to London, Gabriel and I kept up our friendship, but I did not become enmeshed in his deeper circle of admirers and friends. I had my own concerns and the glorious Miss Spartali to court. When Mortimer Winslow, in a dark suit and matching bowler hat, appeared again at my door one morning, I was shaken to realize that it was past time to return to America to seek opportunities of regular employment and the elusive Mrs. Fullerton.

"It's possible," Winslow said once we were seated, "that the life studies will surface at some point at auction or in the hands of private or not-quite-reputable collectors."

"It comes to the same thing," I said.

"Yes, Mr. Stillman, it does." He slowly brushed an index finger across his mustache. "You may understand that I've followed every lead and have had to place the Rossettis' interests aside, by and large, for lack of anything new."

"William himself told me as much."

"We have never been able to draw in the police due to the questionable legality, strictly speaking, of my clients' holding the illustrations in the first place."

"Yes. Certainly."

"To this day I don't know precisely how Gabriel Rosssetti obtained them. But that isn't important to my task. The brothers are scrupulous on that point."

"I understand, Mr. Winslow."

"They have assured me that no one beside William knew Gabriel had obtained them. They were believed to have been destroyed, with all the others."

"Indeed."

"Otherwise, only Miss Cornforth knew of their existence, and she believed they were the product of Gabriel's hand."

"I firmly believe that's true."

"Except for yourself, of course."

"Of course." I was not about to entangle Allegra Fullerton, even if she had let me down. Surely, the less Winslow knew, the better off I would be.

"So you can, I quite imagine, Mr. Stillman, see that such circumstances leave us with two alternatives in this matter: One, that the theft was one of several random acts in the environs. Or two, that you—the only other person who knew about them—managed to abscond with them."

"Theoretically, yes. But we can't forget two facts. First, Fanny herself said the packet was in her room after I left, and second, I departed for Rome without that packet less than twenty-four hours later."

"Miss Cornforth said that there was an oilcloth package in her drawer after your departure, sir. She could not attest to what was wrapped in the oilcloth."

"She could not? Then she must not have looked."

"Oh, but she did."

"And?"

"And a drawing of a certain sort, at a glance."

"What the devil are you saying, Mr. Winslow?"

"Nothing more than the facts we know thus far. To my associates' and my knowledge, no such drawings have emerged on the market, shady or otherwise. I haven't drawn any conclusions yet."

"But you have no difficulty sitting there speculating and intimating all kinds of doings on my part."

"I'm merely asking you to explain why that particular line of inquiry is unfounded, sir. So that I may eliminate it, if you see my point."

"I've explained that fully already."

"If you say so, sir."

"I do say so, Mr. Winslow. Now I have business of my own, if you'll excuse me."

He rose as I did, and I saw his humble, dogged back out the door.

* * *

I departed for America immediately. My separation from Marie began when I sailed that June of 1870 with the children for New York. I arrived to be met by my brother Charles, only to be told my aged mother had died. Her last wish, Charles told me, was to see her namesake Lisa, who had been born during the seven years I was abroad.

For the first time my financial troubles somewhat abated: my photographic book on the Acropolis cleared about $1000, I came into a little family money, and J. M. Forbes of Boston, who was a generous friend of my old days spent tramping about painting the wilds of the Northeast, gave me a commission for a landscape. I sought the best medical care I could for Russie (complete with all his records from the London physician's office). Then I left the other children with Laura's parents and journeyed to the Glen of the White Mountains with the newly naïve hope that I would manage to execute my commission.

Of course before I left for New Hampshire, I went to Boston in search of Allegra. She had not returned to her former address. The old friends I asked in Boston or Cambridge could not offer a word of her whereabouts.

I was far from ready to accept defeat at her hands, but I had a commission to execute. I made for the mountains straightaway. Why this rebirth of hope for my old dream? Was it merely Forbes' friendly assumption that my painting skill could not have abandoned me? Was it some new energy of optimism born of Marie's love? Whatever it was, I willingly returned to the methods of my old days of hunting and painting in the Adirondacks, Catskills, and Berkshires. I lived in a tent on a reduced diet. Memories flooded back of my youth spent tramping through the Northeastern wilds or of conducting my "clients" in the Adirondack Club into the true wilderness of Follansbee Pond, well beyond Saranac Lake, in the 1850s. In the process I came to understand how sick I was of politics, war, and diplomacy.

As on a previous journey to the White Hills, I once again took the time to ascend the greatest peak, Mount Washington, spent a cleansing night in one of the stone cabins, or Tip Top houses—and then over two days of tramping, I worked my way south to Thompson's Tavern in North Conway, where artists had lodged for nearly two decades on the example and blandishments of Benjamin Champney.

These excursions reminded me all the more of those old dreams and adventures I had when Louis Agassiz came to visit me in my mountain retreat, as we had planned he would when I saw him recently at a dinner party in Cambridge.

As he sat by my campfire now his first night with me, he began to reminisce about old times and friends in the Adirondack Club.

"That was a more innocent time, William," he said, poking at the fire with his stick. "And the primeval woodland was to me like some Eden the rapaciousness of man had not yet touched. One felt back at the beginnings of things, the most ancient sources and breathings of nature."

"I recall Waldo hoping to catch some whisper of the secret," I said.

"Which secret he came to believe ever to be sought because never to be discovered." He laughed. The relentless scientist in Agassiz must have had hope for the secret—nay, all the secrets—to reveal themselves someday before the exertions of millennia of mankind.

"I found there, William, as I had in my Alpine explorations, that the truth and the limitations of character are always discovered in such circumstances. The great solitudes strip us of our conventions and put relations on an informal basis unlike anything attainable in society." He chuckled. "This compulsory intimacy of the great mountains and woods causes men to find one another out quickly."

We spoke of our old associates—Emerson, Professor Jeffries Wyman, John Holmes, Judge Hoar, Horatio Woodman, and Dr. Binney—and of what we had discovered of their pure personalities, unencumbered by convention, during those Adirondack summers.

Since the object of my own study in the White Mountains was in part composed of huge boulders dropped into a gorge, it was believed, by an ancient glacier from beyond Lake Superior, Agassiz took interest in the painting when I had shown it to him that afternoon. For

although he had already experienced his first attack of the brain malady that finally took him long before his work was done, he had come
to me hoping to combine the pleasure of our visit in the mountain wilderness with studies of his own.

"So how do you find returning to this painting business again, William?" he asked.

"I hope to execute this one to Forbes' satisfaction, but to be honest—" I hesitated.

"But? But you're feeling a little rusty. That it?"

"Yes. Or more accurately, Louis, from my years abstaining from
painting for official duties and this business of photography, my hand
seems almost paralyzed. I have always had some difficulty of hand that
men like Ruskin and Turner hadn't. At one time I thought practice and
study would overcome it."

"You begin to feel it's too late to catch up or resume."

"You've named it, my friend. My delusion that somehow I might
demonstrate otherwise by this commission is now unmasked."

He looked at me not with false sympathy, but with understanding,
as if he knew from experience the limits of his own dreams. "Could
you not, however, continue your photography and writing?"

"I'll have to find something along those lines, or God forbid, take
another consular post. The truth has fully revealed itself to me—I'll
never make my way as a painter. To be honest, I don't believe I was
ever meant to."

"Understand thyself, old boy. Takes decades of one's life!"

"You've made the journey yourself, Louis?"

"Indeed." He didn't seem to want to talk about his own journey,
however. Instead he said: "I made some inquiries for you, William, as
to the history of this Mrs. Fullerton you're so anxious to find." He looked at me pleasantly with his nonetheless sharp, inquiring eyes.

"Found something?"

"I'm not sure. One acquaintance told me he'd seen or heard about sales of certain of her mountain views—these very mountains here, I mean to say—a few years ago. He sent me on to another who said he believed, though he could not swear to it, that she'd long since returned to England, perhaps three or more years now, 'sixty-six or 'seven."

"England? Anything's possible. I've no idea of her wanderings since we parted in sixty-one."

"Well, if the woman holds paintings or whatever they are that belong to you from the pen and brush of the great Turner, you shouldn't give up your pursuit."

"No one mentioned her presence when I was passing through London earlier this year."

"Perhaps you were otherwise engaged. You asked after her?"

"I thought her in America and was too absorbed in Russie's decline. My responsibilities were to the children. And then, as I said earlier, the beautiful Miss Spartali came suddenly into my life."

He gave me a knowing look. "You've endured a great deal, William."

"I've survived."

"That you have! You are nothing, William, if not one who survives."

We both laughed, a laughter tinged with sadness and loss. I think he knew that he would never complete his own work, that time had begun to undo us all, just as it had undone and killed off his beloved colleague Professor Wyman. Indeed, this was the last time I was to see Louis, because a second attack of the brain malady took him off.

"Have you some idea of what you'll do?" he asked.

"Do? Up here alone, I've had time to think. Thought I might see Dr. Holland about work."

"*Scribner's Monthly?*"

"Yes. Some sort of assignment in his behalf from abroad."

"Good. I'm pleased to hear you have a plan! That you're not growing simply morose up here, frustrated in your painting, dwelling upon your losses and the disasters—as you've described them—of consular duty."

"One must live on. And then there are others one must live for."

"It's good to have purpose to your life. Purpose is a salve to suffering."

* * *

When we parted two days later, I was firm in my immediate plan of inquiry and action. Russie was soon discharged from the Boston hospital as incurable.

"I'll never get better, Papa?" he asked, looking up from his couch.

I looked at him, his eyes still bright but his body wasting from inactivity and pain. "That's what the doctors believe, Russie," I said, "but why shouldn't we have hope? People are cured all the time in spite of their doctors' pronouncements. We shall do our best!"

"Do you think mother watches over us?"

"You know, though we were never much for church-going, your mother had the deepest personal feelings. She loved all God's manifestations on this earth—people, animals, even the plants. She loves and watches over you still."

"I saw her praying a few times, Papa. Do you think she prays for us, for me to get better?"

"I'm sure she does, son."

I had no real hope, but I had to encourage the boy to live another year, another month, another precious day. I also knew that the modest resources I'd gathered would soon dwindle under the weight of medical bills and supporting my children.

Fortunately, J. G. Holland agreed to see me in New York. After a lengthy meeting with him, he hired me to hold the literary agency for *Scribner's Monthly* in London. So I began to make plans to return to England. I had one pleasure chiefly in mind: to again see my secret fiancée.

Chapter 21

I arrived alone in London that autumn of 1870 to begin my work for *Scribner's*. Having gainful work, being in London again with Marie, planning to bring my children abroad with me as soon as I was fully settled—all these prospects began to raise me out of the state of mental depression that had dogged me since Laura's death and that only Marie had been able to mend.

My immediate plans were derailed, however, during my early weeks in London. On the insubstantial authority of Agassiz's friend saying Allegra Fullerton had most likely returned to England, I began to ask around for her. Leslie Stephen, with whom I had business related to *Scribner's*, told me he believed she kept a studio somewhere near Chelsea. I went in search of it immediately, but without success. I was not yet ready to make inquiries of the Rossettis, so I devoted part of another afternoon inquiring of two or three gentlemen in the street whether they knew of the artist's painting rooms. Again, no luck.

I began to realize I would have to try the Rossettis.

* * *

I was about to hail a cab one morning when the figure of a woman ahead of me on the other side of the street entered my peripheral vision. I had noticed this phenomenon before, with Laura, with Miss Spartali, with others. Even if she were a silhouette presenting itself to your merest glimpse, you instantly recognize an attractive woman with whom you've grown familiar, who has so to speak, entered your interior life: the way she walks or turns, holds her hands, raises or lowers her veil, moves her arms, or tilts her head.

I looked over directly at the woman's back as she hurried along the street. This was no apparition, no trick of the eye. I walked faster and then broke into a run. "Mrs. Fullerton!" I called.

The woman turned quickly, looked right at me, confused, perhaps startled, apparently not recognizing me as I stopped running but kept my step hurried. Finally her eyes brightened. With surprise in her voice she called, "Stillman!"

"I've been looking for you for years," I said as I came up to her, my hand extended. "In Boston, in the mountains, through every channel of your acquaintance. And here you are now, the streets of London! London once again!"

She stood staring, as if confronted by an apparition.

"Mr. Stillman," she said and smiled. "How good to see you again after all these years. Calm yourself. We've found one another. As you say, in London again!" She laughed. "I sent you letters. Three."

"I received but one," I said. "In Rome." Her face was beginning to show her age, still filled with light and ebbing beauty, but deepened by years and adventures that no woman could have kept out of her face forever.

"I inquired when I didn't hear from you again, to discover you had moved on to the Cretan consulate. I sent two more letters after you there."

"I never received them. The latter two. Conditions in Crete were appalling. Often only government or official mail got through, and sometimes not even that."

"Something of the sort had occurred to me when I didn't hear from you."

I looked around. "Forgive my abruptness, but I simply must ask. What have you done with the Turners?"

"They're safe, Mr. Stillman. How could you think otherwise?"

"Safe? I certainly hope so. Where?"

She looked around us now. "Why don't we meet somewhere, where we can talk unnoticed and unheard," she said. "Where are you staying?"

"Percy Street."

"Oh, within a walk of the Cremorne Pleasure Gardens?"

"Not far."

"Then reserve us a table for tomorrow evening. We'll blend right in with the diners and dancers." She offered her most becoming smile. "I'll stop by your rooms and we can take our exercise to the Gardens. An ideal place to tell you everything." She pulled a card from her reticule and handed it to me.

"*Tomorrow* evening! My dear woman, I've waited years for this. To hear word—"

"I understand. But please believe me. I can't break off my current engagements. I assure you. You shall be satisfied."

I hated to give up. I looked at her card, then back into her eyes. Could I trust her again? Had she written to me and nothing got through? It was a plausible tale. In the confusion of the moment I relented. I slapped the card against my hand. "If you say so," I said. "Then I shall and without fail see you tomorrow evening, seven o'-clock." I handed her my card.

"Certainly, Mr. Stillman." She looked carefully at my card. "That's my promise to you."

She hurried away on her business, but before I returned back to mine, I walked directly to the address of the painting rooms on her card. I entered the foyer of the building and climbed the stairs to the number indicated. To the door was attached another card just like the one she had given me within a little brass plate. I believed I had cornered her at last. Now she would have to divulge the secret. How could she escape me again?

* * *

I was unfit for work or sleep until the time of our meeting. In my anxiety, I stood outside my building ten minutes early. Soon a cab pulled up and she got out. She had not escaped me; she graciously invited me to walk by extending her arm. Walking calmed my irritability as well as the awkwardness I suddenly felt beside her.

I paid our two shillings as we entered the Pleasure Gardens and made our way directly toward the brightly colored pagoda where an orchestra was playing beside the circular dance platform. There was already a good crowd of men and women performing their evolutions on the floor, and the tables set out under the trees were quite full. I presented my card to the head waiter, and we were soon seated at our reserved table in one of the private supper boxes that overlooked the throng of well-dressed pleasure seekers who were dancing, strolling, and eating and drinking.

"Shall we order a bottle of champagne?" I asked.

"If you wish," she said. "But I might prefer to start with a whisky and soda, if that seems agreeable."

The waiter came by with two menus and I placed our drink order. The orchestral music of popular tunes made a fine background din: the perfect place to be anonymous while carrying on a private and difficult conversation. For some time we simply made ourselves comfortable over the menus and drinks, observing the colorful crowd in constant motion.

When our food arrived I ordered champagne. We sampled our dinners. Then I began by saying, "Well, Allegra, you must know that my first concern is the Turners. Having not heard from you since that letter in Rome, and not being able to find you twice when I returned to Boston, set me askew. I didn't know what to think."

"You thought I had run away with them, sold them on the illegal market maybe?"

"I confess every conceivable idea occurred to me."

"You didn't fully trust me. I had perhaps rushed you into a decision before your departure." I heard no irony or jest in her voice. Now in her fifties, she had not lost her figure, and she had retained her face sufficiently with the aid of cosmetics to exude a certain kind of appeal that any man over forty would readily understand.

"It was no decision, but merely being rushed by accumulated circumstances."

"Yes," she said. "I might've been not quite fair to you."

"Indeed. However—"

"However, how can you believe I would have endangered them?"

"I simply didn't know what to think after applying to your landlady in Boston and hearing of your flight...somewhere...unknown."

"But I am here, prosecuting my art, my business. I've fled from no one. As I said, I wrote to you."

"Thank you. Maybe I—who have been looking back in constant motion for the last decade—I haven't been entirely fair to *you*." I summarized my travels, the death of Laura (whom she had never met), and Russie's accident and physical degeneration.

She expressed her condolences convincingly, adding that the death of her husband of a lingering bilious fever when she was in her early twenties was as fresh in her memory as anything in her entire life. "So I understand something of what you've been through, Mr. Stillman.

Here we sit," she raised her tumbler to me, "two souls severed from their true mates by the hand of Fate. Your health, old friend."

"Widow and widower," I said, putting down my empty whiskey tumbler, determined not to let her enchant me once again. "But I may have found a remedy for my loneliness and pain." I looked right at her as the champagne was uncorked and poured into glasses. She betrayed not a hint of disappointment or concern.

She anticipated me. "Oh, a new woman? How wonderful for you."

"Someone who has it in her power," I said, "to bring meaning and purpose back into my life."

"Do I know this fortunate lady?"

I hesitated. "Say nothing of it?"

"Of course."

"Marie Spartali."

"Oh yes, certainly! The painter. She's quite dedicated, and a marvelous model for Rossetti and the others. You've gained good fortune after all." She smiled.

"I knew her father quite well," I said. "He was the Greek consul-general in London. I met her when I stopped here on my way to Boston with the children from Crete."

"Will you marry?"

"That finally will be wholly within her power to decide." I did not want to speak of my secret engagement to Marie.

"You are to be congratulated on your taste, Stillman."

"Thank you. But please don't keep me waiting any longer. The Turners! You say you have them?"

"Not in my rooms." She placed her champagne glass on the table and returned my gaze. "For reasons that should be plain after a moment of sober consideration, I soon realized that I couldn't very well carry them with me to America. In any case, as I said in my letter, I was not prepared to leave off business here and return until some months after you left. I had not intended delay, but certain circumstances pressed me as well."

"But you did finally return."

"Of course. As you know."

"Then what'd you do with them when you returned to America?"

"Well, my return was briefer than I expected. I was soon traveling more—to Florence and Rome (long after you had left, I discovered), and then back to London. And I've been out painting the British countryside. But earlier, when I left for America, I enlisted the advice of the one man I deemed capable of appreciating the studies—an old friend, Richard Burton. He was just returned from abroad to London on the eve of his own marriage."

"Burton!"

"Yes. At the time I believed he would settle from his constant adventures and travels.. He examined the studies, immediately understood their significance, and offered to keep them secure while I was away. He was the only man I knew broadminded enough, courageous enough, and intelligent enough to take on the task. And over the years I had learned to trust him. He may be questionable in the eyes of society, but he's a man of unimpeachable honor. Once he gives his word, as he did to me, nothing will convince him to deviate from it."

"And now?"

"Now the objects are still under his care. He is far better suited to this task than I. They're mine again whenever I request them, but I haven't."

"We may request them now?"

"Certainly, but he is currently abroad."

"Abroad!"

"Yes. He assured me that he has a secret place for their security when he must travel. It turns out he still does much work for the government. Travels more than I would've expected after his marriage. But if he says the studies are safe, I believe him without question."

"But you don't know where they are, exactly?"

"I don't. It's not necessary that I do. They're safe, I assure you."

"Would he return them to me?"

"Yes, if I told him to."

"And will you?"

"Of course. When he returns, if you wish. But is there much point in your taking them back when he's happy to keep them safe for us? For you?"

"I would like the assurance of seeing them, at the least. I met Burton once. One of those weekend gatherings of Monckton Milne's, at Fryston." Captain Richard Francis Burton. I now recalled the tall gypsy figure in Adele Wholemate's vision. The Burton I had met at Fryston was then a swarthy, fierce looking man with great African spear scars on both cheeks, his thick hair growing low on his forehead, heroically proportioned in body, looking proud and ruthless, but perfect, even charming, in his manners.

"A worthy officer and scholar," I added. "Everyone knows of his adventures and exploits, his brilliance, his great physical strength and endurance. I know that he is esteemed by many as the best swordsman in Europe and probably the best pistol shot, that he is England's greatest linguist, and to many minds her greatest traveler and explorer. He's also a man of exceptional liberality of mind. So I understand why you might turn to him. Still, I'm not sure, Mrs. Fullerton, that I approve your disposition of the Turners. We can't, after all, put our hands on them if we wish. Right now, for instance."

The waiter entered our box to remove the dinnerware and offer desserts. With Allegra's permission, I told him we would just finish the champagne at our leisure.

As soon as he left, she said: "Consider then that he's the man most experienced and least hypocritical. He's traveled the globe, into its most primitive and varied reaches, and has made the sexual practices of other cultures one subject of his ceaseless studies."

"Both from observation and experience, scandal has it."

She laughed. "Oh, he's really beyond scandal, given that his accomplishments range so far outside the dull orbit of our unholy respectability, and given that he's been of such great use as both overt and covert agent for the British government. But that's all neither here nor there. The point is, when pressed by circumstance, I was unable to think of anyone more able to appreciate these works without a shred of prejudice, nor anyone more able to guarantee their security. I knew I'd only have to ask him. I knew his interest would be immediate."

She poured the little champagne left into both our glasses.

"Do you dance, Mr. Stillman?" she asked.

"Not if I can avoid it."

"Shall we walk a little in the gardens then?" She raised her glass to mine and we finished the champagne.

The night turned dusky and the crowd below us swelled as the globe-lamps brightened in the orchestra's pagoda around the dance floor, in the supper boxes, and even in the trees above the tables.

The trimmed lawns and neat flowerbeds of the gardens gave way to the dazzle and flaunt of deep evening. As darkness settled over the city, the gardens brightened in the gas-glare. It was the hour of transition, when the swells and loafers began to arrive in the full array of their dandy evening dress and loose-sleeved capes. They idled about the wrought-iron lamp standards with garnet and emerald cut-glass drops and with globes sparkling against the night, turning the whole area around the dance floor into a crystal platform. The play of lights on the surfaces and reflections seduced yet more participants into the throng of dancers and idlers, and now the flirts were arriving as well in their fine silks and linens.

As we walked toward the Crystal Grotto the sounds of polkas, gallops, and quadrilles gradually dimmed, as did the horns and whistles of the penny steamers ferrying the most respectable clientele of the Pleasure Gardens safely home. The gas-lighted paths, the evening fireworks, the distant orchestra—all contributed to reduce a sense of danger or impropriety. For here the mass of Cyrenaic humanity seemed to restrain itself just within recognizable bounds of flirtation and assignation. The chief complaints against the Gardens were, in fact, the noise the crowds of men and prostitutes made in the adjacent streets after the midnight closing of Cremorne.

"Give me time to think about this," I said as we stopped to admire the grotto, her arm in mine. The grotto was in the form of a tall, three-tiered fountain. A well-worn pathway at its base allowed strollers to enter the womblike cave of understory, protected from the waters flowing and dropping all around them.

"This?" she asked in good humor.

"This Burton business," I said. "And there's one further complication."

"Yes?"

"The Rossetti brothers have hired a man—a Mr. Winslow—to search out the Turners."

She turned to look at me. "I believe I wrote of him to you. Are you saying he's approached you?"

"Twice. Once in Rome, and then when I was in London some time ago. Not recently."

"In Rome! Well, he's certainly had no success. They are safe as can be. As I said, I'm absolutely certain of that. What does he suspect?"

I told her about my two interrogations.

"He's fishing," she said, "but he does seem to have narrowed the possibilities. You'll have to take care. Is he following you?"

"No. I'm quite certain." I pulled her closer on my arm. "Forgive me. But I must have assurances from Burton."

"It's understandable."

"Though it's obvious there's nothing to be done this very moment."

"Then we'll discuss it again, soon." She stopped us and turned to look directly into my face. "Don't worry, my friend," she said and smiled. "You'll see them when he returns."

"When might that be?"

"Who can say? But he will. He always does."

Chapter 22

During the past year, her twenty-seventh, Marie had prosecuted her studies with a fury. Her works were exhibited to greater advantage now. As soon as I returned to England, we began meeting secretly at Mrs. Senior's or at the South Kensington Museum, where Marie would arrive in her hansom and show her veiled face at the glass. Then we would be driven away to some more convenient assignation. In one of these meetings, at the vacated town house of a wealthy friend who knew of our secret appointments, we agreed on the date for the ceremony.

"You may live forever apart from your parents," I said as we held each other by the window.

"In time they may be brought around," she said, "but if not, then that's as it must be."

"I'm still astonished you can love me."

"But I do," she said and laughed. "As you well know by now, dear William."

She gently pulled away from me, crossed the room to her small handbag, and from it removed a rounded item wrapped in lemon-yellow paper. She placed it under her nose and breathed in softly, closing her eyes. "Come here," she said, holding out the package.

"Heavenly soap," I said when she placed it under my nose. "My darling—"

She put her fingertips to my lips; then held up a finger on her other hand to indicate one moment. She went into the adjacent bathroom, leaving the door open. I heard a faucet squeak and water begin to fall into the tub. I returned to the window, still mindful that most of our friends thought us an unsuitable match, with it being highly favorable to me but with very little to recommend the match to her. They did not know—how could they?—our true feelings. Still, I had to admit they were right, but that was not going to keep us apart. I would try to be worthy of "the sacrifice" they knew she was making.

The water kept running. She must want a bath, I thought. I poured myself a drink and wondered how we would manage. She came out of the bathroom wrapped only in a long towel, her hair done up high on her head. "Join me, William?"

I was out of my clothing and beside her in a minute or two more. I cradled her in my arms and carried her into the bathroom and held her over the handsome tub with its mahogany surrounds. She let the towel fall open; we removed it and placed the towel on the mahogany towel rack. I lowered her into the water and then climbed in to face her.

Without a word, she handed me the soap and washcloth, smiled, and leaned back against the tub, closing her eyes. I soaked the cloth and began slowly to squeeze water over her body. Then I soaped my hands heavily, put the soap in the nearby strainer, and began gently to massage her. She murmured sweetly now, and then her eyes closed like a woman dreaming. Finally, she took my hands and held them still. Then she turned that I might wash her back. Later, she turned again and said, "Your turn."

I lay back against the tub while she kneeled between my long out-stretched legs. In her hands the soapy cloth slowly cleansed and stimulated my entire body. A dark thought plagued me for a moment: Had Ranelagh done this with her? Taught her to be so free with her body and her lover's?

I recalled an image Rossetti once drew of her as the dangerous archer Diana-Artemis, goddess of the hunt, of wild things—that enigmatic cult-figure haunting fertility rites and childbirth. But what did any of these thoughts matter? We were simply two people experienced in the ways of love. I pushed the unsettling image of them out of my mind.

Her hands consumed me until I would soon lose control, and then she stopped and stood, bent and picked up the towel. She dried herself as I watched. She motioned me to stand and then she toweled me.

I carried her back to the bed, she reached down to turn the sheets, and I laid her onto the mattress. I stood over her, bending to kiss slowly the length of her soap-scented body—sweet and tangy like sugared lemon. She was instantly aroused and spoke my name. As I prepared to enter her, she spoke again, "No...William, not yet." She turned over, exposing now the entire length of the back of her body to my kisses and attentions. After that surreptitious afternoon together, our betrothal, against all opposition, was sealed.

* * *

Miss Spartali and I were married in the spring, April 10, of 1871. Her parents could not reconcile themselves to it, so we chose a small civil ceremony at the Chelsea Register Office. Madox Brown and his daughter Lucy, Marie's great friend and fellow art student, served as witnesses. No one from my family was present. That right-minded people considered a Register Office wedding undignified, even perhaps a little sordid, encouraged me as a demonstration of Marie's defiance of conventions and her parents for the sake of our love. If need be, we would live our lives alone against the world.

Following the April ceremony and a brief honeymoon on the Isle of Wight, we returned to London and began immediately to make plans for our voyage to America to collect my children and introduce my new wife to my family. We sailed for Boston on June 6 through an Atlantic storm and remained in the States for six weeks. Seeing my two girls again, and poor Russie, was the highlight of our trip. But Marie and I devoted certain hours as well to the museums and galleries of Boston and New York. Marie was enchanted by America and Americans, and she enchanted them. British painters had long earned the respect of Americans. Turner himself was included in an American exhibition as early as 1857, and following Ruskin's *Modern Painters*, had been among the favorites—championed by Channing, Cole, Emerson, and Norton. Marie made arrangements for the American sales of some of her work. But we soon returned, *en famille*, and took a small furnished house at 100 Clarendon Road, Notting Hill.

After our daughter Effie was born there in 'seventy-two, Marie's parents began slowly to relent. Her father called his daughter home twice for serious discussion. Upon Marie's suggestion, I in turn wrote my father-in-law to say that I had the greatest respect and affection for him and Mrs. Spartali, and that I was prepared to reconcile in any way satisfactory to them. Following this combination of efforts, Marie's mother urgently requested that we come to live in a vacant house at 8 Altenburg Gardens, abutting their grounds.

Thus truly began our reconciliation that reached its completion nearly a year later when, appearing I would have to return to America to ensure more regular literary employment, Mr. Spartali settled £400 a year on Marie.

* * *

Although I had not yet told Marie about the Turners, she knew of my acquaintance with Allergra Fullerton, who had begun to speak of sequestering herself in her native land.

"With each year, travel and sojourning abroad grows more inconvenient," Allegra told me. "I look now toward some place in the New England countryside where I can continue my work, out of the noise, the smells, the crowds, the avarice and competition of one international city or another. London especially has grown stale to me. The London art world has lost its magic. I sell my work, but I grow jaded. All I seem to see about me now are hypocrisy, venality, and ignorance."

"*Omnia Romoe venalia sunt,*" I offered.

She laughed. "Oh yes, all Romans are venal. Especially these Londoner-Romans at the center of their empire."

"You'll be giving up your painting rooms, your sustaining income."

"I've put something aside." She seemed to hang fire, her head slightly lowered.

"You're telling me everything?"

She looked up. "Everything you need to know."

"You must trust me by now, Allegra."

She hesitated a moment more. "I haven't been feeling as well as I should lately," she said. "That's all."

"All?" I searched her eyes. "The doctors told you something?"

She returned my gaze. "Something," she finally said. "They rather doubt I have more than a year. I'd prefer not to discuss it."

"I'm terribly sorry!"

She turned her face away.

"Can I do anything to help? Surely there must be something."

She looked back at me, composed now. "Thank you, William. There's nothing, really. All I can do is go home, it seems." She tried to smile. Suddenly I couldn't speak.

"Home where I started," she said, after a moment. "My husband, just before he died in our bed, where he'd been lying for what seemed weeks of a bilious fever, awoke briefly to say goodbye. He told me that when my time came after a long life, I should return to be buried beside him."

I still couldn't say anything, so she continued. "He said I should return to his grave, that he would come to me as a lion to help me over."

I found my tongue. "A lion?"

She smiled again, a wistful smile. "Yes. As a lion who would carry me away on his back. To devour me out of this world. His delirium, no doubt. But—"

"You loved one another very much."

"We married young. We hadn't been married long. There had not yet been years 'tasting the disenchanting days and nights of matrimonial wine.'"

"You have a kind of faith in him though, still. Somehow he will help."

"I try to."

"You love him still."

"I remember our love, our long-ago youth. The love is deep in here, hidden away for decades." She pressed both fists to her breast. "But alive still, like this pulsing heart."

"You stayed true to that love, in your own way."

"Never marrying? I suppose in a sense. Not that the world would see it that way."

"Bugger the world!"

She laughed outright. "You're helping me already, William. You see?"

I couldn't bring myself to ask her what it was, her illness. I knew she didn't want me to. I assumed some sort of cancer, probably of the sort women fall prey to.

"I think you did remain true to him," I said instead. "I think you also, at the same time I mean, remained true to your art. Difficult choices. But you to lived your life as you wished."

"After his death, I simply had to go on as I did. It hardly felt like a choice."

"Don't forget, you had to choose not to marry. Surely there were opportunities."

"Some few." She hesitated, then smiled. "I might have married Burton, once."

"You fascinated him."

"He's never said anything about it. He's a gentleman when it comes to that sort of thing. But I don't mean he proposed. No. It wasn't that, but we had our private, mutual obsession for a time." Then she added: "It might, rather easily I think, have grown into something more. It very nearly did."

"But you each had your own work to do."

"At the time we both knew we couldn't settle down, so to speak. We didn't have to say as much. We knew it."

"Life with Richard would hardly be settling down. But I understand your point."

"There were other men, here and there. Before Richard and after. But he was the only one who could have tempted me to throw over...well to throw over my essential solitude. The solitude of work."

"Maybe you forfeited a great love, Allegra. You made the harder choice."

"When your time comes, of course, you wonder about such things."

"Of course."

She grew silent. It was clear she didn't want to discuss it any further.

"When are you thinking of leaving?" I asked.

"Haven't decided; it may take me some time. My affairs here have grown entangled and deep-rooted over the years."

"You must write to me. Tell me how you're doing."

"I will."

"And the Turners?"

"We should have a talk with Burton. Then you decide."

"When he returns."

"Yes, from Damascus, where he's the British Consul, I discovered." She looked at me to test my response. "I'm not leaving soon, anyway. And as I said, he'll return."

"We don't know when, however. I don't at all like leaving the Turners to chance."

"I've written him a letter, asking him to write directly to you to explain precisely how they came into his possession and what he's done with them."

"Haven't you already told me how he received them?"

"I want you to hear it directly from his mouth. Or I should say his pen. His mouth will follow his pen, I assure you." She smiled. "And their whereabouts, of course. I only hope he receives my letter. If he does, he'll reply."

Chapter 23

I did not have to wait long for Burton's reply, delivered by a government special courier, his consular seal unbroken on the thick envelope. He wrote that he was indeed on his way back to London to answer at the Foreign Office unfair charges against him arising out of certain of his activities in Damascus and its desert environs. After mentioning that he recalled meeting me at Monckton Milnes' and asking pardon for his not being available when I was in London, his letter went immediately to say: "Mrs. Fullerton has asked me to give you a full, confidential accounting of how certain studies came into my hands, where they currently reside, and how you may come at them if you desire." Then he recounted the moment of receiving the studies, making a little narrative that for authenticity's sake I present here intact.

* * *

First, how they came into my hands. It was in December of 1861, if memory serves, that month of tremendous cold and the death of the Prince Consort, that a friend approached me with a dilemma: Mrs. Allegra Fullerton, the American artist with whom I have had an amusing and delicious acquaintance over the years. We met at her invitation in a London coffee room—Rie's Divan, on Strand, I recall—where she explained—disingenuously, I later discovered—only that she had been given a small collection of erotica that had escaped the flames of certain benighted characters. These, she assured me, were all that survived. As she was to be completing business for her English patrons over the next several months and then returning to an America in disorder, she asked if I would be willing to hold the designs—she called them "studies"—until she or the person who had given them over to her would return to claim them. The person she named I remembered meeting once.

She then insisted on coming to my bachelor's quarters uncomfortably close to the time of my marriage.

"My dear Burton," she told me after we had settled to business in my apartment, "you are the one man in England I believe I can trust with these."

"Your old habit of flattering me, my dear!"

She returned my smile and added, "Especially for your loyalty to anyone whose trust you've plighted."

"What do you have then?" I looked at the valise she had placed on the floor beside her. From it she drew out a substantial package wrapped in protective cloth.

As she had expected, I was naturally fascinated by the objects she placed before me. "I can see now why you believe there are few alternatives," I said. "I'd be honored."

"Thank you," she said. "I knew you'd understand."

"How did your friend come to possess these?"

"I've promised never to reveal that." She looked straight at me. "He must tell you himself, if you wish to hear the answer. Suffice to say he was anxious to preserve, by any means, what he could. And he recently had to leave on a mission abroad. You must never mention his connection to these; he runs a grave risk, and he'd consider me a turncoat."

"I see. Nonetheless, whatever devices he used, it took some courage. Plainly, these must have come to you by some species of theft."

"And customs officials here or in my own country, or indeed Italy, might find it a duty to cause either him or me serious difficulty."

"I've smuggled many items by customs in my time."

"It's not something, upon due consideration, I wish to chance."

"It's always risk upon risk for one who would extend knowledge."

"So their illegality," she said, pointing to the package now on my table, "wouldn't daunt you."

"At this point I no longer think of the legality of my private interests or publications. I simply exercise caution." I smiled and began a little joke I liked to tell. "You heard what the chloroformed bride pinned on her pillow on her wedding night for her bridegroom to discover?"

"A little note saying 'Mama says you are to do what you like'." She laughed. "You've told me that one before."

"Ah! I threaten to become a bore. You know I've always been in the business of knowledge in the face of ignorance."

"The pursuit of which, as you've written, is dangerous."

"More so with every passing year, it seems."

"All I ask is that you promise to keep their existence secret. And furthermore, that you must take someone else into our confidence and enlist his aid only if it is absolutely necessary for their veriest security."

"Well, you know of my own impending marriage—to Miss Isabel Arundell? Yes. I should think my life might become somewhat regularized now. But you have my word."

She shook my hand on it in a most manly fashion, placed a chaste little kiss on my forehead as I gave her a bow, and saying her goodbyes left directly, as if to honor my betrothal by not lingering either of us into temptation.

Before I locked the package away in my own study, I considered the illustrations at my leisure. I had not yet seen more truthful depictions of men and women, and of genitalia, in acts of congress, nor better depictions of the secret female parts and their phases of arousal. I myself was about to be newly married, my wildest adventures perhaps over, and I began to believe my constitution fit more than ever for composing works that might synthesize some knowledge gained from world travels and my studies of both Occidental and Oriental languages and literatures.

But understand, sir, that for years since that second meeting with Mrs. Fullerton my leisure for study and literary labor has been limited. Financial imperatives drove me to consular posts in Africa and South America —with and without my new wife Isabel. And Isabel and I traveled for some years more in Africa and India. During most of those years of work, travel, and study, I did not believe I could guarantee my trust to Mrs. Fullerton, unless I deposited the studies in the only place I knew they could remain both secret and secure—the archives of my friend Monckton Milnes, who as you know became Lord Houghton in 'sixty-three. You know him to be a collector of great curiosity and scholarship. Milnes I knew as a man of sufficient courage and catholicity to appreciate these artifacts for what they actually were. It was at Milnes's country house Fryston, moreover, that I believe I once met you, sir. You have my word that I shall keep your name out of any connection whatsoever to these illustrations, unless you direct me otherwise. Please be sure to burn this letter immediately after reading it.

* * *

As Fortune would have it, we were in America retrieving my children when Burton returned to London to exonerate himself at the Foreign Office. But through the intercession of Mrs. Fullerton, Burton and I were able to meet at an appointed time in 'seventy-two at Fryston Hall, an austere and imposing Yorkshire country house that Lord Houghton and his wife had made more inviting upon moving in after the death of his father some fourteen years earlier. Long ago an ancestor had added to the old house of rambling dark corridors and staircases an eighteenth-century façade of pillared portico and white stone slabs. Mrs. Milnes, now Lady Houghton, had also added the lavender gardens and borders of stocks, nasturtiums, and sweet-pea. But the Houghtons had devoted particular and modern attentions to the front rooms: the drawing and dining rooms and the long library.

I was granted an abbreviated tour of the old structure; it seemed that the entire house had been turned into a library. The books were carefully organized and shelved not only in the front library proper but in bookcases running along the walls of passageways and staircases and bedrooms and cupboards. I was being shown one of the most celebrated private collections in England of French, German, English, and Italian literature, as well as beautiful editions of Greek and Latin classics. I remarked on a surprising amount of current American literature, another testimony to Houghton's well-known tolerance. There were also many holographs from previous centuries, and of course his collection of erotic literature (mostly French and Italian), the largest in England.

It was in his long library—smelling heavily of leather and tobacco—that the three of us once again examined the lost Turners. Houghton retrieved them from among his beautifully bound collection of illustrated erotica—Fragonard's illustrations of *La Pucelle*, Laclos' *Les Liaisons Dangereuses*, Caracci's illustrations of Aretino's sonnets on erotic postures, and many others. The illustrated texts seemed to be separately shelved from the non-illustrated erotic books, his collection of

Sade for instance, but I hadn't the leisure to analyze his punctilious system.

To my memory the Turners appeared to be all there—no longer jumbled together in an old oilcloth. They had been preserved in delicate papers, each individual sketch with its own protective soft slipcover and the torn portion of the sketchbook wrapped in lush green felt to keep moisture out. The loose materials were still unbound but now folded carefully into leather and board covers. My feeling at the moment was strangely similar to what one feels upon meeting an old friend one never expected to see again, and in better condition than ever. Suddenly I knew the wisdom of Mrs. Fullerton's difficult decisions, and I made a mental note to write to her in America to tell her so, and to thank her.

Burton—returned from a stay in Edinburgh and a trip to Iceland, and flush with his success before the Foreign Office committee—told us that he had received an appointment as Consul to Trieste and was preparing his wife Isabel and his household to remove yet one more time. The death of his mother-in-law had complicated the arrangements, and now in his early fifties, he was recovering slowly from the removal of a carbuncle. Yet his appearance was still that of a heroic figure: dark, forceful, ruthless, with an iron countenance—his demeanor and appearance gave the impression that if you crossed him he would cut through you like a sword. His enthusiasm over the Turners summoned his vast energies. He began to ponder aloud the idea of putting together a volume of essays with illustrative reproductions on the nature and meaning of these secret works.

"With your permission, of course, Mr. Stillman," he said. "And when I have greater leisure to attend it."

"No one would be better suited to the task, Richard," Houghton said. "Brandy, gentlemen?" He directed us to be seated at a business table where a decanter and eight glasses sat amid sheaves of papers and books in the process, apparently, of being catalogued.

An enormous clock ticked ostentatiously while Milne decanted the brandy. As Milne clipped our cigar tips, Burton again took up his theme.

"I would of course have to make a detailed study of the painter, his life and work, and come to my own conclusions as to the purpose or meaning of these." He waved his hand toward the bookcases where the Turners were again safely stored. "That won't be an easy task, given the painter was something of a confidence man, wasn't he? Operating under assumed names and disguises as it pleased him, keeping separate households going at the same time, disappearing for a weekend, to devil knows where, and the like." He laughed. "But I must say I find all that appealing, as well."

"A kindred spirit," I said.

" 'Indistinctness is my fault,' Turner is reported to have proclaimed," Houghton put in, "and 'atmosphere is my style.' This man who painted the very air, this man of ambiguities upon enigmas!"

"A sort of Will Shakespeare for his own time," Burton suggested and chuckled. "A universal genius shrouded in enigma, enigmas in no small measure of his own doing."

"But these are obviously studies of some sort," Houghton added, gesturing toward the bookcase, "of varying quality as to the execution, and perhaps as to the seriousness of purpose." He lit his cheroot and offered the long match around to ours.

"For some years I've pondered their purpose," I said. "Just one more of the old master's riddles? Sometimes I think they've little more than the purpose of so much erotica, the stimulation of memory, of fantasy and desire. Was he not, perhaps after Rembrandt, pleasing himself as he grew older? Over the past few years I've often imagined Turner in his Chelsea cottage first-floor painting room overlooking the river, luxuriant ivy peeping in at the window full of river lights and hues, some of these studies before him, a landscape painter in the end no longer capable of outdoor expeditions, drawing and painting the landscapes of human bodies as no one before him. A picture of the old man I can't get out of my head. The final work of his life, begun, I take it, in his youth. But toward the end he didn't give a hoot what others thought. So long as they just left him alone."

"If so, one has to assume whatever he might have been painting ultimately was destroyed?" Burton asked.

"Destroyed even before Ruskin got hold of them," I said, "for there's been no word, not the slightest whisper, of a larger project. We know a great many sketches never resulted directly in a finished painting."

Burton flicked his ash toward an ashtray. "Yet we do know from Ruskin's own mouth, and Rossetti's, as I understand it, of the destruction of such studies as these; many more perhaps."

"Yes," Houghton said, "and that might argue for the destruction of any greater work—full paintings, say—if such destruction took place, before the bequest ever made it to the National Gallery."

"We simply don't know," I said. "I've thought the old man might have embarked on some sort of Gnostic transgression, some exploration of the sexual nature of the body, male and female: the energies thereby unleashed."

Burton's eyes lit up. "Ah, you mean the liberation of Eros! Interesting line of inquiry—a sort of Blakean project, perhaps?"

"He was profoundly interested in many of his predecessors," I said. "Blake among them, who certainly had an influence on Turner's *Death on a Pale Horse* and *Angel Standing in the Sun*.

"But ultimately we can't say, can we?" I added. "And if anyone had found some larger body of work left behind he might well have taken it upon himself to destroy it."

"That Mrs. Booth?" Burton asked.

"Possibly," I said. "She might've known what he was up to, and indulged the old man. He no doubt would've kept her particular body out of his final project!"

When Burton laughed his face lengthened and his upper lip rose with pleasure, showing a canine tooth.

"She humored him, I mean to say," I went on. "Just as she was doing when they strolled the neighborhood along the river, boated together, and lived like an old married couple of differing ages come to rest in Chelsea. And perhaps she humored him all the more if these paintings were the grand project toward the end of his life. What harm in it, if it amused him, alleviated his pain, gave him hope and vitality? She knew, if we play this line of speculation out, that she would be able to destroy them immediately after his demise."

"Or perhaps she was not ashamed of them," Burton suggested. "I take it she was a rather voluptuous creature herself, in a matronly, widowly, Junoesque sort of way."

"Aha!" Houghton said, smiling. "A luscious armful to warm a man's bed in his declining years."

"She would have been older and perhaps fuller still by the Chelsea years, after 'forty-six," I said. "But they seemed to cohabitate off and on since the early 'thirties when she became a widow near her fortieth year. By all accounts she was tall, ample, and comely."

"Hadn't she assumed, also, the studio duties Turner's father once performed?" Burton asked.

"So it seems," I said. "His lodging at her house in Kent at Margate overlooked the jetty and beach, a sort of bedroom studio with a view of the land, sea, and skies that had inspired him from his youth when he was first sent by his parents to reside with relatives."

"All amusing speculation!" Houghton said. "Still, gentlemen, I think this idea of Richard's to make a study including reproductions, privately printed of course, is a capital idea. A century or two from now the world may well be able to countenance such a volume, and learn from it." He smiled and waved his cigar in the air, a man growing expansive as he looked toward some enlightened future.

"If you continue to preserve them here in complete safety," Burton said, "then I may return as I can to prepare the book." He slid me a look. "But I suspect it shall be some time before I can take the project in hand."

I agreed to leave the artifacts in Lord Houghton's capable hands, or library rather, for now. I had every assurance from him that I should have the sketches returned to me at any time of my choosing. Burton and I were guests that night at Fryston, and we left together the next morning in a phaeton Houghton provided to transfer us to the railway station. Awaiting the cars for London, we strolled on the platform for the air and exercise.

"You may well be right, Captain Burton," I was saying, "that the best way to pass the legacy on to some future, more enlightened and grateful citizenry is just such a book as you propose—" when he interrupted me by a gradual movement of his hand against the front of my upper arm.

"Don't look around, Stillman," he said in a low, careful voice. "We're being watched. That large man seated on the bench, wearing a shabby workman's coat and cap. You can glimpse him after we turn again and walk past."

I had not seen the man before and I could not imagine how Burton knew he was interested in us.

"Following us for some time," he continued, sotto voce. He gave no indication otherwise—by any suggestive movement of his arms, head, or torso—that we were speaking softly and confidentially. We remained two gentlemen taking their exercise before the railcars arrived.

"To and from Fryston?" I asked.

"Possibly."

Once seated in our car, we remained watchful. "Any sign of him?" I asked quietly.

"No," he said. "But you can be certain he's with us, in another carriage. If we see him again, it'll be after we disembark."

I saw no alternative than to tell him about Mortimer Winslow.

"This man is not Winslow, however," he said. He was completely unruffled by my news.

"No. It isn't. One of his men?"

"My guess is one of the heavy characters he uses for such work, and worse. Just as well you're not traveling alone."

"I certainly can't call in the police!"

He laughed. "We'll see what he does once we get off."

But after we got off the car, the man in his workman's guise never appeared again. Burton and I finally and cautiously went our separate ways. I must be that damned Winslow's chief suspect, I thought. The man and his minions threatened to haunt me the rest of my life. I couldn't rely on Burton's aid anymore either, because he and Isabel Burton soon left for his post in Trieste.

I had my hands full with my new family, my new employment, and my sick son. I often wondered about Allegra Fullerton, who had left for America.

I had very few letters from her over the following year. Then one day a letter arrived from Eliot Norton telling me, as she requested of him when her time came, that she had died and been buried beside her husband in a Lexington cemetery. That night I dreamed of her riding the back of a lion—his dark mane flowing, his roars diminishing as he moved toward the horizon where a lake shimmered among trees in the afternoon sun. I told Marie of her death.

"She's home at last," Marie said. "But she's also left all her wonderful work behind for the rest of us."

We spoke little about Allegra Fullerton after that. Marie and I were consumed by our labors and raising our family.

And in a few short years I would endure the greatest affliction of my life.

Part III, 1875–1890

When everybody steals, cheats, and goes to church, complacently, and the light of their whole body is darkness, how great is that darkness! And...the physical result of that mental vileness is a total carelessness of the beauty of sky, or the cleanness of streams, or the life of animals and flowers.

— John Ruskin, *Fors Clavigera*

There was a rocky valley between Buxton and Bakewell, once upon a time, divine as the Vale of Tempe; you might have seen Gods there morning and evening.... You cared neither for Gods nor grass, but for cash...; you thought you could get it by what the *Times* calls 'Railroad Enterprise.' You Enterprised a Railroad through a valley—you blasted its rocks away, heaped thousands of tons of shale into its lovely stream. The valley is gone, and the Gods with it; and now, every fool in Buxton can be at Bakewell in half-an-hour, and every fool in Bakewell at Buxton; which you think a lucrative process of exchange—you Fools everywhere.

— John Ruskin, *Fors Clavigera*

Chapter 24

When Russie's mother died, I had convinced myself that any death would be more bearable. But in watching my son's youth devastated and the lingering pain of his long leaving, I plunged into a consuming grief that was like nothing in my experience. As I cared for him in his helplessness and prosecuted my futile search for a medical cure, we had become as close as father and son could be.

His poor body had swelled with dropsy; we knew the end was near. I wanted to take him away to some private, quiet place for his life to end. Mr. Spartali kindly offered us a cottage on his Isle of Wight estate, while Marie stayed home with the children and to prepare for an exhibition.

I carried Russie into the hotel room we took while the cottage was being readied. In my arms he looked up at me and said, "I don't want to die, Papa. But do you think I'll see mother again?"

"I believe so, Russie. Yes, certainly. I'm sure she awaits you and the end of pain." I placed him recumbent on a short settle, his feet elevated, his head resting on a pillow.

I read a great deal to him in those final hours together. He took pleasure—the only pleasure left to him—in our long reading sessions, until that evening when his eyes closed and he went into convulsions. The hotel room had become our prison cell; now the violence of his contortions was unsupportable to me. Might not a doctor ease the trauma? Was he in terrible pain? I swept him up into my arms and began our flight home to Altenberg Gardens, requiring a rail voyage of at least a dozen miles. We arrived at late evening. I placed him on a pallet and called for a doctor. But the disease that had long ago entered his damaged bones had written his Fate.

At the age of thirteen, on March 27, 1875, about midnight, he passed from me. I rose from our common pallet, walked out into the night, leaving his deserted body behind, and gave way to my full grief for this child—my pride, my hope.

We buried him quietly in the churchyard at Arreton. A final kindness was the rector never asking for proof of baptism. He knew I was not a churchman and had long renounced the New England faith of my father and mother. Laura and I had refused to encumber Russie's tender life with dogmas, and no one knew better than I the effect of dogma on a developing mind.

For months I was unable to pull myself out of a deep well of despondency. Marie feared for my sanity and my life. She tried to console and distract me from my despair with those small graces of her marital sympathy—trifling with my hair as I lay with my head in her lap, handling the back of my neck as I sat in my favorite chair, massaging my feet as I lay in my bath. But for the first time I could not initiate or respond to such gestures of tender intimacy. Nor could I initiate or respond to impassioned marital relations with this lovely woman who had healed my first consuming grief and returned the possibility of joy to my life. It was as if I had become a mere mechanism, shut out of all human empathy, all feeling for life, all hope of salutary development.

I especially could not shake the self-indulgent feeling that I was being punished. But for what? Betraying Laura once during the years of our marriage? Falling in with Mrs. Fullerton? Conniving to steal the sketches from my friends because I did not trust their judgment? Other decisions that had left my family destitute in the worst of times and sending us about the world seeking the flimsy remunerations of consular posts? My failure to become an artist, to summon the courage, skill, and labor required? Leaving Russie behind while I traveled to Constantinople? Or all my failings together?

Another shadow haunted me. I kept remembering an instance just before Russie's final decline. On our last outing together, I had been pushing him in his wheeled cage in Hyde Park when I glimpsed a dwarfish figure in a shabby black cloak scuttling behind trees. I said nothing to Russie about it. My mother and her mother before her had premonitions, or second sights, usually on the eve of some fatal mishap. I feared this instance was but another foretoken of evil about to befall us. As we perambulated through the park, I could not admit to myself what it might be. I wanted no more apparitions disturbing my fragile equilibrium. But upon my son's death, my mind envisioned that scuttling black shape with frightful repetitiveness and potency.

What was this thing of darkness glancing off my vision? For me, as for Ruskin, Turner had been a divinity, a Mount Blanc floating golden above the clouds near sunset. Unlike Ruskin, however, my discovery of the esoteric studies (for I had begun to think of them as at once secret, cryptic, essential, almost indeed occult) had not reduced Turner in my estimation. But now this—these glimpses of something dark, surreptitious, and foreboding.

I suppose I was half mad—Marie called it my "brain fever"—and I came to suspect Ruskin was by now half mad as well. For we had a bizarre meeting, as I recall it, when he paid Marie and me a visit to express his condolences. I imagine I must have looked and acted like one in a dream. I had a deep sense at that time of being displaced, as if I were moving in some aqueous realm parallel to this one, but not quite of it.

"I only heard of your dear son, William," Ruskin said, once we were seated, "several weeks following his decease. Or I would have paid my respects sooner. My memory is of a bright and lovely child."

"William has been inconsolable, Mr. Ruskin," Marie said.

"Most understandable. You're such a good father, William. Anyone can see your children adore you. You have much to live for."

"If it weren't for Marie and the children, yes, I couldn't go on."

Ruskin scrutinized me, as if studying a person upon first acquaintance. He had not yet taken on the shaggy and distracted appearance of his last mad decades, which began with his first complete breakdown only four years later, as if he were following the perilous path of old Turner. Yet even now, shortly after his young friend Rose La Touche's death, I could see the signs in his face of what Professor Richmond was to describe as "beauty and mad sanity" and the sense one felt of "strife, inward and outward, revealed, and a dreamland yet unexplored."

Ruskin smiled as if he were about to float a little joke. "The consolations of marriage and children, I'm sure, surpass those of philosophy."

We spoke of Russie and the aftermath a few moments more, and then Marie left us to see about tea.

"I haven't heard much from you, William. I thought perhaps you might be harboring some animosity against me." He smiled again, but it was an odd sort of smile, even for him.

"I knew you were busy with your Oxford professorship and your books," I said.

"Still, one might trouble to inform an old friend." He stared at me, subdued his voice, and added in a low, almost dramatic whisper, "and child's namesake."

I said nothing. He spoke of various matters that concerned him, perhaps against the awkward silence. He rambled from one topic to another and began to speak of his anti-vivisection work. He mentioned Isabel Burton, who had organized many women in the cause, as noble a captain in this sphere as her infamous husband was in his. This thought turned his tumbling words to other matters on which, I now realize, he had been working.

"Given the state of England, I rather despair," he went on. "No professorship, no school of art can be of least use to a public and a government that blast mountains to ruin and blacken riverbeds with foam and poison."

I understood that his turn to political and economic writings had consumed his genius, and the more he looked into what his friend Thomas Carlyle called the dismal science, the angrier he got: above all, apparently, for the removal of all moral questions from the consideration of the scientists. Perhaps it was my still-dazed reticence—I suppose I remained in some sense in a state of shock—but he was like a man talking to himself about his latest passions. "Education," he said, "is not teaching people to know what they do not know. It means teaching them to behave as they do not behave. We need not more money, but better men as the fruit of our educational systems."

It was not that I disagreed with him entirely, for I had read like so many others his "Letters to the Workmen and Labourers of Great Britain" that were to become collected into *Fors Clavigera*, and I agreed that the British system of capital and empire—a system America had been doing its best to emulate—had resulted in grotesque cruelties, terrible working conditions, and pollutions across the land, all the while pretending to a punctilious Christianity and national superiority. It was no wonder such a system generated doomed Utopian experiments as counterpoise to the despoliation. But for some reason, I challenged him.

"I wouldn't disagree, John, that all ethics, Christian and otherwise, have been removed from considerations of capital and industry. It's rather that the insertion of a narrow moral evangelism restrains only a very few from utter descent into greed and violence, the sheerest egoism. I've seen that in the East as well as the West. A fanatical, narrow dogmatism is, finally, ever destructive."

"Oh," he said and slapped the arm of his chair. "I for one have been horribly plagued and misguided by evangelicals all my life!"

"And you've seen the damage of which you—we all—are capable, as a result."

His gaze, one eye roving a little, penetrated me. I had said nothing of the Turner legacy, but he seemed to understand my meaning immediately for all his fine frenzy. Marie came in pushing a tea tray just at the moment he stood up to leave. He made a little bow to her and said, "I must be off. I fear I've overstayed my welcome."

Marie began a polite protest, saying certainly he could stay for a cup of tea, but he was on his way out and there was no restraining him.

As I opened the door for him he handed me two sheets of paper, folded together. "Excerpts from a letter to my father I had thought to be of some interest to you," he said. Then he turned and walked down the front steps.

I closed the door and turned to Marie, who had stood just behind us with a questioning look on her face. I unfolded the sheets. "Two fair copies. Each a portion of a letter sent to his father," I said. "Dated August 29, 1858."

"Please read them to me, William."

I began to read:

"Men ought to be severely disciplined and exercised in the sternest way in daily life—they should learn to live on stone beds and eat black soup, but they should never have their hearts broken—a noble heart, once broken, never mends…. The two terrific mistakes which Mama and you involuntarily fell into were the exact reverse of *both ways*—you fed me effeminately and luxuriously to the extent that I actually now could not travel in rough countries without taking a cook with me!—but you thwarted me in all the earnest fire and passion of life. About Turner you indeed never knew how much you thwarted me—for I thought it was my duty to be thwarted—it was the religion that led me all wrong there; if I had the courage and knowledge enough to insist on having my own way resolutely, you would now have had me in happy health, loving you twice as much—…and full of energy for the future."

"My goodness," Marie said. "Why would he have given you such a portion of his former life and thoughts?"

"That was about the time I believe fearful doubts began to trouble him," I suggested. "Let's see what the other says." Once again, I began to read:

"The Mistakes which bring about the evil of the world are mainly:

1. Teaching religious doctrines and creeds instead of simple love of God & practical love of our neighbor. This is a terrific mistake—I fancy the fundamental mistake of humanity.

2. Want of proper cultivation of the beauty of the body and the fineness of the senses—a modern mistake chiefly."

I looked up at Marie and handed her the two sheets. "Perhaps he planned to discuss these with me?"

"It seems some sort of, what would you call it? Some sort of offering? As if to make peace between you," she said, "as if to demonstrate that in the essentials he didn't disagree with you."

"It's true in that earlier time he couldn't, or wouldn't, reveal to me the degree of his doubt, the inner voices of self-criticism."

"Should you write to him, tell him you understand all that now? He wouldn't want forgiveness, not directly, but some sort of understanding perhaps."

"Would it make any difference now? He seems no longer quite rational. In some deeper way he confronts his own folly: at times recognizes the terrifying chasm between his beliefs and his actions throughout his life."

"Well, think about it anyway."

"I will," I said. But in truth, I doubted I would try for some sort of reconciliation.

* * *

At this time, after Russie's death, it was only by a device of my father-in-law, who no doubt feared for my own soundness of mind, that I returned to work. He arranged for me to serve as correspondent to the *London Times* to cover the beginning of the Herzegovina insurrection in 1875, which by '76 had spread to Bosnia, Serbia, and Bulgaria. Thrown back into the correspondent's metier I had come to master, forced to witness daily the cataclysms of history, I began to regain my life through work and travel.

Over the next three years Marie and I were often apart, and she, bless her, cared for her stepdaughters with the same attention and affection she lavished on our daughter Effie. Yet determined and resourceful, Marie never ceased her study and painting. Her work was appearing at the Dudley, the Grosvenor, the Royal Academy, and in America. Often, she spent long rather isolated periods at family property on the Isle of Wight with only the three children for company and a busy easel and paint box. Though I regretted our long separations during the wars and alarums of the 1870s, and missed the children, our tenuous prosperity depended on my absence as Special Correspondent.

During this separation, as I reflected on the circumstances of my marriage to Marie, I recalled that Laura and I had been young together. Our intimacies, if not fervid, were full of youthful energy, sufficient and fruitful. But Marie was still a young woman, a woman of passions and dedication, married to an older man with the many scars of his longer life all too apparent. It troubled me that although I was capable of enchantment, my ardor nonetheless might well no longer be capable of matching hers. In my absence, I was neglecting, as well, the full range of her needs as wife and mother.

While stopping in Montenegro at one point in my journalist's travels, my thoughts turned to how my employment disturbed our marriage. I sat down to write her a letter, including these lines: "I stand the roughing it here very well so far, though I fear I am looking like a wild man and very brown—I begin to realize that I am getting old, dear, and to think it a great shame that your life should be wasted on such a wreck as I am. If only I could be sure to keep you happy as long as you live or even as long as I live, I shouldn't so much regret the fruitlessness of my life. But sometimes I am much saddened by a fear that I rather marred your life than otherwise, and perhaps if you had not seen me you might have found a truer life elsewhere."

* * *

My first years working for the *Times*, I traveled to and from the Balkans through Trieste—that small, civilized, polyglot seaport where winds and temperatures range in the extremes—where I was finally able to catch the Burtons recently returned from the East.

In their earlier years in Trieste, Isabel and Richard kept a sprawling fourth-story apartment. Its reception rooms were brightened with trays and dishes of gold, silver, and brass, and adorned with oriental hangings, with Persian enamels, and with fine English and French porcelain. Without carpets or sofas, the rooms were instead set with brilliant Bedouin rugs and divans covered in silk. Indeed, in this setting it was Isabel's grand piano and their endless shelves of books that seemed out of place.

A talkative, dark-haired, bright-complexioned woman, Isabel was both eloquent and animated. She gave Richard no favor in their discussions and debates. They were often quite playful and self-deprecating on both sides, by turns exaggerated satirically one against the other. She had a ready and rather loud laugh. Her hands moved as she spoke and her eyes flashed. By reputation she was highly adventurous and yet a quite orthodox Roman Catholic, as Burton could never be. Her Catholic votaries could be seen amongst the Oriental hangings and objects. Devoted to him yet always holding her own, it seemed, it was clear she helped him in his work, just as he helped her in hers—her recent book on Syria having proved a better seller than many of Richard's own books.

Over lunch, she spoke for some time about researching her book, particularly the difficulties of getting around and of hiring pack animals and reliable horses.

"Some of the available ones were not in very good shape to begin with," she said, frowning slightly.

"As we've found in so many travels," Richard put in. "In my experience, Africa is the worst place for cruelty to animals. But whether in Algiers or Damascus or anywhere else we've traveled together, Isabel, unlike most of the English who merely complain of it, never averts her eyes. Rather, she's very practical; she sets about gathering donations from the English colonists and their ministers to buy, feed, and treat ill-used beasts."

"Then I embark on a mission to educate the owners of the animals that a well-fed, well cared-for animal is a better investment," she said, "better capable of the labors they would set them to."

"She thereby alleviates some small degree of pain and suffering in our world," Richard said. "And she's been very active as well on behalf of abandoned or orphaned children."

"Very admirable, Mrs. Burton," I said. "I've been astonished and disheartened myself by spectacles of cruelty. And I say that as one who hunted game all the years of his youth and early manhood. Attaining meat is one thing, but mindless and vicious cruelty, especially when prolonged, is quite another. You've perhaps heard that Mr. Ruskin threatens to give up his hard-won Oxford professorship due to the 'ghastly moans and howls' as he put it, emanating from the university's vivisection laboratories? You know, Turner himself had great empathy for suffering human beings and other creatures."

"I hadn't heard Ruskin's threat," she said. "But I respect him all the more for it. It seems, Mr. Stillman, he extends his concern for the abuses of labor to this other arrogance and cruelty."

"To be honest," I said, "I've never known a man so admirable in so many ways who is likewise so limited, so incapacitated, in others. I named my first-born after him, but now we barely speak."

"It'd be difficult for me to speak to a man who had burned Turner's work," Richard said.

"Of course," Isabel said, "we don't know what he found. Something reprehensible, unimaginable, severely damaging to the painter's good name and memory?"

When Richard did not respond, I realized that he hadn't shared with her yet his intention to make a study of Turner on the very point of what Ruskin had found. I knew he shared his work with her. But I took my lead from Richard's silence and look and changed the subject.

After our light lunch, Burton led me into one of the workrooms for a private talk while Isabel went to her nap. "Isabel and I rise to our tea and work about dawn," he explained, "lunch lightly, as you see, and after a brief nap we take our exercise together— fencing, walking, swimming—according to the season. She's quite accomplished with the broadsword, and an excellent swimmer."

There were, I soon discovered, three such workrooms within the large apartment: deal worktables for writing, more endless bookshelves containing volumes in every language imaginable, and collections of guns, spears, pistols, swords, masks, and scientific equipment tucked into every corner.

He had already begun planning with Forster Arbuthnot and Edward Rehatsek his Kama Shastra Society—a protective front for the publication of his translations of ancient erotica.

"You see," he explained, his eyes flashing amusement, "The Obscene Publications Act of 'fifty-seven was only to stop those who published and sold pornographic materials in the very agorae of London. It never intended to suppress private collections, scholarly and artistic materials, or even closed societies from private circulation. Hence we intend to skirt the law by creating our own private society, and by working with subscribers only." He stopped to laugh. "Beating the arbiters of public morals at their own game."

"Then Ruskin was wrong to invoke the terrifying shadow of the Act?"

"According to my legal advice," he said. "Of course to give him some credit despite his crimes, Ruskin was no doubt responding in part to the ninety- eight percent successful conviction rate from prosecutions under the Act brought by the Society for the Suppression of Vice." He chuckled. "Those Mrs. Grundies of every county magistrate's office and those middle class, respectably pious, water- swilling prats of every town and city."

"So you see your Society as the publisher of your proposed book on Turner?"

"Nowhere else to go. But it'll be some time before I can turn my full attention to it. That's why, as you noticed, I haven't discussed it yet with Isabel. Too much other work before us, and there's no need to offend her with these drawings. She's tolerant of all my stranger work, but there are limits to what even she'll countenance. Anyway, all in good time."

"You'll have to wait till retirement from the Foreign Office?"

"The book would require constant travel to Lord Houghton's, as well as preparing the images for exemplary reproduction." He gave me a significant look. "And beyond my consular duties and not infrequent requests for travel on behalf of the Foreign Office and the government, I do have other work to hand."

"Your translations."

"Yes."

It was widely believed that Burton had been given Trieste as a quiet—some would say harmless—sinecure for his long and brilliant service to England, but that he was too outspoken, too public a figure, and had made too many enemies in the government to be granted the more exciting and remunerative posts he desired, or the full honors any honest citizen would have deemed equal to his courageous service. As a result, he now filled his adventurous soul with private travels and escapades, with foreign service emergencies no one else was capable of handling, with his own bold studies of esoteric subjects, and with translating Eastern and ancient erotica from original texts.

"You don't see a suitable period of extended leave?"

"Well, since they"—I assumed he meant the Foreign Office—"appear to have abandoned me to this little corner of the world, I expect to take what leave I can in other travels and in London. I have an excellent deputy here in Mr. Brock. But as to your question, no, I don't foresee frequent and sustained encampments at Fryston sufficient unto the work. And not at the expense of my other travels in the service of the translations underway." He looked weary. I had never seen that look about him. "I'd thought," he continued, "to request of you, at some future day, permission to travel to England and return here with the Turners under my personal care and protection. Then to fully launch into the projected volume."

He was probably the only man I could imagine into whose hand I might entrust their removal. But I said, "I can't even think of letting them out into the world again, not yet, given the years I suffered searching to reclaim them."

"It would require great trust, I agree."

"It's not that I would ever question your word. It's more fear of some accident, beyond your—beyond anyone's—control."

"We never know what Fate has in store. We can only exert ourselves, and perhaps ingratiate ourselves with Fate." He laughed softly. "I've survived several deaths by my exertions."

I laughed with him. "Your idea, however, would take some getting used to."

"I don't myself feel hurried about a Turner book. But it entices me greatly, shimmering there, so to speak, on the crepuscular horizon."

I stayed for dinner, after a long walk up into the high ground with them. They had their eyes on renting a particular high palazzo, should it ever become available. After dinner he took me into another work-room where there were several projects on tables. Red handkerchiefs, to be used as wipers, were tied to each table's leg. The projects included travel books, translations, whatever. He handed me two of his most recent publications: *Etruscan Bologna* and *A New System of Sword Exercise*. "Let me ask Isabel, come to think of it, to make you a gift of her *Inner Life of Syria* as well. She's a wonderful writer, you know."

Then we spoke of my own work for the *Times* and Richard's view of the mess in the near East.

"Serbia and Montenegro declaring war against Turkey will prove a disaster," he accurately predicted. "The thing will spread to Bulgaria, Turkey will respond as it always does with massacres and atrocities, and before long we'll have Turkey and Russia at each other's throats."

I told him of my and Laura's earlier experiences in Crete and of my broken efforts later in Constantinople. All he could do was shake his head. "That Britain is still in political collusion with the Turks is a sin against humanity we shall one day have to answer for."

That evening as I took leave of them, the three books tucked into my satchel, I assured Burton that we would later consider some means of providing him full access to the Turners. I did not say that at the moment I was thinking of a time after he retired from all consular posts and all capers on behalf of the Foreign Office.

Chapter 25

The misfortune truly threatening Burton's study of Turner occurred within months of our visit in Trieste—Lord Houghton's Fryston caught fire. Due to my own travels, I heard of it some time following the disaster itself near the end of 1876. But the moment I heard it, I thought: the Turners are lost! To think we had saved them from Ruskin's fire, only to have them consumed in the conflagration of a congenial private library! A generation from now would anyone even know of Turner's secret work? Very, very few had ever seen any of it. The cognoscenti now knew of Ruskin's arrogance and audacity. I imagined that if word of the "obscene" work ever surfaced among future generations, it would be disputed as a mere rumor. There would be those who wished to protect Ruskin's reputation, and those who wished to protect Turner's. Each camp would happily feed the censorious motives of the other.

The following year when I was able to make a brief trip to London to conduct some business with the *Times*, I arranged to meet Houghton for an hour at his club. The man was disconsolate, of course. "The entire house was not consumed," he told me, "mostly the front."

"The front library?"

"Yes."

"Utterly destroyed, sir?"

"Not utterly. But a great deal of water damage to the books. And much destruction and loss otherwise. From flame and from the rough treatment from our exertions to suppress a holocaust. There was, I hate to admit, some looting as well."

"Good Lord."

"On the other hand, many people in the neighborhood turned out to save what they could."

"There's no full accounting yet? No inventory of salvaged materials?"

"Not yet. Only partial, sorry to say." His face was like that of a man ravaged by the loss of a daughter or son. "To tell you the truth, I'm not sure I want to know. Understanding the full extent of the loss will, I fear, be but another terrible shock to my ancient frame."

He did appear now to have suddenly aged.

"I'll write you soon as we uncover the survival or demise of the Turners," he continued. "I'm terribly sorry, Stillman. Sorry for us all. Please give me your card."

"I'll send you my change of address," I said. "My wife Marie and our children should be joining me in Florence soon, and we shall no doubt settle in new quarters. Be sure to send word to Burton too, please."

* * *

In late April of 'seventy-eight, I moved Marie and the children to Florence. It was the city closest to her heart, especially for its associations with the artists and poets of the early Renaissance, and far more convenient than London to my own activities as war correspondent and photographer of antiquities.

At some point during our first year in Florence together I received the best possible news. A letter from Lord Houghton assured me that the Turner sketches were among the materials salvaged from the

Fryston fire, "having endured," as he put it, "a small degree of damage, however, in the miraculous process of their salvation."

Several months later when I returned to Florence from the front lines of the Eastern conflict, I found a wire from Burton: *Received Houghton's news of miracle. All more reason Sketches safer here and to hand for book.*

I hesitated to allow the sketch studies out of England. Fryston was being restored. I didn't answer Burton's wire for some time, assuming he might expect I was away for weeks and months fulfilling the duties of my post. I asked Marie what she thought. She had never seen the material in question, but I had told her about it and my long struggle to reclaim it.

"Lord Houghton's house and library are going through a long process of restoration," she said. "Can you guarantee their security in the meantime? And don't forget, Houghton's not a young man anymore."

"I can't guarantee anything from here. But short of their being in our hands—."

"There you are, then," she said. "And you've been talking for months now about reclaiming them yourself."

"Yes."

"Do you think you'd be a better person than Captain Burton to bring the Turners secretly to Italy?"

"It's just the idea of getting and keeping them in my own hands."

"But Burton could not write the book if you did."

"True."

We had been standing in her studio, a perfect workspace overlooking the Arno between the Santa Trinita Bridge and the Ponte Vecchio, on the Lungarno degli Acciaiuoli. She was now thirty-five, pregnant with our second child, Michael Spartali Stillman, or Mico, and never more productive— growing daily in her painterly accomplishment—and never more beautiful to me. Out of her own happiness in Florence she had created a home for herself and our children.

She turned fully toward me. "Do you want him to write it or not?"

"I do."

"Well then?"

I didn't speak at first but made up my mind at that moment. Then I said, "It's more important to have remnants of the old master's leavings properly studied and reproduced than to worry over them while they molder at Fryston."

"Or suffer a worse Fate eventually at the hands of Houghton's executors and heirs."

"None of whom, of course, I can vouch for."

"It's your decision, William, but you should at least see things clearly before you decide." She thought a moment. "Are you sure the safest way wouldn't be to have them yourself, kept under lock and key?"

"Then Burton's book would never get written. At best, they'd likely become nothing but yet more artifacts lost to the obscurity of private and secretive collectors."

"That may be," she said, "but now you must choose one risk or the other."

I wrote to Burton to arrange a time for me to return to Fryston, collect the Turner materials, and meet him at Portsmouth for a transfer so he could smuggle them into Europe and across borders all the way to Trieste. Between my labors and his, it took many months before we could set a date to meet. But finally I found myself at Fryston, well under restoration by then. Houghton handed me the Turners in a clean portfolio, which I placed in a large handbag. A day later I arrived in Portsmouth, rented a room overlooking the port, and began my vigil. I expected Burton within seventy-two hours.

That very first night in Portsmouth, however, I sensed something was wrong. I couldn't put my finger on it, but the old instinct was stirring again, intimating trouble. Had I glimpsed something askew? Thinking back on it, I believe I must have been followed from Fryston. I can't imagine by what mechanism of watchfulness. But the following morning, Burton not having appeared, I went for a walk in the sea air. Perhaps by getting out rather than holing up in a room, I was convincing myself of my courage. I carried the valise along with me—in fact, I never let it out of my sight. The day proved uneventful, and I began to disbelieve my forebodings.

That evening, just before going down to supper, a heavy knock at my door convinced me Burton had arrived. I opened the door and was confronted by a large man who looked familiar in some way I couldn't explain. His overcoat, derby, and walking stick suggested a rather shabby gentility, an impression reinforced by traces of Cockney in his speech, as if he were a man born to it who had tried to suppress it from his voice. "May I 'ave a word, sir?" he asked.

"I'm just on my way to dine," I said. "Can you tell me what this is about?"

Close to him now, I could tell he had shaved recently, yet his heavy beard still cast a shadow on his face. He was thick-set, solid as a stone monument, and just a shade shorter than I, who am a wiry 6'3".

"William Rossetti sent me, sir."

"Rossetti? How does he know I'm here?"

"May I come in, please? So's we might speak?"

In that split second, confronted by him, I made the kind of flawed decision anyone can make at times. I stepped aside.

Once I had closed the door, he turned and said: "It wasn't a secret you're here, were it?"

"Not a secret. But I'm here briefly on business and hadn't told any of my old friends—and certainly not Rossetti—because I'd be unable to see them. Now, sir, would you do me the courtesy of stating your business, please."

He had removed his hat, and for the first time memory began to open. I *had* seen this man before. Where? On the railway platform with Burton? Winslow's man?

"It's not that Mr. Rossetti knew you'd returned, but my employer works at 'is pleasure. 'E asked me to contact you about some art work belongs to 'im, Mr. Rossetti."

I knew William himself didn't truly suspect me, for after so many years of our friendship, he would have asked me outright. But I also knew that this man Winslow, hired by the Rossettis to pursue the Turner sketches down the years till something turned up, did indeed suspect me, even if he couldn't fully explain why.

"I don't know what you're talking about," I said.

He slid a look at the valise I had placed on the bed table.

"Look here," I said, "have you been following me?"

"I won't keep you in doubt." He pointed to the table. "I've come for those paintings and such."

"I don't have any paintings…or any such."

He walked over to the valise and gripped it in his hand. When I moved to restrain him he unsheathed a blade from his walking stick more quickly than I could cross the room to him. "Sorry, sir; I'll just take these, if you don't mind."

"But I do mind! Those are my personal papers. You've no right—"

"Careful now, sir," he said and flipped the exposed blade toward my face. He calmly walked around me, valise in hand, and opened the door. "I wouldn't follow along, I was you."

"I'll call the police!" I said.

"Don't think you will. Better not to anyways." He gave me a cruel smile and slipped the cover back over the cane blade as he closed the door behind him.

I probably hesitated just long enough for him to descend the stairs to the front door of the inn before I grabbed my coat and fled after him.

Just out the door I spotted him turning into a small side street. I followed cautiously at first, trying to make up my mind what to do. As he turned into an alleyway behind the houses and storefronts of the main street, I saw another figure hurrying as if to meet him—a tall man in strange headdress.

In my own confusion and outrage, nothing of these events made much sense to me, but I followed along as if somehow I might recover the stolen property. It was, of course, an absurd plan. The man was armed, perhaps with more than the deadly cane. He was obviously of a pugnacious and fearless nature. As thoughts do in such tormented moments, it flashed across my mind that he had been a pugilist—that Minotaur's neck and shoulders, that off-kilter nose. And now there were two of them!

I heard a voice from the alleyway cry, "Halt!" I began to run. Turning the corner into the alley, I saw the man in the headdress—a sort of desert or Arabic affair wrapped to obscure his dark features—confronting the thief, who had turned to face the Arab. With a quick movement, the thief again unsheathed the cane blade, and the two men began to circle one another slowly like wary fighting dogs.

When they stopped, the Arab was facing me now and the thief's massive back was to me. Then abruptly something happened. In a single flowing movement, the Arab pushed aside his coat and a gleaming streak struck the thief against his ear, causing him to stagger. I saw now it was a broadsword whose flat side had struck him, and just as I was seeing that, the Arab's right foot shot out to catch the thief's feet and propel him forward. With another lightning smack from the flat side of the broadsword across his back, the thief fell forward onto his face, spilling the bladed cane as he fell. In a half-second, the Arab stood with one foot on the thief's shoulders, the tip of the broadsword held firmly against the back of his neck with just enough pressure to draw a small trickle of blood.

"Release the valise," the Arab said, and I recognized Burton's booming voice, despite the Arabic accent he was feigning.

The thief, without protest, did as told. By now the thin trail of blood had leaked down around his neck to stain the sides and front of his shirt collar.

"How much Mr. Winslow pay you for this Portsmouth operation?" Burton demanded.

The thief remained silent.

"The slightest movement severs your brainstem from your backbone," Burton said. "Self-defense, of course."

"Five pounds," the thief said.

With his free hand, Burton reached into his overcoat pocket and pulled out a small bag closed tight by a drawstring. He motioned me toward it, told me to remove five pounds, and tucked the bag back into his pocket. He flung the coins on the ground by the thief's head.

"Your name," Burton said.

Silence. The sword, by the most delicate application of pressure, released a thicker stream of blood that began to drip onto the pavement.

"Monk Ballaster," the man said.

"The prizefighter?" Burton asked, a touch of delight in his voice.

"Your service."

"Well, my friend, Mr. Ballaster," Burton said, retaining his accent. "You return to Winslow. And you tell him that after long, long searches and pursuits, and after confronting Mr. Stillman, you've found no evidence of the artifacts you've been pursuing. Clear?"

"Yes."

"Because if you cross me in this, you cross the Brotherhood of Gabriel. Do you know what that is?"

"No, sir."

"A Muslim alliance that will find you no matter where you are and put you to death in such a slow painful manner that you shall indeed be sorry for—you will curse most terribly—the very day your mother was born."

Silence.

"You understand me."

"Yes."

"Five pounds for your trouble on the ground by your head. Everything between us perfectly clear, yes?"

"Perfectly."

"And be absolutely certain you report to Winslow what I told you. Much preferable to reporting defeat."

Silence.

"Understand?"

"Yes." By now the bloodletting had been considerable, but the thief no doubt believed himself fortunate to have his brain and his spine still connected.

Burton motioned to me to collect the valise and return to my room. I did so with alacrity and saw nothing more of what transpired in the alley.

Ten minutes later, Burton was at my door, his headdress gone, smiling, holding out to me a long, thick cigar.

"I arrived a day before you did," he explained, after I asked him how he had managed this feat. "I believed if there were to be an effort from this ever-persistent Winslow fellow you'd told me about, this would be it. I had no idea whether an effort from that quarter would materialize, but it wasn't a time to chance it."

"And by following me yourself, you'd keep me and the Turners safe from whoever was, or might be, on to me?"

"That was my plan. You see how well it worked, my friend!" He laughed, showing his canine tooth again. He was no longer young, but the encounter seemed to have put blood and joy into his ruddy face. His physical strength and quickness of reflex had been tested, and this confirmation of his powers gave him pleasure.

"The Brotherhood of Gabriel?" I asked. "As in Rossetti?"

"Appropriate, don't you think?" He laughed again. "But Gabriel is, of course, also the angel God chose to make his final revelation to Muhammad, the revelations of the *Koran*. 'In the name of God the Compassionate the Merciful.'"

"Very clever, Richard."

"Make it up as I go."

"He never even saw what was in the valise," I said. "That Monk hooligan."

"No? He must have assumed then. Steal now, assess later. They've been keeping an eye on you, no doubt, longer than you think."

"You believe that's over now?"

"I'd say so, yes. And the materials will be out of your hands. They won't track me, or not for long if they try." He opened the valise placed on my bed, removed the neatly bound packet of sketch studies, untied and inspected them briefly, and wrapped them tight into two compact bundles within another cloth each. He then tucked the neat bundles into two pocket-like pouches sewn deep inside his overcoat.

We went downstairs and Burton inquired about the hours of the ticket office for tomorrow's boat to France. Satisfied, he began to usher me out the door, saying, "You stay a day longer. Watch my back tomorrow as I board. It's better to travel separately."

"Understood."

"Very good. Well now, Stillman. My appetite's up! I'll let you shell out for supper."

Chapter 26

Burton departed the following day. I began my journey to Florence the day after that, happy to be aboard the ferry, free of the sketches and somehow quite certain the Rossettis, by Burton's stratagems, would forever be convinced the Turners were lost to them by hands other than my own.

Back in Florence, I entertained Marie with the whole story. That summer, however, she was ready to return to London, as she occasionally did, to see her parents and her London colleagues, to show her work and sit yet again for others. I think nothing improved the bloom of her womanhood and her artistry more than her being in these years able to avoid the English winters, which had frequently caused her to be ill. Marie's Florentine disposition was a tonic to me whenever I returned from my travels. The city, as we expected, proved to be the most salutary for her development, for she found there an intellectual life and serenity she found nowhere else. These were the years of her great quickening as an artist: she was never more engaged, never more productive.

But the Italian summers' pestiferous heat would send us northwards into the higher elevations. We became convinced that the city's water supply was contaminated by waste water flowing into the Arno and back into the city's wells. That summer she decided to return to her parents with our three youngest—Bella, Effie, and Mico.

I didn't begrudge her those homecomings; I was after all often away myself for my correspondent's work. But I had grown a little uncomfortable with her frequent talk of Gabriel Rossetti, her willingness to sit for him at his pleasure, and the stream of letters between them that seemed to flow in and out of Florence. It may have been her keeping these letters private, never allowing me to read them, seldom enough telling me some news that had arrived by them, that began to discomfort me. And then I knew Gabriel too well to convince myself that he would refrain from making love to my wife, a woman he had openly praised for her beauty and teasingly "courted," merely to save me the pangs of cuckoldry.

"Please try not to become too entangled with Gabriel and his coterie," I said before she left. "I don't think his influence is beneficial to you any more, Marie."

"I don't plan any entanglements," she said, "but I can hardly ignore the Rossettis."

"I agree. But he's, if anything, grown more unsavory, even less stable, over the years."

"You don't trust him with me?"

"Frankly? No."

"And me? Do you trust me?"

"Of course, but I know how he can be. I wouldn't trust any woman he finds attractive with him, to his 'life of passionate intimacies.' Not for the woman's fault, but for his, I mean to say."

"Give me more credit than that, if you please, William. My vessel is not so weak."

I thought it better not to bring up the letters. I placed my trust in her strength and our love.

But following yet another family tragedy, I felt my suspicions flare once again. You see, as I knew it must, Gabriel's body finally gave out. His death shortly after Marie's return to Florence set off a bout of melancholy, unusual for her. She placed all his letters to her into a heavily bound package and locked them in a drawer. I don't know what she was planning, but then just two weeks later our third child together, another son named James (or Giacomino) who had been born in August of '81, succumbed to bronchitis and fevers nine months later.

I had been away in Athens on assignment through most of Marie's pregnancy with James. But we were together in Florence again by the time of his final illness until his burial in the Anglican cemetery that terrible spring. Almost as soon as we had buried little James, Marie burned all Gabriel's letters to her. I dared not reproach or question, for she was at the time in no condition to be plagued by my jealousy, and neither, to be frank, was I in any condition to voice my suspicions. I had known Rossetti too well, perhaps; his erotic obsessions and power—not unlike Turner's?—that had pulled women into his glowing orbit and spurred his productivity as an artist. Marie herself had succumbed to his gravitational pull, as had so many others, had perhaps burned with the same fire—a woman too often abandoned by her own aging husband. I spoke none of these thoughts to her. Yet the stain of suspicion, for my part, marked our marriage thereafter. The disturbing fissure that had cracked open between us after Russie's death and had grown during my travels abroad, now seemed to darken and gape wider still.

My own state of mind grew bleaker, even as the battles in the Balkans finally began to wane. Without the danger and adventure of war reporting, I again sank at times toward a darkness that ever threatened to consume me. I now realize I was haunted by my own habitual use of chloral and my efforts to escape it, by my doubting Marie, and by those memories of my dead wife and sons, Russie and James. All the disappointments of my life rose before me.

* * *

Burton and I remained out of contact for some time following his flight to Trieste with the Turners. It was not until 'eighty-three, when I had returned from the Balkans, that I found a gift copy of Burton's *Kama Sutra* and short note explaining that they had taken the Palazzo Gossleth above the port as their new home in Trieste. "You may recall from our walks," he wrote, "that this residence has the appearance of a museum—a perfect repository of artwork!" In his characteristic humor he added: "We come to like it in Trieste, and yearn for our returns from other, sun-scorched travels. Besides, between Mrs. Grundy, Widow Brown, and Mr. Gladstone, England is no place for an Englishman."

I opened the beautiful privately printed copy of the book. Marie had read here and there in it, finding sometimes humorous its depictions of sexual athleticism. But she had great respect for the labor that went into it as an excellent translation and visually appealing book. As I leafed through the text, I recalled what Burton once told me about his travels on research or on the business of his government. "Being amongst Moslems has often been a kind of repose to me; I find the atmosphere of Christendom dominates and distresses me. I feel, for example, more comfortable with Sufism," he had said, "than in anything I've been taught from boyhood."

He had always refused, however, to romanticize the Moslem or the Hindu. If he had made friends, lovers, confidantes, teachers, and comrades-in-arms in Africa and the East, he was all too aware of Eastern peoples' warring sects and tribal enmities, and the horrors of their slave trade.

"From Darfur and the Sudan," he once told me, "men, women, and babes in arms are driven by the thousands through endless marches to be imported into Arabia, Egypt, and Turkey." He could still remember the price of "a harem-bound beauty" or "a eunuch." The boys, he explained, had to receive their operation by the age of ten to ensure a chance of survival.

"The parts are swept off by a single cut of the razor," he said, "a tube inserted into the urethra, the wound cauterized with boiling oil, and the patient put in a fresh dung hill to be fed on milk." The surviving eunuchs, he recalled, would then fetch five to ten times their original value on the slave market.

"And though pederasty is forbidden by the *Koran*," he went on, "the Kurds and the Iranians have deeply rooted traditions of pederasty, and even in the monasteries of Morocco and Damascus I've seen them keep their catamites. Trying to write about this now. You've heard of *The Scented Garden?*" Yet if he could not behold the East falsely as all sweetness and light, his deeper knowledge never tarnished his love for Eastern culture, art, and literature.

I turned his gift book to the Preface where I found his translation of a description of "the perfect woman": "Her face is pleasing as the full moon: her body, well clothed, her flesh soft.... Her bosom is hard, full and high. Her eyes are bright and beautiful as the orbs of a fawn...her nose is straight and lovely...her *yoni* resembles the opening of a lotus bud and her love-seed is perfumed like the lily which is newly burst...her voice is low and musical as the note of the Kokila bird. And she is respectful and religious as she is clever and courteous."

* * *

The following year I wrote to suggest a visit to the Burtons' Palazzo. The Balkans had entered a period of relative stability, and my correspondent's work declined precipitously. But Burton's return note begged off. He had taken ill with heart failure in his sixty-third year.

Despite his illness all that spring, he wrote, he was nonetheless able to see his preparations for publishing his translations of the *One-Thousand Nights and a Night* through to near completion. "Mutilated in Europe to a collection of fairy tales, my *Nights*, on the other hand, shall be a unique study of anthropology: an accurate picture of Oriental life told through its shiftings from boldest poetry to baldest prose, a marvelous repertory of Eastern wisdom and earthly praxis from the making of eunuchs to marriage ceremonies, sodomy, and other cultural and sexual exotica. Mrs. Grundy will howl on her big bum till she almost bursts, but will, like many an Englishwoman, read every word with intense enjoyment!" I could see him laughing as he wrote those lines.

His *Kama Sutra* and his *Nights* inaugurated the production of his texts so often banned or censored in the West, particularly in Britain. He wrote that he didn't know how much time he had left, how long his heart would hold out. He blustered awhile about overcoming much worse physical ailments and sufferings in the past, but I felt somehow that he had for the first time truly sniffed the depths of his own mortality. He would no longer be able to fall back on that great physical strength and willpower which had carried him through so many dangerous adventures in far-flung places.

I wished him well, but I began to doubt he would ever complete his book on Turner. Nonetheless, I had my own necessity to consider. We left Florence for England, and then from the spring of 'eighty-four till late summer the following year, I spent in the United States, accompanied by my eldest daughter Lisa, where I looked for work.

But I had little luck and couldn't stay in America, so Lisa and I returned to Marie and the children. When, several months later, *The Times'* Rome correspondent died, I was asked to fill his place at a salary of £600. I was to cover both Rome and Athens in the first permanent

salaried position of my life, at age fifty-eight. This good fortune, however, was to have another side—some further years of intermittent separation from Marie. For she had become indispensable to her aging parents, who had suffered irrevocably from the death of Marie's sister
Christina, and from a period of deep financial reversals for her father:
the latter a combination of unwise speculation on the Alexandrian market, his brother's dishonesty in handling funds to cover debts, and the
Greek government's calling in credit extended to him for several
projects.

Moreover, Marie felt her first necessity was to provide a stable
home and proper English education for Effie and Mico. So off I went,
returning to Rome—a city never quite congenial either to Marie or
me—with the two older girls: Bella to help me in certain historical art
research and Lisa to continue her art studies under Ernest Hebert of
the French Academy in Rome.

We settled in and began work in Rome. I hoped for an opportunity
to visit the Burtons during my travels in Italy and Greece, but just as I
began to make plans, Richard had returned to England, his health momentarily improved, on the occasion of his Knighthood. He visited
Marie briefly to hear news of me and wrote me a letter saying that he
was pleased to report more of his translations were coming out. "With
the death of Houghton last August," he added, "it was propitious for
us to have met in Portsmouth to have our adventuresome evening."

Chapter 27

With his letter, Burton enclosed a little surprise for me: a portion of an early draft of the introduction to a book he had finally begun, entitled *The Turner Erotica*, which introductory material I present below.

1

This treatise on a small but valuable collection of curious visual studies in Eros and anatomy by the British landscape painter J. M. W. Turner assesses work that came by a strange route into my hands. I wish to consider throughout this volume the works themselves, including their provenance, by outlining the results of my researches and cogitations, as well as by speculating on the purpose of these studies through a careful analysis of them in relation to the painter's lifelong work.

I have devoted one portion of my life to collecting, translating, and making available to the West the religious and erotic literatures of the East. That, indeed, is the task I find myself devoting ever more time to during my reclusions here in Trieste, even as my time on earth grows shorter. I have long contended that just as greater honesty toward human sexual practices would produce salubrious effects among English men and women, so also is it necessary for our Foreign Office to shed the ignorance in which they presume to establish empire and govern in the Middle East, Asia, and Africa. My Englished version of *The Book of a Thousand Nights and a Night* alone appears to have begun the work of opening English minds to a simple fact: we constitute the greatest Mohammedan empire in the world, yet the study of Arabism and Moslem life is still completely neglected in examinations for the Civil Service and in the education of our empire's leaders.

Is it any wonder then that wherever we are called upon to handle governmental problems in Moslem lands, we fail in such wise as to scandalize our very few friends and earn the contempt of both Europe and the Eastern world? And nowhere has our misinformed state seemed more signal than in our finding offensive and obscene what other peoples embrace as natural or divine.

Our women complain they have no knowledge of their own physiology; at what heavy price must this fruit of the knowledge-tree be bought by the young first entering life. Shall we never understand that ignorance is not innocence? Respectability unmakes what nature made. Moslems and Easterns, on the other hand, study the art and mystery of satisfying the physical woman. Mock virtue, the most immodest modesty of England and the United States, pronounces the subject foul and fulsome. Throughout the East, however, such inquiries are aided by a long series of volumes, many written by learned physiologists, by persons of social standing and by religious dignitaries in high office.

Whenever in later years I cared to study the Turners, I applied to Lord Houghton. After his death I made my appeal to the appropriate persons and obtained these materials on loan. However, it was here in Trieste, in my seclusion, as I fitfully approached my seventieth year, that I proposed to complete this study and to reproduce the illustrations in question for the edification of all who would understand the more secret, fertile corners of the Master's genius.

2

What, then, is the work Turner was about with these studies? There is no doubt in my mind that it is at times serious preparatory work, at other times private pleasure. It is nothing like the satiric, playful delineations of, say, a Rowlandson, whose purpose is the amusement of the pornographic and humorous impulses among selected viewers, and which caricatures I doubt not Turner knew. No, I judge most of these illustrations to be not an end in themselves. They appear to me, rather, to be "studies" of some sort: studies of an heroic artist with an inexhaustible appetite for observation. My first thought, perhaps because of my own work of translation—having published my *Kama Sutra* in '83 and my *Ananga Ranga* and my *Nights* in '85—was that Turner himself had somehow happened upon knowledge of such texts and had ambitions to turn out his own manual of love and transcendence, a manual for which these studies were but the partially preserved tailings. Since we know that he consulted Hindu and Eastern sources and made notes regarding the worship of Priapus, might not that be the grand project to which this most prolific of painters had turned? For even as I was preparing for publication from the French *Perfumed Garden of the Cheikh Nefzaoui, A Manual of Arabic Erotology*, I had at times the Turners before me. But I did not entertain my initial theory for long.

Why not? The author of the *Ananga Ranga*, for example, begins: "And thus all who read this book shall know how delicious an instrument is woman, when artfully played upon; how capable she is of producing the most exquisite harmony; of executing the most complicated variations and of giving the divinist pleasures....How the husband, by varying the enjoyment of his wife, may live with her as with thirty-two different women...rendering satiety impossible." There seemed to be no effort on Turner's part, the more

I looked at them, to use such studies in preparation for a published pleasure manual. But I began to wonder if his purpose might be more personal—a sort of record through his art of his experience of the nature of sexual congress, not incidentally with intimations of Kalyana Malla's devotional purpose in his *Ananga Ranga*. For after the fashion of the Vedanta, every stanza from these Eastern works has dual reference to both the amatory and the mystical. Where, moreover, male and female forms in their complementarity adumbrate the mystery of the Over-Soul in the same way that physical and psychic forces through copulation are joined in divine worship.

Turner of course would never have put it that way, or anyway close, but I begin to believe I have struck a path toward understanding his project. His bold sweeps with brush and palette knife are not merely the techniques of a man reveling in the pigments newly available in the second and third decades of our century, nor are they the gestures of a radical theorist and chromomaniac. That is, in some sense his whole project is to be discerned as both erotic and eschatological. Just as in so many Turner paintings light—as if divine—momentarily confutes our presumed solidity of the material world, and just as his public paintings so often display objects washed clean by light, shimmering (so to speak) in the iridescence of their ceremonious identity, Turner in these secret studies, I theorized, sought some rapprochement of the old Western, Christian sundering of the soul from the body. As in the *Upanishads*, there is no Christian concept of original sin, no connection between Eros and shame, but rather the promise of transcendent sexual energies by way of the body; and as the female sexual athletes of the Indian temples are both *apsarases* and *devadases*, or metaphysical and physical beings in one; and as sexual activity is conjoined with aesthetic arousal and response —so do these depictions of Turner's (some masterly, some rough or coarsely or glibly executed) intimate a similar attitude toward what the West forbids, shrouds in darkness, or denies. Or fears.

How many respectable English husbands would fall into confusion were their undefiled wives to unleash the darker powers of their sex upon these very husbands who made of them idols or angels? What the prostitute pretends, the husband is trained not to countenance in his untainted spouse. Her soul and her body must never be one. Might Turner have been engaged in some grand project of unification?

If so, it was a synthesis in his work as well as in himself. He is a man who strove to employ the full range of himself in his work, the mature and the immature: a device of genius for seeing things through new eyes, for pursuing his belief that "every look at nature is a refinement of art." For his depictions of genitalia and coupling are done with wonderful accuracy at times, as if for a medical treatise; at others they are suffused with darkness and light and obscure atmospheric forces swirling around the lovers who exercise their passions in a variety of postures; at others still they are close-up depictions of human sexual anatomy and physiology, often, to be sure, of the human female. It is no doubt the anatomy and physiology of the human female that the English stand most in anxious ignorance. Was Turner planning some great and secretive work—never to be shown in his lifetime—a future corrective to that ignorance? Or was he preparing to use, and in fact already using, the structures and functions of human physiology in his visions of macrocosmic energies? Or was he embarked on a project, or projects, that united both goals?

One sees throughout his work allegories of the human form—especially the genital—in the natural world: these towering, perpendicular masses of cloud, building, ship, and lighthouse; these conjunctions of fire, heat, and blood; these feminine clumps, mounds, clefts, and whorls. And when we espy these forms in counterpoint within a single work, we feel their supernal energies released, the very energies of creation that issue in the act of procreation. Opposites interact, contend, unite. Counterpoint and synthesis.

As I was also working on my translations into English works of Italian and Latin eroticism—Basile's *Il Pentamerone*, the Latin *Priapeia*, and previously suppressed texts or portions of texts by Ariosto, Catullus, and Juvenal, I found when comparing the Turners that they seemed more in harmony with Eastern than Western composers. In the spirit of the West, the Turners are bold, brash, unprintable, unshowable, earthy, bawdy, or whatever; but they also speak of something else, something more, of something larger intended. Had he ever created greater, whole works on this theme? Works of completion? Works that are the more direct and recognizable fruition of these studies? Had such greater works been hidden away somewhere? Or—perhaps more likely—destroyed?

Here is a mystery. You shall see from the text that follows, however, I lean toward the conclusion that the master was not likely to have been preparing, say, some large canvasses across which he would splash images of human genitalia and congress at their most physiologically realistic. Might he have tried out a canvass or two? Well, of course: he might have tried anything. But such was not, I believe, his true purpose. His purposes with these studies are closer to what I have suggested above—call it a lifelong study of the geometries of anatomical mechanics and sexual physiology, as painterly observation and information in the first place, and as personal pleasure in the second. Like all his geometrical, mechanical, and architectural studies of the works of man and God, these too are but preparations for the understanding and depictions of the greatest, most universal Creative Energy. The energy he felt within him and within all nature.

The more immediate question I put myself is whether my health and my other work would keep me from demonstrating my solution to this mystery of the Turner Erotica. I have asked myself whether it might be more productive to put someone else on the case.

Why not Leonard Smithers, for example, my co-translator and co-conspirator in Anglicizing erotica of the ancient and modern world? He has the education, the energy, the interest, and the solicitor's knowledge of the booby-trapped mazes of the law and legalism. I've come to trust him completely. I am, under his advice, asking that in the case of my death, Smithers shall complete and publish what I have thus far accomplished.

It was here that his draft pages ended, an adequate sample to appreciate the nature of the project on which he had embarked. A final paragraph in his letter explained that his *Nights* had by massive subscriptions earned him more than any other book and more attention than any other publication or exploit (here he exaggerated, surely), but "now that I know the tastes of England, Lady Burton and I need never again be without money."

I was delighted to see this Turner book at long last underway. Would he have the time and health to finish it? I threw my trust into his great powers once again, like a boy trying to ignore fears invoked by the reality of disease, age, and death.

The draft of Burton's introduction recalled to mind a clue Ruskin himself had once offered. We had been standing before a painting considered one of Turner's most esteemed and derivative: *Crossing the Brook*, an oil executed in 1815. Ruskin told me he had been studying this work for some months and had begun an essay in which he would take the painting apart, so to speak, piece by piece to unsettle, rather than to confirm, the complacent prejudices of the public and the critics' views of it. He had, in fact, found considerable feminine sexual imagery in the painting. But because the artist had handled his themes emblematically or allegorically (that is without the blatant erotic intensity of the troublesome sketches), Ruskin was much more prone to praise than to blame—as if this public painting confirmed his view of his artist-hero, just as the disturbed and mysterious obscenity had undermined his view of Turner.

Everyone, Ruskin had explained, saw *Crossing the Brook* as Turner at his most Claudian. Even the generalized title seemed innocuously to derive from similar works of de Loutherbourg, Thomson, and Reynolds—idealized images of girls crossing a body of water. "But," Ruskin hurried to explain, "here we have surely something more. To begin, the girls are Turner's own illegitimate daughters, Evelina and Georgiana."

"I would never have known that," I said.

"But beautiful and delicate young women for all that, to judge by this. And, more to the point, on the verge of womanhood. He'd made a tour of the West Country in 'thirteen, and this certainly looks to me to be the River Tamar and Calstock bridge."

"A perfect idyll."

I recalled Turner's oil *Saltash with Water Ferry* from his earlier tour of the area in 1811, a painting set also on the Tamar that Ruskin had described as "what the mind sees when it looks for poetry in humble actual life."

"There are any number of classical qualities and references to the idyll," he continued, "but it is not merely echoes of Claude—or of Theocritus and Virgil, for that matter. For if the dark grotto behind the girls is the ancient symbol of the sacred springs of life, it is here a womb-like opening with a well-worn path leading our eye to the girls, especially Georgina (the younger of the two) seated on the bank with a white bag, while Evelina, the elder, crosses over the water holding her wet red bag."

"A rather obvious reference to puberty—crossing to womanhood? Baptismal."

"You take my meaning."

"Is this perhaps the only grotto painted into a finished work?" I asked.

"They're rare, in oils. Have you seen *Weathercote Cave*?"

"No."

"A watercolor, a rather gushing grotto!"

Later, when I first saw *Weathercote Cave*, the rather vaginal form of the grotto struck me.

But now I began to see the painting before us anew—every element of it as an emblem contributing to the theme: the well-worn grotto, the body of water to be crossed, the bridge itself, the mature and fertile trees towering above Evelina and the saplings near Georgina. And the red bottle with its stopper inserted leaning against the younger girl's still white bag, reflecting moreover the white cloth draped across her lap as she watches her older sister make the crossing. And then I noticed that Evelina's red bag was reflected in the water between her legs, not in its shape but in a shape at least as phallic as Turner's lighthouses, at Eddystone and elsewhere. And the sun, casting long shadows, was not setting but *rising* in the east. All this and more I now saw, and then two final emblems struck me. They were obvious but I had hardly noticed them before: the cleft rock and the dog. These two emblems were aligned: the rock, I now saw, unmistakably reflecting the female sexual cleft, and the dog, crossing the water between the girls.

"The dog," I said, "a reference, it would seem, to the animal life Evelina is now entering—as much a natural force as the trees, water, and sun."

"It seems rather clear now, doesn't it?" he said, his voiced pleased. "How could it not be a loving celebration of female awakening and fertility? Interpreted through, in this instance, the two female beings he most loved, as their father."

I did not then mention that I now saw this most approachable painting as of a piece with Turner's strong sexual curiosity. I said, instead, "It seems, then, an affirmation of yet one more element of the natural world that interested him so deeply." There was, however, nothing overtly sexual about Turner's treatment of the girls. Rather, the whole feeling of the painting struck me with a paternal tenderness.

"And in this instance," Ruskin said, "in the beauty of the natural forms—the trees, the river, the light, and the very girls themselves—we see his belief in the organic life humanity shares with nature."

Why, I wondered, hadn't this man, for all his awareness and insight, been able to see that mass of sketches he had destroyed with such righteous violence as part of the same impulse—and equally significant to our full understanding of the mysterious Turner? Was it merely because the beauty of all those womanly parts was not, as in this painting, idealized, not shown, as it were, through the filters of pastoral light and allegorical allusion? *Ut picture poesis.* Had not Turner himself, said to Ruskin's pleasure no doubt, that "Idea is the noblest part of art," that it is the "connecting metaphors" that reveal not slavish replication of nature but those powers that animate the particulars of the natural world, the invisible within the visible, which the imagination only is fitted to perceive?

His sketch studies, I mean to say—whether erotic or "innocent" of Eros—are his depictions of what he discovered with the exactness of architectural geometry to address the *eye*, while his finished paintings are his depictions of what through mere eye addresses the *imagination*. The sketches were then the tracings of the eye through memory; the paintings, the synthesis of the particular and the universal. If one was the basis of the old master's art, the other was the end of art: the essential reality behind the optical appearances carefully studied through thousands of sketches. Wind, clouds, sea, ships, animals, people—these were to him all of an energetic whole; all interactive, dynamic, flowing, and unified; all expressions of that divine energy that drives our world and cosmos; all one, if we would but see it. In the geometry of a flagrantly available vulva or an erect phallus is the physical basis of the cleft rock and aqueous reflection, the allegories of puberty and sexual awakening. But as it was those merely "optical" studies—those erotic sketches that served as the foundation for allegorical ends—it was into *that* world of the physical mechanics and architecture of sex that Ruskin could not follow his master. Yes, it was here that he had averted his eyes and conscience; it was here his genius failed him, or forsook him, in favor of the compunctions of his precious and dogmatic upbringing, the scruples of the very nineteenth-century British culture he so eloquently and brilliantly reviled.

Was that after all what had happened? He had simply turned his childish incapacities, his outrage and his shame, to violence? Ruskin was a product of his time and place as his master Turner could never be. And bound to his era—for all his prescient prophecy—he failed both himself and his beloved Turner. An image flitted to mind: Ruskin as the moon, aloof from human lovers whose fleshy passion his cool light ensilvered from on high. I had witnessed, perhaps, a personal as well as historical tragedy.

* * *

Another letter from William Rossetti reached me in Rome that year. "Of course you know Wilfrid Blunt," he wrote, "England's Great Fornicator, who seduced Janey Morris at his Sussex estate in '84, and God knows how many times thereafter. Well, he's set his sights, I fear, on Marie, and for reasons of her own Mrs. Morris appears to collude with him. I don't for a moment doubt our dear Marie's constancy, but as your old friend, I believed duty bound me to mention his tireless offensive. As you can see from the enclosed, Marie is the center of attention everywhere she appears now: dinners, the opera, gallery openings, garden parties, etc., etc. Blunt has proclaimed Marie to his friends to be 'the most beautiful woman who ever lived or ever will live in the world, though she can't be less than forty-five.' He sends her gift poems and books, and otherwise has laid his formidable siege against her ramparts, like the Chevalier of Eros he so famously is."

This epistle ran on to other matters, including his sharp interest in my and Bella's researches in Agrigento, Sicily, of the fifth century Greek temples—"Pindar's most beautiful city of mortals." After reading it, I opened the carefully folded article from the May 11 issue of *London Illustrated News*. The author wrote of Mrs. Stillman's "beautiful picture-like head...so familiar in Mr. Burne-Jones's pictures" at an Academy opening. In life, too, the author continued, "she looks like a figure from the artist's canvas, as she stands clad in a black and gold matelassé cloak reaching to her feet in straight folds, her hair gathered in a great mass at the back of her head held up by a comb, and a wreath of green leaves on her brow."

For some time, on brief visits to London and by the post, I had been asking Marie to join me and the two girls in Rome. I now wrote a more forceful request, adding: "William R. has given to understand that the Grand Sybarite Blunt has been sniveling and snuffling about your skirts. I know he has for some years been a friend of yours, or ours, but William would be pleased to honor a request from me to warn him off. In any case, my Dear Marie, surely it must be time at long last to join us in *Civitas Dei.*"

Her response was soon at my door:

My Dearest William,

I hope to join you, Lisa, and Bella this year, having made progress settling my parents at #42 Earls' Court, and have placed a large placard on the house "To Be Let Furnished or Unfurnished." I'm sorry to hear of your bouts with gout and despondency.

I have nearly finished arrangements to have Mico continue his schooling by staying on in Hampstead with Miss Cave. My plan is to come to you in October, if possible.

As for our friend Mr. Wilfrid Scawen Blunt, please do not trouble yourself. It's true he paid me rather assiduous court, as if I were a widow, but as I came to see he was going too far in his devotions-turned-to-entreaties, I told him quite plainly that he "must not talk to me of such things and not look at me as you do." Since no more of his love letters and poems to me have issued from his pen, I have every reason to believe he understood me completely. Moreover, word has spread that I am to leave England this autumn. Hearing of my intent to remove, he called on me once and was quite pleasant and witty. We parted with promises to remain friends; he offered to look in on us when next in Rome. I know you have found him amusing before, so please try to forgive him his harmless "enthrallment," as he calls it....

Chapter 28

Marie's letter gave me comfort. But not two months after her arrival in Rome, Blunt and his wife Lady Anne appeared on their way to Naples for a steamer to Egypt and their Arabian horse stud at Sheykh Obeyd. Perhaps because a man's pride is furbished when another man desires his wife, or perhaps because I had always found Blunt a man of culture and wit, I tolerated him. During their visit I was temporarily back in Rome working on article and book assignments resulting from my travels, so Blunt knew, of course, I was able to keep an eye on him. His behavior toward Marie whenever we were together was respectful. I was involved in my own work, so I did not intercede when he arrived alone to escort Marie to the galleries she had offered to tour with him. But as the days wore on and their touring continued—a morning here, an afternoon there—I asked Marie one morning as we were finishing breakfast why Lady Anne seldom seemed to accompany them.

"Oh, she has, on occasion," Marie said. "But she hasn't shown the interest Wilfrid has. Prefers, apparently, to meet her round of obligations to polite society."

"Given his attitude toward you previously, do you think it wise to, well, to encourage him?"

"He behaves himself. It's the galleries and museums that gather his passion now." When I didn't rejoin immediately, she began to rise and clear away her cup and breakfast plate.

"His sustained attention and his contriving for you to move about alone together don't bode well," I said. "God knows his reputation alone would put anyone on guard."

"You prefer we stop seeing him?"

"Alone. I think yes, you alone. If you must go, make it a point to invite—to insist—Lady Anne come along."

"I'll cancel my plans this afternoon, then. I'll invite them for dinner or tea instead."

Something in her tone troubled me. "Marie, you know I've never tried to restrict your movement in any way. We've always given one another ample latitude." She stood there, her breakfast dishes in hand, looking at me. "I acknowledge that I suffer the trials of a husband whose wife has such beauty and allure. I myself am her captive. But I simply don't trust Blunt. He might try to corner you."

"Here," she said, reaching over to pick up my breakfast plate. As she moved to carry the dishes out of the room, she said, "I'll send a note around to them this morning. You've got work to do."

At tea that evening Blunt did nothing by look, glance, or innuendo to further my suspicions. Perhaps, I thought, Marie had, as she asserted, deflated his dreams of conquest.

Later that week, however, as I was taking my exercise in the direction of the Campagna, I saw an open fly carrying a man and a woman pass rapidly by. I felt quite certain it had been Marie and Blunt, perhaps headed for the Campagna. I decided the time had come to confront him.

But he was not in when I called later at their apartments. Marie was by then home, however, and I couldn't hold my tongue.

"Then it was you!" I said when she admitted the two of them had driven out together. "I thought we'd agreed you were to avoid being alone in his company."

"As I said, darling, he came by when you yourself were out enjoying the glorious early afternoon. He'd rented the fly and it seemed an innocent pleasure to be off, as he said, for an hour or two."

"An innocent pleasure."

"As indeed it was, William!" Her eyes never wavered, but instinct told me I hadn't the full story.

"Marie, I know this man all too well. I'm not placing blame for his impertinence on you. But I'm asking you to trust me, to please disclose completely what's going on."

"If I were betraying you, do you believe I'd disclose it? No, don't speak; it's my turn to speak to you." She paused to ensure I would listen. "But here is the truth, if you want the truth so badly. First, here we are in Rome, finally together again. We've been having a lovely time when you're not traveling, haven't we? Is there anything in our intimate relations to give either of us cause to doubt the other?"

"That's true my dear, but—"

"Let me finish. And along comes Blunt again, of his own volition. I'd offered him little encouragement to seek me in Rome. But we were courteous; we didn't spurn our compatriots when they approached us." She paused a moment. "Yet that old instinct you are always falling back on hasn't been entirely wrong. It has, rather simply, led you to distrust me. For the last two weeks he's observed all the proprieties and courtesies in his relations with me. But this much is true: today—perhaps because they'll be leaving soon—he did, much to my chagrin, renew his efforts to convince me to surrender to him. I had misjudged his offer of an innocent ride in the air. But I rebuffed him once again, and with great finality."

"He accepted this rebuff?"

"You don't believe me?"

"I believe you, Marie. But how did *he* take it?"

"He was sorry, he said, that we couldn't come to an understanding, given our mutual affinities and interests, and sorry for having troubled me with his love. 'But I will remove myself from my feelings, Marie,' he told me, 'so that we may remain good friends'."

"He's sorry!"

"Yes. It was a heartfelt apology, and a plea for continuing friendship. He understood finally—I believe this now—that I'll not relent."

"That you do not want to? Have no desire to?"

"That I value his friendship. Nothing more."

"You're sure he accepts this now."

"I am. And they're leaving, in any event. When he apologized he said he couldn't help himself because for him always love had been what the dram is to the drinker."

"We're well rid of them."

"I enjoyed their company. But I'm tired of this disunity."

"Then there is no more disunity."

"It's neither my fault nor yours that he pursued me so tirelessly. But that's over now. Can we get on with our lives and work here? You suffer too much from the insecurity of a man your age."

"You can't blame me entirely."

"We'd do better to heal over the openings left from the months and months we've been apart these several years. That should be enough to command our full attention."

We stood there looking at one another, neither of us wavering, both of us speechless suddenly, as if demanding that each grant the other now his or her unquestioning trust. What choice do I have, I thought, if I am to continue this marriage? The loss of Laura had devastated me. I was certain the loss of Marie's love would destroy me.

When Marie had burned Gabriel's private letters to her, I wondered whether I had reason to doubt her constancy. Now, despite her protestations, a sort of sickening pain—terrible love, terrible fear—slithered through my entrails. I turned away, unable to speak. Some hardness of mind and spirit in me was renewing itself, some mechanism of separation from Marie I had begun to feel, quite irrationally, upon Russie's death.

Was it possible for a woman to feel love, lasting love, for her husband and yet feel unsatisfied as a woman? Or worse, to feel lasting love of her husband and still seek a woman's satisfaction elsewhere? That I could not find the answers did not keep the questions from haunting me.

Rome was never entirely congenial for Marie, and our strife had made Rome less so. But she continued her own painting, especially on Italian subjects. Marie pursued her painting through everything. Just as I could no longer match her carnal heat, I had not been capable of matching her ceaseless dedication and devotion as an artist. I told myself now that I had mistakenly thought to regain through her beautiful body something of what I had lost as a failed painter. Art through Eros. But my time had long since come and gone. I had never been like Ruskin—loving women but repulsed by, fearful of, their secret flesh. Quite the contrary. But as to carnal passion I was a solar system away from Turner; I was not even on the same planet as Gabriel. Or Burton.

We should have left Rome. Like Marie, I would always love Florence as I could not love Rome, that city where my consular hopes had been dashed, where Laura and I had found ourselves in desperate circumstances on the eve of our fatal posting to Crete. But Marie and I lingered in Rome for some years. Marie made occasional overtures toward reconciliation and renewed trust. But wrapped in my doubt, my own sense of folly, my ever more disturbing view of myself, I was unable to drop my guard and respond adequately to her openness, her love.

While Marie studied and painted and painted, I turned to my own labors, gathering what I had learned across many years and lands into my salaried pieces for *The Times*, my essays on art and history for journals and anthologies, and my books on Ulysses, the Italian masters, and Italy's struggle for unification. Through it all I had maintained a sporadic correspondence with Richard Burton, whose illness had begun to lay him low and impede his final work.

His last letter to me in 1890, when he had entered his seventieth year, described the long process of his physical failing. He had exhausted himself in his illness by the effort it cost to complete and publish his last works of translation: *The Beharistan* and *The Gulistan*, and just recently scheduled for publication the original *Scented Garden* and *The Priapeia*.

"Despite our scrupulousness in regard to private publication," he wrote in his letter, "whenever Isabel is in England making the necessary arrangements or going over proof, she is dogged by some snooping minion or other of the Society for the Suppression of Vice. Her landlord has noticed the house where she stays being watched, and during one of her visits to England as my agent, a pious evangelist actually took a nearby room in the same building. And now detectives have been making inquires about Smithers and Nichols' print shop. But I'm firm in my belief that we operate within the narrow legal straits. We have good legal advice, and if it comes to that I'll walk into court with my Bible and Shakespeare and Rabelais and show them that before they condemn me they must cut half of them out. What a national disgrace is this revival of Puritanism with its rampant cant and ignoble hypocrisy!"

He had, he assured me, made progress on the manuscript of *The Turner Erotica*. "But," he wrote, "this new doctor, one Baker who has served me since a second attack in Cannes in 'eighty-seven, now believes I haven't much time left. So, my good colleague, it is time for me to return to you your hard-won property. Can you come here to pick up the originals? If you prefer, I can give them to Leonard Smithers, my trusted advisor and associate publisher in the Kama Shastra Society, for transport to Rome. The reproductions I will have executed as soon as I hear from you."

I wanted to see Burton again before his illness advanced further. I wrote that I would leave Rome for Trieste myself at the very first opportunity. His line about the revival of Puritanism prompted me to add this paragraph. "Yes, my dear Richard, I find, in the end, that the years spent following Turner have made me cynical, suspicious of the English race generally. Everywhere I see the bigotry of a hollow, a sham and narrow-minded, morality. For the general run of English men and women it all comes down to an acquired distaste for the body, that most inconvenient bundle of carnality, that unfortunate brother ass who connects us all irrevocably to Mother Earth and the grosser realities of the animal kingdom. We of British extraction, including my compatriots and my own family with our old New England roots, seem to assume that our highest purpose in life is to leave behind—nay, to deny—our animal selves. Is our only hope that in every culture there are those few who rise above the narrower prejudices of their fellow citizens?"

* * *

I did not arrive at the Burtons' Palazzo Gossleth, Largo Promontorio, however, until just after October 19 of that year, 1890, the day Sir Richard Burton's great heart finally failed him.

I had seen the Palazzo before on one of our earlier walks together. Their home since 'eighty-three was a large stucco villa with Palladian façade. It was situated on a high, wooded knoll with beautiful views. The steep hill divided the older parts of the city from the Bay of Muggia. There were pleasant gardens and shade trees, and the large entrance with a polished marble staircase provided access to the twenty rooms of the palazzo, many with high ceilings. Their residence was filled in every room with the furniture and objects collected during their world travels. Bookshelves ran everywhere, and maps, prints, paintings, and photographs filled every wall space not taken up by the shelves. I read later in a newspaper account of a major portion of the library's removal back to England that the original library consisted of some 8,000 volumes, not including the boxes of untold numbers of manuscripts, diaries and journals, and research materials.

His wife Isabel was, of course, in deep mourning, and she herself had been diagnosed three years earlier with ovarian cancer. "If I live to do anything at all," she told me through her black veil, "I shall write the biography of this great man, my long love and husband, who has never been fully honored in his own land."

It was, in fact, my understanding that whatever honors he had finally received came to fruition mostly from her own exertions on his behalf. "But it will take me two or more months to prepare everything for removal and final disposition," she added. "Strange as it may seem, it took Richard's death for the choruses of appreciation to begin. The whole civilized world is ringing with his praise. 'No man of action—Sir Walter Raleigh alone excepted—has equaled Burton in purely intellectual and scholastic gifts.' That's the sort of thing one reads now. And I have hundreds of telegrams and cards. Why has glorious appreciation come so late?" Here she stopped as if her throat had turned to stone.

"Perhaps," I said, "because while alive he was too threatening to their frenzy for propriety. And he knew, I take it, many a government secret. Now he is rendered harmless to them."

She looked at me with apparent warmth, but could speak no further. Out of respect for her feelings, her bitterness and mourning, I kept my first interview brief and did not mention the Turners I had come to claim or the manuscript I had come to read. I left Richard's letter in my pocket. She no doubt assumed I had arrived, like others, merely to pay my respects. I told her I would say my goodbye tomorrow.

But Dr. Baker, who was still on hand to help, pulled me aside as I was about to leave for my supper. "Mr. Stillman," he said. "Leonard Smithers told me about Richard's Turner project."

"I didn't want to ask Lady Burton about the illustrations on first meeting to express condolences."

"I appreciate that. But I have something to tell you." He looked at me steadily. "I don't know where they are."

"Don't know?" I said, not sure I heard him correctly.

"Yes. I'm sorry to say. I've looked about as much as I dare. She has not asked me to arrange his papers. She has rather politely tried to keep me away from them. She had long planned, I've come to understand, to arrange them herself, no doubt with her biography of Richard in mind."

"Then she must have them, or know where they are."

"I believe she knows, but she may not have them."

"Please be clear."

"I don't know what she has done with them. But I can tell you this much: Sir Richard's death has completely unhinged her. She has burned certain of his papers—so far as I can tell the whole of *The Scented Garden*—that she feared would be found, exposed after her death, and severely tarnish his reputation, which had been already tarnished enough, in her estimation. And a number of other papers, books, and illustrations. And once she returns to England, I'm certain there will be more conflagrations."

"Good Lord, man! You're suggesting that she might have burned his book on Turner? Even the Turners themselves?"

"I'm saying that given the black mood she is in and her determination to polish his reputation to the high point that she believes he never succeeded in polishing it himself, and that he so very much deserved, she is probably capable of anything. She knew Richard was at work on *The Turner Erotica*; I don't think he ever told her the provenance of the studies he was actually using. I rather doubt she ever saw them before his death. And she has no idea how much longer she has to live, you see. All her thoughts and actions in regard to his papers, works in progress, and publications have an air of urgent desperation about them."

I fear I stood there, mouth open, looking like a man struck about the head with a bat. For it occurred to me that it was the long train of my own folly that had led to this last disaster, if disaster it proved to be. I knew only that I would have to speak to her about it tomorrow before taking my leave, show her Burton's wishes as to the Turners, and have the truth from her own lips.

"I'm sorry," Baker said. "Please let me know if I can do anything."

"I'll speak to her tomorrow. Can you prepare her a little by telling her Richard wrote to me to come here to reclaim the Turners? I'm sure she'll tell me where they are. It was one of his last wishes by letter that in light of Houghton's death they be returned to me."

* * *

Late the next morning in Richard's study, a dozen votive candles fluttering on a shelf behind her, Isabel sat in her widow's weeds with a large, bejeweled silver cross hanging around her neck—the very picture of determined misery. But already my empathy for her pain, empathy arising yesterday out of my deep sympathy with what she felt, had fled from me. I asked her early on about *The Scented Garden* manuscript. Was it true, as reported by some of the inmates of the house, that she had destroyed it?

"Yes, Mr. Stillman," she said. "Along with sundry other materials I didn't wish to see in the hands of anyone who might hope to bring down the memory of Richard. He'd made his enemies, you know."

I must have looked dumbstruck; she didn't say anything more.

"Had you his permission to do so?" I asked.

"I had his permission for certain materials, but before his death neither his permission nor his admonition against the *Garden*. He too, however, expressed anxiety over what others would make of his life and work after he was gone."

"Did you include the Turner manuscript?"

"Yes, with the illustrations he was having made from the originals."

It occurred to me again that Burton himself perhaps protected his wife and long-time colleague from close knowledge of his more dangerous work.

"It was only after I was offered £6,000 for the *Garden* that I sat down to read it," she went on in what was beginning to feel like a fit of self-justification. "It treated, among other things, a certain passion. He

261

was dissecting that passion as he had dissected others, as a doctor dissects a body to study it. Had he been alive to justify himself against the calumny that would surely follow, that were one thing. But he is gone, unable to defend himself. Moreover, he'd been ill and debilitated throughout his last labors on this project; it was not up to the standard of his other work." She searched my eyes through her veil. "You may believe me or not, Mr. Stillman, but I saw Richard—I mean he appeared to me—and asked me to burn both manuscripts of *The Scented Garden*."

I was prone to believe this latter point a desperate fantasy. But I also recalled Burton's telling me his *Garden* would examine, among other practices, pederasty and sodomy. "Lady Burton," I said, "do you know anything about the original studies he was using for a proposed book on Turner's erotic art?" I handed her my letter from Burton. She read the letter with care and then handed it back to me.

"I burned them, along with his manuscript and reproductions."

I leapt to my feet, a completely involuntary reaction. Had I a weapon in hand, I believe my leap would have terminated with my shooting or bludgeoning her. "But these Turners were not his!" I shouted. Then I added with some restraint: "As you see, he had written to ask me to come fetch them, or send them with Mr. Smithers."

"Smithers is not trustworthy," she said, unmoved by my excitation. "I hadn't seen the sketches until I discovered them among Richard's papers. I knew he was at work on some kind of Turner manuscript. I did not know to whom they belonged or how he had come by them."

"He said nothing tangible about them to you?"

"I knew of course about the destruction of the Turners in the National Gallery and Ruskin's hand in it. The event is by now rather infamous, is it not? But Ruskin was right to try to save the reputation of his master, who himself had many rivals and mean-spirited colleagues who would have liked to bring him down, and who would have not hesitated to use such illustrations to do so. What I did with certain of Richard's work was done in the same spirit, and but continued Ruskin's own decision to protect his old master from himself as well. I was, you see, protecting two men from the jaws of their enemies and the gaping mob. And the fickle pronouncements of posterity." Her face looked like a statue's behind her mourning veil. "No," she went on in a fervor not displayed till now. "I will not have it. I will not give them the satisfaction. No. No."

I don't recall whether either of us spoke beyond that. I recall a sort of seizure in my chest and my staggering from the room and out into the afternoon, unfeeling of the midday sun. I remained by the side of the Palazzo to catch my breath, then turned toward a bush, feeling a rush of nausea. But in my trepidation I hadn't eaten breakfast; nothing stirred from my stomach. I felt my heart beat rapidly, continued pressure at my chest, and I began to sweat. Perhaps, I thought, now past my sixtieth year I was finally about to meet my own death.

Somehow I began to make my way down toward the seaport and my lodgings. Not far along I stumbled and dropped to my knees. The full weight of the loss Isabel Burton had inflicted kept me from rising. I recall shedding tears of frustration; then out of that very same frustration I finally began to laugh the laughter of futility and helplessness.

Still on my knees in the footway, I thought I heard, as if echoing in the distance, someone else's laughter. I looked up and turned my head toward the sound. As the laughter drew closer, a shadow emerged from a grove of trees, standing there at the margin of the clearing, a mere silhouette shimmering like a mirage of a short man in a top hat. Had he come to usher me into the next world? Was I now completely mad? He seemed not the dark dwarfish figure or the faunlike youth glimpsed before, but a healthy man in his middle prime. This time he did not elude me from a corner of my vision. As I looked directly at the figure he gradually became more distinct—more corporeal—until I could see his face and then his raptor's eyes looking across the field into mine. Was it a look of triumph? Triumph over my failure, ultimately, to fathom and live by the darker mysteries of human passion, that joining of bodies and souls the old master had so long pursued through his life and his work? It was a look altogether unsettling, a look engendering the conviction that I had been defeated. I had betrayed friends and family by convincing myself that my motives were the highest. Now all of it—the years of searching, the collusion with others, the desperate desire to preserve the last secret of a great man's legacy—amounted to this. To nothing but ashes.

Still on my knees I looked away and closed my eyes. "Marie!" I heard myself say. "Marie."

The laughter ceased. I could look away no more. An aura of small dark flames began to shimmer around the now silent figure. Soon the flames were leaping outwards in the stiff breeze running up the hillside, and as they grew and increased in fury the figure was consumed before my eyes, leaving no trace, no sound, hardly a memory of what I had seen, as if it were nothing more than a half-forgotten dream.

I struggled to my feet and continued my way down toward the town, tears blurring my eyes. I stopped a moment to regain a small degree of composure. What was the loss of the sketches, after all, to the loss of one's child—or spouse? Marie—her tactful *tendresses* as well as her vehement intimacies, her artist's expansive soul, her beautiful love for my children and for our children together—possessed, it struck me, the very thing I had sought all along, and which had entered my life through her, as perhaps it had entered Turner's life through Sarah Danby and Mrs. Booth.

Eyes closed, I saw Marie's face, her smile encouraging me to keep on (as it had so many times since she had blessed my life), to render her finally my utmost trust, to accept at long last the loss of my self-imposed duty, and to take hold of a new life together, free of the afflictions of my old burden. "Marie," I said again.

I opened my eyes and made my way toward the town, knowing only that when I got back to my hotel the first thing I would do, even before packing my bag, would be to buy passage for my journey home.

Acknowledgments

I'd like to thank several people for their generous reading of the manuscript of this book in various stages of its development: Linda Begiebing, Merle Drown, Loftus Jestin, Lawrence Kinsman, Diane Les Becquets, Wesley McNair, Jack Scovil, Don Sieker, and Moira Sieker. My thanks also to Southern New Hampshire University for a sabbatical grant to work on this book. Editor John Lemon not only took this book on with enthusiasm, he read it with a sharp and helpful eye.

Any work of biographical fiction that employs characters based on the lives of people who once walked the earth has, it seems to me, a duty to be as true as its author can make it to each consciousness now deceased and unable to defend itself. To that extent I have tried to preserve the spirit and the general life-structure of the historical figures whose lives intersect in this tale: Stillman himself, Turner, Laura, Marie, Ruskin, the Burtons, the Rossettis, and others. I have boldly used their own words at some points as those words appear in their autobiographies and other works they themselves have published. I have also at times borrowed their words from their diaries, journals, letters, and their biographers. I'd like to acknowledge especially two indispensable sources: William James Stillman's *The Autobiography of a Journalist* (vols. I & II, 1901) and David Elliott's *A Pre-Raphaelite Marriage: The Lives and Works of Marie Spartali Stillman & William James Stillman* (2006).

Yet passing through the cauldron of the novelist's imagination, even characters who carry the names of those who once lived are a species of invention, and not to be confused with the actual persons. Invention in a purer sense, on the other hand, lies in the areas of incident or scene and in the interrelations among historical personages and fictional characters. Such ingredients make for a profligate stew, but a stew that has always offered readers the pleasurable flavor of historical drama and fiction.

Photo: Linda Begiebing

Robert J. Begiebing is the author of seven books, a play, and thirty articles and stories. His books include a trilogy of novels spanning 1648-1850. His novel *Rebecca Wentworth's Distraction* won the Langum Prize for historical fiction. *The Strange Death of Mistress Coffin* (reviewed by Annie Proulx in *The New York Times* as the work of "a gifted writer with an extraordinary feeling for the past") was chosen as a Main Selection for the Mystery and Literary Guild Book Clubs and is currently optioned for a film. His fiction writing has been supported by grants from the Lila-Wallace Foundation and the New Hampshire Council for the Arts. In 2007, Governor John Lynch appointed Begiebing to the Council for the Arts. In 2009 he served both as one of the inaugural faculty members at the Norman Mailer Writers' Colony and as finalist judge for the Langum Prize. He is the founding director of the Low-Residency MFA in Fiction and Nonfiction at Southern New Hampshire University. To read an interview with the author about *The Turner Erotica*, please visit the author's website at www.begiebing.com, or visit the Ilium Press website at www.iliumpress.com.

ILIUM
PRESS

If you have any comments about this title, or if you would like to be notified of upcoming releases from the Ilium Press, please visit www.iliumpress.com.

CPSIA information can be obtained at www.ICGtesting.com
Printed in the USA
LVOW080252210213

320930LV00001B/71/P